FINISHED OFF IN FONDANT

Peeking around the door, I saw a pool of blood on the carpet and smears of blood across the floor where Skylar crawled to the door. I lifted my gaze to a five-tier wedding cake sitting on the coffee table.

The round tiers, smashed and broken, leaned to one side because the cake topper was too heavy. Push-in pillars littered the floor. Instead of an ornate or thematic decoration sitting atop the smallest layer, someone placed a bride across the cake.

Decked out in a gorgeous wedding gown, the young woman lay faceup askew in the confection like she'd fallen asleep in a bed of buttercream. Judging from the pool of blood on the floor and the knife stabbed into her chest, she wasn't snoozing.

She was dead.

Books by Rosemarie Ross

COBBLERED TO DEATH

FINISHED OFF IN FONDANT

Published by Kensington Publishing Corp.

Finished Off in Fondant

ROSEMARIE ROSS

KENSINGTON BOOKS
www.kensingtonbooks.com

KENSINGTON BOOKS are published by

Kensington Publishing Corp.
119 West 40th Street
New York, NY 10018

All Kensington titles, imprints, and distributed lines are available at special quantity discounts for bulk purchases for sales promotion, premiums, fund-raising, and educational or institutional use.

Special book excerpts or customized printings can also be created to fit specific needs. For details, write or phone the office of the Kensington Sales Manager: Kensington Publishing Corp., 119 West 40th Street, New York, NY 10018. Attn. Sales Department. Phone: 1-800-221-2647.

First Kensington Books Mass Market Paperback Printing: December 2020
ISBN-13: 978-1-4967-2277-5
ISBN-10: 1-4967-2277-9

ISBN-13: 978-1-4967-2278-2 (ebook)
ISBN-10: 1-4967-2278-7 (ebook)

10 9 8 7 6 5 4 3 2 1

Printed in the United States of America

For my BFF, Lisa Koolstra, whose friendship with me
is now literarily murder.

Chapter One

"Welcome to *Cooking with the Farmer's Daughter*." The corners of my lips trembled before I pushed them into a wide smile. Pulse pounding in my ears, I kept my focus on the camera filming me and not on the faces of my live studio audience. My colleagues from *The American Baking Battle*, another cooking show I'm involved in, peppered themselves throughout the studio audience to show their moral support.

You wanted to do this. My internal reminder did nothing to stop the apprehension weakening my legs. As much as I wanted to apologize, and set the record straight to my fans, I knew my confession could end two careers, mine and my producer, Eric Iverson, and result in job losses for all of the behind-the-scenes employees of the show.

I drew a shaky breath. We'd planned my confession right down to my wardrobe. Instead of a bright gingham or eyelet blouse, I wore a pale-yellow T-shirt under a darker yellow denim vest with matching capris because the network found research that said if you are apologizing to friends, you should send yellow flowers. I consider my viewers my friends, and although I can't send each and every one flowers, we chose my outfit around the research. My long black hair, pulled into a high pony tail, hung down my back. I exhaled. It was now or never.

"On today's show, I'll be preparing various side dishes using the root vegetable parsnips." I allowed my smile to fade. "Before I begin cooking, there is something I need to tell you." My gaze remained focused on the camera. "It has to do with my own roots," I said. I moved around the counter and stopped on a small piece of tape. We'd blocked the shot earlier in the day so the cameraman could catch a close-up for the at-home viewers, yet still allow a full view of me for the live audience. Eric felt an honest apology and explanation shouldn't have a counter barrier between me and my fans. I agreed.

"As I'm sure you all know, I'm also a host on *The American Baking Battle* filmed here at the beautiful Coal Castle Resort. Tomorrow, we start filming the second season of the popular baking competition." I stopped while some people applauded.

"A sad turn of events happened during the taping of our first season." This time when I paused, a few people murmured or nodded their heads. I continued. "I became a target of an investigative reporter and his murderer because of a secret I'd been asked to keep by my network. At first, the secret seemed innocent and harmless. As time passed, it began to wear on my conscience. Maybe not all of you, but I fear a great many, believe the title of my cooking show, *Cooking with the Farmer's Daughter*, reflects my personal background."

I stopped because a knot of emotion thickened in my throat. It's never easy to admit deception. I broke my gaze with the camera and sought out my friend, Shannon Collins. Shannon, star of *Southern Comfort Foods*, is also a cojudge for the baking competition. Her hot-pink, cold-shouldered blouse made her easy to spot. She occupied an aisle seat in the third row on my left. Her gentle nod and warm smile encouraged me to move forward with my apology.

Swallowing hard, I said, "I am not a farmer's daughter."

This time audible gasps from the audience stopped me. Tears sheened my eyes. "I am so sorry for misleading all of my fans. There are many legalities surrounding a television show. One of which for me was a gag order to keep my true background a secret because it was in direct opposition with my cooking show persona. The truth is, I was born and raised in Chicago. My father is a doctor."

I took a few seconds to search the audience faces to discern if any were angry. I saw angry and shocked expressions. Not as many as I'd expected. I drew another deep breath and stared straight into the camera.

"I am sorry. Please forgive me if you feel deceived by my true background versus my on-air persona. Recently,

I was told that I may not have been raised on a farm, but I had the heart of a country girl." I smiled, remembering Shannon's words. "I cherish the compliment. You have welcomed me into your homes, treated me like family and made me a part of your world. Again, I hope you can forgive me and help me to learn even more about your wonderful way of life."

Breaking my gaze with the green camera light, I chanced a look at Eric. He smiled and gave me a thumbs-up. Next, I sought out Harrison Canfield, a renowned chef whose cooking show, *At Home Gourmet*, enjoyed high ratings and landed him a gig as a cojudge on *The American Baking Battle*. Seated in the middle of the back row to my right, he wore a sober expression while giving me a nod of approval. Lastly, I searched the faces for Skylar Daily, who shared my cohosting duties on the competition show and hosted his own game show, *Grocery Store Gambit*. He sat in the middle of the front row to my left. When my gaze found his, he smiled and winked.

Buoyed by their support, I looked directly into the camera and said, "I hope you continue to enjoy my show. The format will not change. We'll continue to bring you recipes that celebrate our country's heartland and tips to save you time in the kitchen." I smiled and hoped it looked genuine versus nervous, which is how I still felt. "When we return, I'll show you how well lemon pairs with parsnips."

The green light went out on the camera. I started to round the short counter in my makeshift kitchen built inside a conference room at Coal Castle Resort.

"Is that why we had to sign a gag order?" a voice called out.

I jerked my head toward the audience. Eric quickly moved to the blocked spot in front of the counter and said, "Yes, it is."

A woman stood up. She crossed her arms over her chest and frowned. "Just why did you feel the need to lie to the public?"

Eric held up his hands, taking his tablet with them. "There will be time for questions later. Right now, we are going to film the show." He turned to me. "Courtney?" He raised his brows.

I nodded my readiness to continue, although my body still reacted to my internal jitters. I hoped my sweaty palms didn't cause me to drop any food or kitchen utensils. I reached for a kitchen towel and wiped my hands, then stowed it under the counter in the event I needed to use it again. Eric nodded at the cameraman; the light went from red to green and I launched into the preparation of the first of three side dishes using parsnips.

The cooking preparation calmed my nerves. Before I knew it, I was actually looking at my audience. I noticed Kinzy Hummel, the director's assistant on the baking competition, seated beside a man wearing an Armani suit and stern expression. He'd occasionally lean her way and whisper something. Was it about me? Or did he not like parsnips?

The taping ended on schedule. The price of the ticket to view my on-location filming included a question-and-answer segment. I braced for the worst, yet was ready to defend my show and my apology.

The woman who'd spoken up earlier was the first to stand. Eric cast a look in my direction before he walked the microphone to her. Staring daggers at me, she said, "I don't know about these good people, but I feel tricked. I'd like my money back and I want to tear up that gag order I signed."

"I'll see that your money is refunded," Eric answered before I had a chance to respond. He backed away from the woman and addressed the crowd. "As for the gag orders, they're binding and will not be destroyed. The network plans to air this show as the season opener next month. If this admission and apology is leaked to the press before then, we can trace it back to one of you and you will be sued. Is there another question?"

"Yes." A man stood. "It's not a question really. I just want to say that I'm not angry at your admission. I understand people play characters on television. I am disappointed, though. I thought a country gal made good." He sat down.

Another woman stood. She cast a disgusted look at both the other woman and man who'd spoken before looking at me. "I don't care about your background. I just love what you cook and the tips you give. Now, can you tell us how to store parsnips?"

"I can." And I did. I answered several more questions that revolved around cooking and only one about my background. The entire audience seemed impressed I was a trained chef with an emphasis on fruit and vegetable carving. I even had time to demonstrate a decorative carving on a lemon peel. By the time we'd wrapped the filming and questions, relief had replaced my panic. Telling the truth was the right thing to do. True fans would stick by me and my show. Judging from their oohing and aahing over my carving skills, the show Shannon and I planned to develop would be a success too.

Once the audience was ushered from the room, I turned to Eric. "What do you think?"

"This was a small sampling of your fan base." He shrugged. "I think it went well, though."

"I agree," Shannon drawled. "Y'all have nothing to worry about." She flopped her hand through the air in a dismissive manner.

Harrison and Skylar wore expressions that matched Shannon's confidence. "We are hoping for the best for you," Harrison said. He brushed imaginary lint from his suit.

"Right." Skylar emphasized his support with a nod of his head. His scraggly beard and free-flowing hairstyle kept him incognito when not in front of the camera.

"Excuse me." Kinzy approached our small group. "I'd like to introduce Quintin Shepherd." She held her palm out toward the Armani-clad man. "He is the producer of *The American Baking Battle*."

Quintin must have seen the surprise on all of our faces. He had produced the first season of the show from an office in New York City. "I am here to keep the show on budget." Grim expression intact, he made a point of looking each of us in the eye. I surmised it was to emphasize the seriousness of his statement.

Before anyone could respond that extenuating circumstances caused the show to go overbudget during the last filming, he extended his hand to Harrison, who also wore an Armani suit, only double-breasted. "Mr. Canfield. It's an honor to meet you. I enjoy your restaurant in New York City a couple of times a month."

Harrison opened his mouth to respond when Quintin released his grasp and turned to Shannon. I caught Harrison's eye and raised my brows. He responded with a slight shrug.

"Mrs. Collins, the camera loves you."

Shannon's smile widened, then faded when Quintin dropped her hand and went to move on to Skylar. Shannon touched Quintin's upper arm. He stopped and turned his head in her direction. "You didn't give me a chance to thank you for the compliment." The sweetness infused in her tone probably raised our blood sugar levels. "Where I come from it's not polite to take a compliment without saying thank you. Thank you, Mr. Shepherd."

Quintin's droll expression remained while he answered her with a brief nod of his head, then once again turned to Skylar while brushing his hand over his sleeve where Shannon had touched.

Shannon leveled a look my way. I grinned. I knew she'd intentionally tried to point out his rudeness. I wasn't certain he'd caught on, though. And what was brushing off his sleeve all about?

"It's very nice . . ."

"Yes, nice to meet you too, Mr. Daily. You look much different when not on television." Quintin pulled his hand from Skylar's and his lips into a frown as he gave Skylar a once-over. I doubted Quintin owned a pair of faded jeans or a button-down flannel shirt.

"And you, Miss Archer," Quintin said while he captured my hand in a halfhearted squeeze, "are very brave."

Albeit limp, his hand continued to hold mine, so I knew he expected a response from me. I puckered my brows. “Brave?” Was he talking about last season when I stumbled upon a dead body?

“Your confession.” He shook his head while pulling his lips into an even grimmer line. “You may be dealing with disgruntled fans and bad press for a long time.” His gaze focused on something high behind me. “Your admission could affect your career in more ways than one.” He let go of my hand.

My eyes widened. His words reignited panic in my heart. Was this a passive-aggressive threat concerning my cohosting duties on the show? Or given my emotional state, was I overreacting? I followed my natural response and looked at Eric. His lips pulled into a deep frown as he studied Quintin. I wasn’t overreacting. I needed to find out exactly what Quintin meant.

Of course, I didn’t get a chance to ask. Quintin turned and strode toward the door with Kinzy following at a brisk pace to keep up.

“Guess I’m chopped liver,” Eric said as the door closed with a bang.

“The nerve!” Shannon’s tone and expression reflected her displeasure. She smoothed a hand over her blond hair and fingered the side braid hanging over her right shoulder.

“I’ll say.” Skylar rubbed a hand over his scruff of beard. “At least he complimented you and Harrison. He ignored Eric. I don’t know how you feel, Courtney, but I think he got a dig in at us.”

Skylar had stated the obvious, which whipped up my panic. I knew my admission could tank my show, yet after seeing more support than disgruntlement from the studio audience, I'd felt relieved and hopeful. Now, not so much. I wanted to talk to Eric, get his opinion. We needed to be alone.

"Time for me to slip out of wardrobe. I'll see you all tomorrow in makeup." I smiled. Tomorrow started the first day of filming on the new season of *The American Baking Battle: Wedding Edition*.

"Of course!" Shannon waved her hands to herd Harrison and Skylar toward the door. "Bright and early."

Skylar sneered, "Why a wedding theme? Why not something else?"

"Because weddings are fun." Shannon continued to steer the men toward the door.

"You think everything is fun." Skylar looked over his shoulder so Eric and I could see his eye roll just before they were all out the door.

I turned to Eric. "Do you think what Quintin said was a veiled threat about my cohosting duties?"

He shrugged. "It meant something. Quintin seems like a man who doesn't waste time on anything that doesn't benefit him. He didn't want to engage in conversation with the others. He did expect a response from you."

"I was relieved with my audience reaction. After speaking with Quintin, I'm worried about our careers."

Eric rested his hands on my shoulders and locked his eyes to mine. "Don't be. The network supported your decision to tell the truth about your background. I'm sure they're formulating an aftermath plan. They have people, even departments, to handle these types of things. Don't worry. Do your job for both shows with the same enthusiasm you always have, and everything will be all right."

My eyes searched Eric's and found they held the same reassurance his tone had, yet neither brought me comfort.

Doubts and questions raced through my mind. Had I done the right thing in telling the truth? Would my ratings drop? Would the show be canceled? Was Quintin on-site this season to fire me from the baking competition? Would my insistence to be honest turn into the biggest mistake of my life?

Chapter Two

With my mind on the events and conversations last night, I hurried into the workshop intent on getting to the makeup room to voice my concerns and fears with my coworkers. In my haste, I almost ran over Kinzy.

"Good morning!" My tone showed my surprise at Kinzy sitting sentinel inside the entry door. Henry Cole had built a workshop in a thicket of trees about a mile away from his home, Coal Castle. A coal mining magnate in the gilded age, Mr. Cole built Coal Castle as a private home. Also an inventor, he'd built a large workshop that now housed the baking competition set.

She smiled. "Good morning, Courtney. Quintin is implementing changes in an effort to avoid going over-budget by filming delays. Security opens the set, sweeps the room to make certain there is nothing suspicious."

She stopped and raised her brows at me. "I come in fifteen minutes prior to the talents' arrival. This way if someone is late, we can alert Security and they can find them. Quintin says it's much more efficient."

I, for one, could get behind this change. I preferred to have trained personnel find anything suspicious, like a dead body, instead of a layperson like me. I peered around the shadowy room. "Why aren't the lights on, then?"

"The set lights go on when the crew comes to get everything ready for the day. According to Quintin, it'd be a waste of money to use more than the security lighting before that time."

This was *not* something I could get behind. The crew reported to work thirty minutes after we did. It's not like the building would be lit up twenty-four/seven. Kinzy shouldn't have to sit in the dim lighting that cast shadows, which created a creepy vibe. Since the security lighting lit up the staircase well, I really couldn't complain, and Kinzy wasn't the person to voice that concern to, anyway. I forced a smile, nodded, then made my way to the staircase that led to our second-floor makeup and wardrobe room. I had a feeling I'd grow tired of hearing "Quintin says." I opened the door to find I was the last of our foursome to show up.

"Courtney!" Harrison threw his arms wide. "How are you this fine morning?"

"I'm great, and a little surprised by Kinzy sitting beside the door." I looked around the makeup section of the room. I knitted my brows at our new surroundings.

"We've had an update." Shannon stood back and crossed her arms over her chest. "I'm not sure I like it."

Where a round table once sat in a corner of the room,

the long makeup counter and mirrors had been installed. A quick glance around the room showed no sign of the table and chairs where our quartet sometimes shared breakfast.

"I don't like it." Skylar circled around the three of us. "Our backs are to the only entry and exit." He slipped into a chair and swiveled it to different angles. "And the door isn't reflected in the mirror. It's unacceptable. Who thought of this?" Skylar exited the chair so fast, it spun around a couple of times.

"What difference does that make?" Harrison asked.

Skylar stared at Harrison for a few seconds, wrinkled his brow, and said, "Bad feng shui." Skylar fisted, then released his hands. "I don't need negative energy. Neither does the show."

"True. I'd hoped for a much better experience," I said. An inadvertent shiver quaked through me. During the filming of the first season of our show, I'd discovered a dead body. One of the contestants had been murdered with my cast-iron fry pan filled with cherry cobbler, making me a person of interest in the murder.

"It's going to be a great season." Shannon clapped her hands together. "Why don't we make a cup of coffee and catch up while we are prettied up." She pointed to the combination espresso/coffeemaker sitting on a narrow counter attached to the wall that last season housed the makeup area.

Once we all had the beverage of our choice, we sat down in the makeup chairs. Skylar twisted sideways with one eye on the door and the other on us.

"I think your apology went well last night." Shannon set her coffee down while her stylist snapped a cape around her neck.

"Yes, only a few naysayers. That was to be expected." Harrison downed his expresso so his stylist could start her work.

"I'm not having my back to the door." Skylar swiveled his chair with his left foot and looked up at his stylist, who drew his brows together and secured a cape over Skylar's upper body. Now Skylar stared directly at the door.

Taking a sip of my coffee, I wondered about Skylar. His nervous behavior was uncharacteristic. Usually he was laid-back. Now, he seemed on edge. Did this turn of behavior have anything to do with finding evidence during the filming last season? He'd been shook up, physically sick really. Had the experience left him paranoid?

My stylist appeared behind me. I placed my coffee on the counter so he could cape me up and get started on my hair.

"So, we need to catch up." Shannon's drawl held excitement. "Harrison, you first."

"I paired Tabitha with my top chef and moved them to one of my fledgling restaurants. In the short time they've been there, we are showing an increase in reservations, which we all know helps the bottom line. She has a signature dessert on the daily specials."

The makeup mirror showed a satisfied smile stretch across Harrison's face. "Her dad would be proud."

We all murmured our agreement thinking back on Tabitha, a contestant last season, who had a temper and a past connection to Harrison.

"What about you, Skylar?" Harrison asked.

Skylar didn't bother to turn toward us or the mirror. "Nothing." His answer, sharp and tight, snapped through the air like our capes before they were secured around our necks.

Shannon, Harrison and my mirrored expressions reflected our surprise. Skylar seldom said a cross word or used a terse tone.

"Well, we know what Courtney did, and we are so proud of her for standing her ground with the network and telling her fans the truth," Shannon said.

She was good at deflecting tension in the room or creating it, if necessary, with her Southern charm. Traits I admired in my friend.

"So, I'll tell y'all what I've been up to. My new line of cookware is ready to release. Next week as a matter of fact."

"Terrific!" Harrison flashed a smile toward Shannon. "An October release means the cookware will be on store shelves in plenty of time for Christmas."

"I know." Shannon squealed the words. "It took so long to get them developed. Courtney helped by trying the fry pan out in the development stage."

I tried to push the envy from my heart and a smile to my lips. I am happy for Shannon. I really am. I knew what a line of cookware meant to your career, another stream of income. I wanted my own line of knives. I'd planned what I should include in the set. I knew what type of metal and weight I wanted. Eric had a company lined up, but the company backed off when they heard I was coming clean on my background. As disappointed as I was, I couldn't blame them. It would be hard to sell a product with a canceled network star's name on it.

"They're great pans." Which was the truth. I loved the one I used. "I predict they will fly off the shelves." I smiled, a genuine one, but Shannon didn't see it because my stylist turned my chair so he could straighten my bangs. He'd teased, ratted and pinned my long dark hair into a French twist.

Shannon also sported a festive style. Ringlets framed her face while a stylish bun rested on top of her head. A netted bun snood dotted with rhinestones covered her hair and gave it a festive sparkle. Judging by our hairstyles, fancy dresses awaited us in the dressing room once our makeup was applied.

Harrison and Skylar were finished. Both of them wore their hair combed back off their forehead with just enough makeup to enhance their complexion with some color. They were up and out of their chairs already. Skylar turned his back to the door long enough to walk close to the mirror to inspect his hair and makeup. He even turned to his best side and gave his head a nod. He must have liked what he saw.

I almost snickered. Skylar was a terrific person with one slight flaw. He was shallow. Last season he complained about colors washing out his skin and insisted his camera angles captured his best side. Was that why he was acting weird? Had he thought he'd been filmed from the wrong side last season?

Both men left the area to slip into their wardrobe.

"Isn't this nicer than last time?"

Shannon's question snapped me from my thoughts. I wrinkled my brow.

"I mean," she drew the word out, "no tension in this area."

"Right. Yes, it's so much better. Who knew Harrison was such a nice man?" We both grinned ear to ear. Circumstances around Harrison's past created very tense moments, and for me, one frightening confrontation in this room during the first season of filming. At this point of filming for last season, neither of us would have referred to Harrison as a nice man.

Our stylists finished up at the same time. After Shannon and I admired ourselves, we turned our attention to each other.

"I feel so pretty." Shannon giggled. "And a little underdressed."

We both wore yoga pants and zip jackets. Shannon wore red and white, while mine was green and navy.

"Imagine how we'll feel in our dresses. Judging by our hairstyles, they must be formal." I patted the side of my hair. Although it looked fantastic, the pins keeping the twist in place dug into my scalp.

"I hope we can step into them so we don't mess up our hair. A wedding show is going to be a blast. I hope we get to dress formal for every episode."

Kinzy popped her head into the door. "Brenden wants you on set in fifteen minutes."

Both of our eyes widened. "But we're not dressed."

"Quintin said we are all to be on time. No more delays."

Not again. I'd been on set for just over an hour and was very tired of hearing "Quintin says," yet I didn't argue. I ran toward the dressing room with Shannon on my heels.

When Shannon and I made our way down the stairs, with the assistance of our stylists due to our evening gowns and stiletto heels, I felt like we should be announced.

The sequin-covered gown Shannon wore sparkled silver under the now-well-lit set. The dress fabric and design hugged Shannon in all the right places. Her gown sported cap sleeves, a jeweled neckline and cowl-draped back that stopped a few inches above the small of her back. She looked stunning.

My strapless chiffon A-line gown with a rucked Empire bust line matched my elegant and classic hairstyle. The wine color accentuated my fair complexion. The asymmetrical dropped waistline, salted with beadwork, gave way to a full gathered skirt.

Easy to pick out in the crowd, Harrison and Skylar wore tuxes: Harrison in gray tails and a top hat, Skylar in black with a wine cummerbund and bow tie. Both of their lapels were adorned with white rose boutonnieres.

We joined the group standing by our respective castmates. Our stylists headed back upstairs when Brenden approached the group, clapping his hands—his signal for the crowd to quiet. "As I'm sure the crew and cast noticed, we didn't have a meet and mingle last evening." He encompassed the group with his gaze.

A diverse group of six males and six females huddled together at the edge of the set. Their wide-eyed expressions told the story of their nervousness. The crew filled in the other areas to complete a circle around Brenden.

"Instead, I have decided to throw a wedding brunch. I believe we'll have a smoother filming schedule than last time." Brenden focused his attention on the cast and crew. He turned to the contestants. "I strive for my group to be one big, happy family. So during the filming of the wedding edition of *The American Baking Battle*, feel free to help one another out if you are ahead of baking time and someone else is falling behind."

Brenden stopped talking while Kinzy parted some of

the crew members to allow the resort's catering staff to push three tables into the center of the group, where Brenden stood. One table held a beverage service of punch and coffee, the second an array of mini quiches and fruit, the third a beautiful five-tiered wedding cake. A cascade of dark pink buttercream roses twisted down the square tiers at an angle over a lighter pink flawless fondant. A custom-made cake topper of a man and woman, clad in aprons and chef hats, stood erect and proud.

Brenden walked to the beverage service, lifted a plastic flute filled with punch and held it in the air. "May the best chef win! Now mingle like good wedding guests at the reception." Brenden sipped his punch and moved to the quiche cart.

Skylar took his cue and moved over to the contestants, shaking hands and encouraging them to move out of their huddle to the food before patting a few of the catering staff on the back in greeting. This was the Skylar I knew. I shrugged. Maybe he was just having a bad morning.

I snagged a coffee with one hand, lifted my skirt with the other in an attempt to follow his good example. I glanced over my shoulder at Shannon. "Come on." I walked toward the contestants still standing in a nervous group. Shannon, punch flute in hand, followed.

"Hello!" I smiled at the group. "Pretend this is a receiving line. We'll shake hands, make introductions, then you can move on to the food line." My greeting and instructions were met with tentative smiles from the contestants.

"What a fun idea." Shannon flopped her hand. "Y'all come on. We don't bite."

An older man, in his mid-sixties I'd guess by the gray in his beard and embedded laugh lines around his eyes, looked around at the group, shrugged his shoulders and stepped forward. He shook my hand. “Michael Phillips, amateur baker.” He ended our handshake and extended his hand to Shannon. “Nice to meet you both.” He then did as instructed and moved over to the food. As I watched him go, I noticed Harrison stood by the beverage table ready to greet the contestants.

“I think Brenden is getting his wish,” I whispered to Shannon, and pointed toward Harrison.

Shannon didn’t have a chance to respond. A man and a woman, both tall and slender, stepped up to us. They wore matching pastel-green T-shirts. His accentuated his fair hair and complexion, while the green popped her cocoa-colored skin. The man spoke. “I’m Miller Smith and this is my wife, Mary.”

“Y’all are married and competing against each other?” Shannon’s drawl held a mixture of awe and disbelief.

“We are.” Mary shook my hand, then extended the same greeting to Shannon.

“We thrive on competition.” Miller followed his wife’s lead on the handshaking, then put his hand to the small of her back and guided her over to where Harrison stood.

Shannon giggled and leaned close to my ear. “That is going to be interesting to watch. Clever choice on Brenden’s part.”

I nodded in agreement while another contestant, a very young man, extended his hand. “Marco Martino.” His black hair curled over his shirt collar. Other than a weak handshake and halfhearted smile, he shared nothing more.

I’d need to reread the contestant bio sketches the show provided to us to learn more about him. All of them, I guess, since Michael was the only one who’d divulged his cooking background.

A line had formed for the contestants left to introduce themselves. A young girl, sans makeup, grabbed my hand and overshook it. "I'm Donna Ray. My grandmother taught me to cook and bake. If I win, I'm using the prize money to attend culinary school."

Finally, someone shared why they wanted to be on the show. Donna hailed from the South. Her drawl, though, was distinctly different than Shannon's.

"Are you from Georgia?" Shannon asked, and took her proffered hand.

"Yes!" Donna giggled. "I know you're from Texas."

"Our Southern states are being well represented."

Donna smiled and nodded her head. She stood in front of us for a few seconds. Was she awestruck or bad at small talk? Finally, she said, "It was nice to meet you."

The next two in line were a young Hispanic man and a woman with perfectly coiffed white hair. They were heavy into a conversation.

"Oh, I'm sorry." The woman extended her hand. "I'm Lynne Doxtad. This is Diego Garcia. We both run family-owned bakeries."

"Nice to meet you." Diego had a firm handshake. "We are talking about our business plans and the struggles of running a small family business."

They quickly greeted Shannon and moved on, picking up their conversation where they'd left off. Shannon giggled before she whispered, "They certainly aren't starstruck. Their conversation is much more interesting than us."

I laughed, then turned my attention back to the receiving line. A taller woman, who appeared to be in her thirties, shook our hands before introducing herself. "I'm Afton Suzy. I'm taking gourmet cooking classes."

After a quick handshake with both of us, she made a

beeline toward Harrison. “Nice to meet you,” I called to her retreating back.

“Jeremiah Roberts.” A shorter man in the same age category of Afton, offered his hand to me, then Shannon.

I blinked. “The Cupcake King of Chicago?”

A wide smile stretched across his features, yet I wasn’t sure if it was from my recognition of this name or his interest in Afton. He hadn’t taken his eyes off of her. “I am,” he said.

“I enjoy your shop.”

“Thank you. I’ll let you get to the other guests.”

I watched him retreat right over to the area where Afton stood. It appeared we have another interesting turn of events, and how apropos for a wedding-themed show.

“Hello?”

I drew my gaze back to the line of contestants. There were only three left, and two of them stood in front of us. “Nadine Holt, nutritionist,” the short blond woman said. “Carla Johnston. I’m a cook at a private school,” the redhead said. Both women appeared to be somewhere in their sixties. The show had chosen a nice mix of contestants.

“Nice to meet you.” I shook their hands. Like good wedding guests, they moved on to Shannon.

“We found we have a lot in common and hope our cooking stations are close together,” Nadine told Shannon before the women stepped away.

A tall, attractive man stepped forward. “I’m Alex Williams.”

His commanding stance and tone indicated, at least to me, that we should recognize him. Involuntarily, I must have knitted by brows. An exasperated expression crossed his features. “Of the maple syrup Williamses.”

Aw! A well-established family-owned business for generations and a common household name. I stuck my hand out. Alex looked down at it, arched a brow and walked away.

"Oh, brother," Shannon said.

Before I could respond, the heavy wooden door of the workshop banged open. Bright, natural sunlight illuminated the room and created a silhouette of a man standing in the doorway, legs splayed and hands fisted to his hips. His deep voice rumbled with anger. "What's going on here?"

Chapter Three

The set fell silent. Quintin stepped into the room and out of the glare of the sunlight. He wore a sour expression while his gaze searched the small gathering, seeking out Brenden. All heads had snapped in his direction.

Hurrying toward Quintin, Brenden said, "I can explain." Kinzy followed close behind her boss.

Quintin looked past Brenden and Kinzy. The frown on his face deepened. He eyed the five-tiered wedding cake and the quiche cart. I guessed he was making a mental tally of the cost.

When Brenden reached Quintin, he spoke in a hushed tone. Quintin rolled his eyes and in a voice everyone could hear, said, "All right." Then he strode off toward the area of the building where Skylar and I usually shoot the opening sequence of the episodes.

Turning to the group, Brenden said, "Please continue to enjoy the reception and mingle." He wrung his hands, sighed and followed behind Quintin.

"What do you think that was all about?" Shannon turned to me.

"Money." I quirked a brow. "We'd better get some breakfast before Quintin orders it removed from the premises."

Shannon and I managed to eat some bite-size quiche while visiting with contestants.

A shrill whistle sounded in the area. Skylar removed his fingers from his lips. "Gather around, everyone, time to cut the cake."

"Aren't we missing a bride?" a crew member called out.

"I don't need a bride to cut the cake." Skylar punctuated his answer with a sneer.

I wondered if Skylar realized how snippy he sounded when he answered. A young man in a catering smock made a big show of presenting a serrated knife to Skylar by balancing it on his gloved hands like he was presenting a sword to a knight. Skylar took the knife, gave a slight bow and stabbed it into the top layer of the cake. The young man doubled over in laughter. Was I missing an inside joke? Skylar had befriended some of the catering staff during the filming of the first season of our show. I recognized the young man, but his name escaped me.

Skylar began cutting and laying nice-size chunks of cake on Styrofoam plates while the young man handed them off to reaching hands.

Hands clapped behind us. Brenden. He and Quintin had returned to the set.

"Everyone, please give me your attention. I'd like to

introduce our producer, Quintin Shepherd." Brenden placed his hand out in front of Quintin. "Now, if the talent would step over here, I'll make formal introductions."

"Not necessary." Quintin clipped out the words. "I met them last night."

Shock set into Brenden's features. "What?"

"Kinzy and I attended the on-location taping of Courtney's show."

"Well." Brenden huffed out a breath and gave Kinzy a narrow-eyed stare before he refocused on Quintin. "Had I known I wouldn't—"

"We need to start filming," Quintin interrupted. He looked at the catering staff. "Leave the beverages and cake for later." His eyes bore into Brenden. "Get started."

"All right. Well. Everyone." It was obvious Brenden was flustered by Quintin's presence on set. Or maybe intimidated was a better word. Finally, he clapped his hands and hollered, "Places."

Catering placed the remaining quiche and fruit beside the beverage service, then rolled the empty table through a side door exit. The contestants looked for their assigned kitchenettes. On the first day of filming, a piece of paper with their names was taped to the countertop. Wine tulle swags decorated the front of the counters. A silver bow topped the peak of each shallow scallop. A white honeycomb paper bell hung under each bow. The back wall of the set was festooned in the same fashion.

Skylar and I found our tape marks under a flower-laden arch. Greenery and white tulle intermingled with burgundy peonies and white roses over white plastic lattice. Not only was it lovely, it smelled nice too. I wondered if Quintin realized Brenden gave the set designers the okay to order real flowers.

"What is this?" Michael held up an apron and frowned. "There must be some mistake?" He looked around at the other kitchenettes.

"I don't think so." Jeremiah laughed and slipped on an apron screen printed with a version of a sweetheart bodice wedding gown complete with a bride's neck, arms and hands holding a bouquet. He mocked a model pose.

Michael looked around at the rest of the contestants and so did I. All of the contestants received a novelty apron of a variation of a tux, three-piece suit or bridal gown. Finally, he shrugged and aproned up.

I chuckled. "Cute!"

Skylar grunted.

When I looked at him he eyed the arch with a disgusted look on his face. "What's wrong? Are you allergic to one of the flowers?"

"No." Skylar looked at me. He pulled his mouth into a perturbed line. "People make too much of weddings. Women fantasize about them for years. Why are women so caught up in one day of their life? One day does not the marriage make."

My brows shot up in surprise. It seemed like an odd statement from the son of a socialite.

"Don't look so surprised. Not everyone loves a wedding."

I didn't know how to respond, so I kept quiet. I knew most grooms weren't as enthused about the wedding planning as the bride-to-be. Society had deemed it her day, after all. Yet, his statement about weddings was edged with anger and had a personal feel rather than just an observation or opinion. Really more like something a jilted lover might say. Was Skylar nursing a broken heart?

"You can all relax for a moment," Brenden hollered

with no hand-clapped warning. “We have to fix a camera.”

Skylar took off to the catering table and poured himself a cup of coffee. I found a chair and gave my feet a rest from the stilettos. Shannon and Harrison, who were not needed for the opening shot, were nowhere to be found on set. I suspected they were seated at the bistro table on the small outdoors set, filming the discussion session of the second challenge of the day.

I studied the wedding decorations on the set and thought about my own wedding dreams, the colors, the style of dress and tux. My opinions changed as I grew from a girl to a woman. I realized the wedding was about two people, not one. I thought of Eric, my business partner, producer, friend and possible love interest. According to Shannon, he had feelings for me. I wasn’t so sure, but her revelation did cause me to look at him differently. If he were my groom, I’d plan a wedding much different from if Drake Nolan, the Head of Security on the baking competition and All-American Hunk, were my groom.

I closed my eyes and envisioned Eric standing beside an altar, a large stained glass window reflecting candlelight throughout the sanctuary. With his blond hair cropped short and trendy, he’d wear a white tux with tails. His cobalt-blue cummerbund would accentuate the sunflowers in my bouquet and match the ribbons tying the flowers together. I’d wear my mother’s gown patterned after Princess Diana’s, only with a much shorter train and my hair in an updo. We’d be surrounded by family, friends and colleagues, a traditional wedding at its finest.

I sighed. I pictured a wedding with Drake very differently. More rugged than Eric, Drake seemed more of an outdoors person. I pictured a sprawling yard. A natural wood gazebo lined with white lights and backdropped with the setting sun. He'd wear a sharp black suit, while I'd walk down the aisle in my grandmother's tea-length wedding gown with cap sleeves, an illusion neckline and corded lace appliqués. Only family would attend.

"Courtney!"

My body jerked at the sound of my name. I opened my eyes to find Skylar looking down at me.

"Were you asleep? I said your name three times."

"No." My face started to heat with a creeping blush. I didn't want to admit to Skylar, of all people, I was fantasizing about getting married and that I had growing feelings for two very different men.

"Well?" I knew by the expectant expression on his face, he'd asked me a question I obviously didn't hear.

"Can you repeat the question?"

"Will you come with me to talk to Quintin? I mean, I need to talk to Quintin, in private. I don't want to approach him alone, though." Skylar swayed a little from putting weight on one foot, then the other. Was that from nerves, or were the tux shoes too tight?

I craned my neck, spotted Quintin leaning against the wall with his arms crossed and a sour look on his face. I understood why Skylar needed reinforcements. Quintin had perfected intimidation. I nodded and stood. We took two steps when Marco Martino approached us with a pen and the paper. The paper bore the logo of the show and his name, so I knew it was his kitchenette placard.

"Excuse me, Mr. Daily. Could I get your autograph?" Marco held out the pen and paper.

"Sure. Call me Skylar." Skylar smiled. "Would you like it personalized?"

"Yes, my girlfriend is a huge fan of yours. I'd say your

biggest fan. She is so excited I'm on the show with you." Marco threw his hands in the air, palms out. "Sorry, I rambled. I'm really excited to be here. Her confidence in my cooking abilities and suggestion to try out for the show spurred me into action. I plan to present this to her when I propose."

Skylar smiled politely. "Whom should I make this out to?"

Marco covered his face with his hands and shook his head before lowering them and looking at Skylar. "Sorry. I'm kind of nervous. Please make it out to Lisa."

The color drained from Skylar's face. His eyes darted around the room; then he craned his neck to look over his shoulder. When he turned back to us, I noticed fear clouded his eyes. His hand trembled so badly the pen danced across the paper, leaving sporadic ink lines in its wake.

What was going on with him? I'd seen him sign many autographs and interact with fans with kindness, humor and gratitude.

"Are you okay?" Marco asked with a lilt of humor in his voice.

Skylar and I both looked at Marco. I narrowed my eyes. I didn't like the cagey look on his face. Had he figured out Skylar didn't like weddings from the cake-cutting incident? Was he goading Skylar because his girlfriend was a fan?

"Yes." Skylar snapped out the response, hastily scribbled across the paper and pushed it toward Marco. Glancing over both shoulders, Skylar turned. Not addressing either of us, he mumbled, "I need to talk to Brenden and Drake." In an instant he was gone.

I watched his retreating back and realized my mouth

was agape. What was going on with him? A minute ago, he didn't want to approach Quintin alone, now he practically ran over to him.

"Wow! What a weirdo. I don't see what Lisa sees in him."

I opened my mouth to defend my friend. Before any words came out, he gave me a devious smile.

"I have a question for you too. What's it like to find a dead body?"

Drake burst into the room before I had a chance to answer the rude, and macabre, question.

"You can tell me later," Marco whispered. He avoided looking at Drake and scurried back to his kitchenette.

What was with everyone's odd behavior today?

I turned my gaze to Drake. My heart fluttered a few times at the sight of him, which put all ponderances of Marco and Skylar's strange conversations and reactions out of my mind.

"Where's Brenden?" Drake called over the muted roar of voices.

A few seconds later, Brenden appeared from the back area with Quintin and Skylar following behind. "Here we are." Brenden extended his hand. Quintin pushed it down.

"Who are you?"

"I'm Drake Nolan. Head of Nolan Security."

Expression blank, Quintin stared at him.

"He's our private security company," Brenden interjected, and held his hand out again.

Drake shook it, then turned to Quintin. "You are?"

Quintin had the good manners to shake his hand.

"Quintin Shepherd. I produce this show." He glanced at a large clock on the wall. "That should have started filming an hour ago." Quintin pointed a sour expression toward Brenden.

"Well, I need to speak with everyone." Drake turned his expectant expression on Brenden, who flinched under two sets of scrutinizing eyes.

"Okay." Brenden looked at Drake. "Make it quick, though."

I knew he added the last part to appease Quintin.

Kinzy gathered the group around Drake. I noticed a petite woman in a peach Nolan Security polo shirt and black jeans standing a few inches behind Drake. The color of her polo accentuated the winter undertones of her skin and the natural highlights in her chestnut hair, which she wore in a cute pixie.

"First, I'd like to introduce my new second-in-command, Pamela Mills."

The woman stepped forward. The crowd clapped, including me, while I wondered just how much security a woman about my size could provide. Hopefully, we'd never find out. No one wanted a repeat of the first few weeks of the filming of our first season. Investigative reporter Bernard Stone had used a pseudonym and fictional background to land a contestant spot on the baking competition. He'd planned to expose Harrison's background, but hadn't planned on a family member of someone he'd previously investigated and ruined being on set. It cost him his life. It cost me a frantic few days of worry since he was murdered with my cast-iron fry pan filled with cherry cobbler. Because the murder weapon had my fingerprints all over it, I became a person of interest in

Bernard's murder. Obviously, it turned out well for me, but not poor Bernard.

"Now the introduction is out of the way, I have a few more 'housekeeping' items." Drake air-quoted the word "housekeeping." "In light of the situation last time, I've added more security staff. Coal Castle Resort increased security on their facility by adding more night lighting, especially on the walking path." Drake paused. His eyes found mine. "They have also limited the number of guests staying at the resort during filming. Both these measures should allow everyone peace of mind and better use of the recreation areas of the resort."

Coal Castle Resort was built in a valley surrounded by the Pocono Mountains. It sported indoor activities, a bowling alley original to the building, spa and mini-gym, as well as outdoor activities, tennis courts, golf course, fishing pond and numerous hiking paths. I hoped to use some of these facilities during my time off.

"Thank you." Drake waved off the crowd.

Quintin pointed to the clock. Brenden nodded and went to check on the status of the repair or replacement of the broken camera.

I planned to use this time wisely and started to walk toward Drake. Pamela stepped in front of me. Not a smart thing to do to a woman wearing stilettos and a long gown. I wobbled. She reached out and steadied me.

"Thank you. I'm Courtney Archer."

"I know. I'm assigned to your show. I need to speak with Eric Iverson. Is he here?" She surveyed the area.

"He isn't. He's probably in the conference rooms that house my set. Is there something I can help you with?"

"I don't think so. I've been assigned to your filming

sessions of *Cooking with the Farmer's Daughter* to ensure nothing happens like it did last time."

I scrunched my features because again, I wondered if she was the best choice to keep me or anyone safe.

"Drake's orders. I need to see your practice and filming schedules and layout of your set."

I'd stopped listening after she said, "Drake's orders." Drake wanted to keep me safe. My heart raced. I looked past Pamela to where he stood talking with one of the crew members. We'd never managed to go out on a date due to scheduling conflicts. We'd kept in touch via numerous texts and a couple of FaceTime sessions, though. I provided the suite and Eric's cell phone numbers to Pamela. She immediately bid me goodbye.

I didn't mind. I set my sights on the handsome hunk of a man wearing jeans and a green polo. He'd trimmed his dark hair. It now rested at the top of the polo shirt collar. "Drake." I smiled as I approached him.

"Courtney." He took my outstretched hands and leaned in close. "You are rocking that gown." His warm breath tingled my skin and weakened my knees, which isn't a good thing when you are wearing stilettos.

"Thank you." I squeezed his hands before we released our grip. I got control of my wobbly legs. "It's nice to see you again."

He shot me a look.

"In person, I meant."

"Oh." Understanding covered his features. "Right." He smiled. "I've looked at the filming schedule. I think we'll be able to finally have a non-work-related dinner." He tucked his hands into his front pockets and flashed me a hopeful smile.

"I think you're right." I smiled wide. "And thank you for the extra security for my show. I don't know if it's needed, but I feel safer already."

Pulling his hands from his pockets, he held them up. "Don't thank me. Sheriff Perry insisted one of my security staff was on-site anytime anyone was on your set since you attract trouble." Drake patted my shoulder. "One of my guys is beckoning me over with his hand. Duty calls."

I huffed out my breath. I didn't bother turning around to watch the retreating view, which was good, believe me. I was too annoyed with myself to enjoy it. Once again, I'd read too much into Drake's actions concerning interest in me when he was just doing his job. For some reason, I couldn't get a good read on him, or his body language.

Yet what really steamed me was that Sheriff Perry thought I attracted trouble. Guess Sheriff Perry and I'd have to have a little talk next time I saw him. Which I hoped wasn't soon.

Gathering up my skirt, I pulled off the pumps and I stomped toward my set chair.

Me, attract trouble?

Never.

Chapter Four

By ten o'clock, with a replacement camera in hand, our cameraman stood a few feet in front of Skylar and me. Our toes on our tape mark, we'd be filmed up close by the cameraman on the floor and from a distance by a camera on a boom to give Brenden plenty of shots to edit. We all waited for our cue. Kinzy, who usually sat beside Brenden, pulled her chair close to where Quintin sat on the sidelines. I'd noticed her title this season went from assistant to assistant director. Did that mean she had to split her time between Brenden and Quintin?

"Get ready. Action."

We turned our heads to flash a smile into the camera. "Weddings are not only a big day for a couple in love." Skylar and I turned our heads to face each other, and smiled big, like we were the happy couple. I turned back to the camera. "They're also a big day for catering and food."

"The wedding edition of *The American Baking Battle* will lead our bakers through each event that requires food."

I breathed a sigh of relief. Skylar had inflected a happy lilt in his tone and flashed a genuine smile while talking about a wedding. I wasn't sure he could accomplish that feat based on his earlier comments.

I picked up the instructions. "The first challenge you are faced with today is three appetizers perfect to serve at an engagement party. They should be finger food with a festive flair."

Together Skylar and I said, "The baking begins now."

The contestants rushed to the pantry and refrigerator area of the set.

"Cut." Brenden beckoned us to him with his hand. Both Skylar and I stepped away from the flowered arch. "You'll be interviewing the bakers today. All twelve. Your cameraman will keep rolling, and I'll edit the conversations we want to air."

"So, just like last season," I verified.

"Only formal." Skylar chuckled at his joke and managed to get a smile out of Brenden. The first one I think I'd seen on his face since Quintin had entered the building.

We allowed the contestants' time to get their cooking supplies before we headed into the kitchenettes.

"Start on the front right and work your way back." Brenden gave his orders, then walked over to Kinzy and Quintin.

"You can interview the first contestant. I'll hang back."

It was obvious Skylar didn't want a repeat conversation with Marco. "Okay." I walked over to the counter where Marco boiled water. "Refresh my memory, what is your cooking background?"

Marco winked into the camera. "I have an Italian bakery business in Los Angeles. Best cannoli in California from a family-owned business."

The confidence of youth.

"What are you preparing for appetizers?" The contestants always know what the first challenge of the day is to give them time to perfect their recipes. The second challenge of the day is always a surprise chosen by the judges. The third challenge revolves around technique.

"Right now, I'm working on individual spaghetti and meatballs."

Knitting my brows, I asked, "How is that finger food?"

"I'll line a mini-muffin cup with spaghetti." He held up a pan. "Then fill it with marinara and a meatball, and top it off with Parmesan cheese. I am also making an antipasto appetizer using salami, ham, provolone cheese and an olive spread wrapped in a pizza crust and baked to perfection." Marco stopped talking, put his fingers to his lips, kissed them and pulled them back. "Magnifico sliced into individual wedges. My last appetizer is crostini with a roasted eggplant spread topped with fresh mozzarella cheese."

"Sounds great. I am curious to see how the spaghetti and meatballs turns out."

"Plan to be impressed." Every inch of Marco's expression screamed arrogance.

Next up was Miller and Mary Smith. We managed to tag-team an interview with them while they talked smack to each other. "Won't this cause problems later?" I addressed my question to Mary after an especially harsh "smack" aimed at what Miller prepared, burnt ends on toasted rounds of garlic bread.

"Nope." Mary smiled up at me before turning her attention back to her vegetable pizza on a cauliflower crust.

Halfway through the interviews, I was ready to ditch my shoes. I soldiered on. Had Quintin not been on set, I might have asked Brenden for a short break. The varied appetizers prepared by the contestants were interesting. I hoped they tasted as good as they sounded. When we moved to the last contestant left to interview, Alex Williams, I saw Shannon and Harrison take their seats on set.

I was ready to get this interview segment wrapped and not just because of my shoes. Shannon and I had agreed to finalize details on the cooking show we wanted Eric to pitch to the network, *City Meets Country*, after we gauge the fallout from my telling the truth about my background. Although the comments Quintin made last night filled my mind with doubts, I'd decided to press on with my future plans.

"What are you making?" Skylar took over the interview, which was okay with me since I found Alex arrogant on our first meeting and I could tell I'd be taking the lead on all interviews with Marco.

"The one I'm working on is individual bacon and egg frittatas with a maple drizzle." Alex sprinkled bacon over a scrambled egg mixture already in a mini-muffin pan. "For a vegetarian choice, I'm making a maple and pecan cracker with a roasted butternut squash hummus. Lastly, I'm making a maple sausage bite out of phyllo dough."

Alex kept working while he spoke and glanced at the camera only once, which surprised me. I noted the theme with his ingredients. I hope he knew better than to plug his family's brand name, because Brenden would edit it out.

"Sounds great. I can't wait to taste one." Skylar turned to the cameraman and pulled his thumb in front of his throat while saying, "Cut." He handed off the microphone and walked with determined steps to the exit door. Did he need air?

"Hello! How'd the interviews go?" The cheerful greeting Shannon gave me as I approached my chair lifted my spirits.

I dropped into the chair next to hers and slipped my shoes off. My feet immediately felt better. I'd have to speak with wardrobe about shorter gowns, which required shorter heels. "The contestants interviewed well. I think Brenden will get some good footage. Shall we discuss our show?"

Shannon wrinkled her nose and shrugged. "Sure."

Not quite the response I thought I'd get.

"Is there something wrong? Are you concerned about what might happen once the network airs my apology?" I doubted that was it. She'd always been so supportive of me even when she'd known me only a few days.

"No, no, not at all. I don't think your fans are fickle enough to leave you over telling the truth. It's not like you said you were a farmer's daughter. It was just implied."

"Were you an attorney in another life?" Shannon's superpower was her perception of most circumstances. I still thought she was wrong about Eric having romantic feelings about me, but she is the one who told me I was a farm girl at heart and that is why people believed I was really raised on a farm.

"Me, an attorney?" A giggle erupted from Shannon,

which turned into a full-fledged laugh. Shannon grabbed my hand and squeezed. "I needed that. I didn't realize how long it'd been since I was tickled into laughter. So, what do you want to discuss?"

"In light of my current show situation, I think we should tread lightly on the country versus city theme. I know urbanites throw posh dinner parties, but I'm sure people in the heart of America do too. I don't want to step on toes or, well, treat any of our audience demographics differently. Maybe we could preface the recipes with a story, like we were at a dinner party and here is what they served. Or refer to the guests at the dinner party and their preferences."

I waited for an answer. Shannon stared off into space, a faraway look on her face.

"Shannon, did you hear me?"

Giving her head a little shake, she said, "I'm sorry. I'm a little preoccupied with my cookware line coming out, planning the apron line and missing my husband."

I'd felt perturbed until her last admission. It had to be tough being apart from her husband, even if it was just a couple of weeks.

"Courtney." Kinzy hurried toward me. "Someone texted you." She handed off my cell phone. I'd given it to her to hold during filming since I had no pockets on my gown.

I woke up my screen and tapped an app. A text from Eric popped up. I read it. Then reread it.

"What is it, Courtney? You look troubled."

I held my phone up so Shannon could read the text while I said the words out loud. "Eric is wondering if everything is all right because he just heard Skylar and Drake having a serious and tense conversation."

"Why is that concerning?"

"Because a serious and tense conversation to Eric means an argument to anyone else."

I quickly texted Eric everything was okay here and that the men had shown no animosity while on the set together. I hit Send, then decided to add another message. My imposed thumbs drummed out my thoughts about Skylar and Shannon not quite acting like themselves. I hit Send and sighed. With all of the stress the cast, crew and contestants were under during the murder investigation last season, did I really know what acting like themselves meant when applied to Shannon and Skylar? Everyone might have been on their best behavior trying to stay under the law's, and murderer's, radar.

My phone jingled. I read Eric's brusque reply: **Busy with Pamela. Talk later.**

Two parts anger and one part hurt simmered inside me. Eric had blown me off for Pamela. Was the unexpected emotion stabbing into my heart jealousy? My eyes widened at the thought. Pamela was following orders and Eric was obliging, I was sure. So, why did his words make me resent her presence on my set?

I knew why. Shannon planted the notion Eric had romantic feelings for me, which in turn led me to examine my feelings for Eric. Surprisingly, I learned my interest in Eric wasn't just business and friends. He was my first and last, as in person I spoke to either by phone call or text in the morning and evening. He was definitely the person I wanted to share the good and bad events happening in my life. While shooting the last season of the baking competition, I'd planned to discuss my feelings, and our relationship, with Eric. Once we returned to our regular lives, we fell back into our easy and comfortable routine. I needed to clarify our relationship before I went out to dinner with Drake. First chance I had, I was talking to Eric.

The workshop door burst open. The sound and bright sunlight streaming into the room startled me, drawing my attention from my thoughts to the door. Skylar, leaning on a Nolan Security employee for assistance with walking, wobbled onto the set. Harrison stood and hurried his chair over for Skylar to sit down. Shannon snapped out of her reverie when I jumped from my chair. We joined Harrison surrounding Skylar in a bubble of coworker support.

"I don't feel so good." Skylar hung his head. "I'd like a drink of water."

Catering was setting up the lunch buffet for the crew. The young man Skylar had joked with in the morning must have heard Skylar. He came running with a plastic bottle in hand. I read his name tag to refresh my memory: "Justin Henry."

"Here, Skylar, drink this." Justin twisted the cap off the water and held it out to Skylar, who guzzled about half the bottle in one gulp.

"Thanks."

"Sure, I hope you feel better." Justin backed away. I noted an emotion in his eyes, worry for his friend, no doubt.

"Brenden," Harrison called before the security staff member told us Skylar had stumbled on the path. He'd helped Skylar to his feet and assisted him with walking to the television studio. His story ended with him believing Skylar was ill because there was no evidence to suggest he was imbibed. Then he took his leave.

"What?" Brenden asked on his way to where we stood and Skylar sat. Kinzy and Quintin followed behind.

"The nerve of that guy! Why would he even bring that up if it wasn't an issue?" Shannon spoke too clipped for much of a drawl to hang on her words.

Confusion settled into Brenden's features at Shannon's outburst. Shannon, ever the loyal friend, was ready to defend Skylar against any disparaging remark, even though there wasn't one. Seeing our coworker, and friend, not himself rattled us all making it easy to lash out. In my mind, we needed to focus on the matter at hand. Skylar. "Shannon, the security guy wasn't being insulting when he implied he couldn't smell liquor on Skylar's breath. He was trying to let us know something is wrong. He believes Skylar is sick and so do I," I quickly added, returning the focus to Skylar, who was distressed. I touched his forehead. No fever.

Brenden put a hand on Skylar's shoulder. "What's wrong?"

Skylar shook his head, then lifted it with effort. "I don't know. I suddenly feel very tired and very nauseous." He cupped a palm over his mouth. "I want to go to my room and lie down."

Brenden nodded and then started to speak.

Quintin cleared his throat. We all looked at the unpleasant presence on our set. His gaze was focused on the clock. "They need to call time in five minutes. Then he can break for lunch and do whatever he wants."

Brenden, lips drawn into a perturbed line, squeezed Skylar's shoulder. "Do you think you can make it for a few more minutes?"

"Yeah," Skylar said through a slow, shallow breath.

"Get into place." Brenden looked at Harrison, Shannon and me. "I'll get the cameraman ready." He glared at Quintin. "Try to get this in one take."

The three of us managed to get Skylar over to the arch. Shannon had carried his chair so he could sit until it was time for us to film. Harrison helped him stand, and I looped my arm around him for support while we stood waiting for Brenden's cue.

It took all of my strength to keep us both upright while wearing the stilettos since more than half of Skylar's weight rested on me, including his head on my hair.

"My good side," Skylar whispered.

"I'll make sure. Do you think when Brenden says action you can stand straighter?"

"Yeah." The word seemed more of a breath than an answer. This was crazy. Had Quintin not been on set, Brenden would have filmed without him or called lunch.

"Ready?" Brenden asked, concern etching his features. "Courtney, you call time. Skylar try to smile. Action."

Skylar straightened but leaned against me for support. I glanced at him. Although he smiled, his eyes drooped. I hoped Brenden used the faraway camera shot for this time call. "Bakers, time's up. Step away from your counters."

"Cut. Shannon and Harrison, get ready to judge the food. Courtney, you can accompany them. Skylar, go lay down in your room." Brenden turned to Quintin. "You realize we are going to have to use the far shot on that time call."

Brenden hurried over to me when Skylar wilted on my side. "Let's get him into a UTV. I texted Drake and he said Security would be waiting to take him to the resort."

I nodded, kicked off my shoes and helped brace Skylar up. To Brenden's credit, he shifted Skylar so most of his weight fell on Brenden's shoulders. Once Skylar was strapped in with the seat belt, Brenden and I walked back to the door. I really wanted to go along to make certain Skylar managed to get to his room safe and sound, but I knew if I was missing from the set it would create consequences for Brenden and me.

"What is wrong with Quintin? Couldn't he see how ill Skylar was?"

"I'm sure he did. Quintin is only worried about money and coming in under budget. I'd hoped for a less tense shoot this time, but with him on set, that is not going to happen. We need to get inside," Brenden said, tone resigned. He picked up his pace and held the door open for me to enter.

I found my shoes and joined Harrison and Shannon beside a counter. After a once-over from my stylist, the cameraman flicked on the green light. We were moving back to front for the judging segment.

"Nadine, what did you prepare?" Harrison perused the appetizers she'd arranged on a three-tier silver serving tray.

"Well, I'm a nutritionist, so I tried to keep my appetizers healthy and tasty." Nadine burped. "Oh!" Her eyes rounded. Her hand flew to her mouth while a blush tinged her skin a bright red. "Excuse me. I'm sorry. My stomach is a little upset."

"Mine too," Carla, who got her wish and worked across the aisle from Nadine, said loudly. "I could really use some ginger ale or an antacid."

I looked from Nadine to Carla. Both women now rubbed their stomachs. Nadine slumped against her counter, skin ashen, while Carla paced the short area behind her kitchenette, face scrunched in discomfort.

"Brenden," I called. "I think we should postpone the judging. We have two contestants who feel ill."

First Skylar and now Nadine and Carla. I glanced over at the catering table. Although their symptoms weren't an exact match to what Skylar was experiencing, it didn't take long to connect the dots. Something on the serving table had poisoned them.

Chapter Five

Despite the glare Quintin shot me, Brenden hurried over to the area where we stood. "I think it's food poisoning," I whispered.

Brenden spoke to both women in hushed tones and surveyed their body language. He beckoned Kinzy over with his hand and released Nadine and Carla from the judging segment with instructions to Kinzy to get them back to the resort and see if their on-call nurse practitioner could check them out.

"Don't worry," Brenden told Nadine and Carla. "Harrison and Shannon will judge your food with you present later today if you're feeling better. No decision will be made without judging your appetizers first."

"I think I can make it," Carla said.

Brenden, lips set in a straight line, gave his head a firm shake.

After Kinzy hustled them from the room, Brenden turned to us and whispered, "If this is something other than food poisoning, like a norovirus, we'll pitch their food and they will have a chance to re-create their appetizers when they feel better. If they have a bug, the cleaning staff will have to scour all the kitchenettes. I don't want this to spread further." His eyes flicked to the area where Quintin stood. "An illness epidemic would cost quite a bit in delays." Sucking in a deep breath, Brenden squared his shoulders and walked toward Quintin.

I knew he was bracing for the worst. Quintin couldn't be so hard-hearted, or money-driven, that he'd make ill people try to cook? Or insist Shannon and Harrison taste germ-infested food?

"Yikes," Shannon drawled close to my ear. "You think they ate some bad sushi last night at the resort?"

I didn't even try to fight my smile. Shannon wasn't a fan of sushi and steered clear of that restaurant. "Food poisoning attacks a person's system faster than that." I perused the rest of the people in the room. No one else showed any signs of distress. I shrugged. "It could be a virus."

Shannon drew her mouth into a grim line and swallowed hard. "I don't have time to get sick."

Her and me both.

After his short conversation with Quintin, Brenden inquired on how the remaining contestants and crew felt, which was healthy, so we resumed the judging segment.

Michael displayed his creations on faux Acadia cutting boards with rugged edges. It fit perfectly with his choice of appetizers.

"What did you make for us?" Harrison perused his boards.

"Sausage pinwheels, cremini pizza and buffalo chicken bites."

"I like your presentation." Shannon pointed to the pinwheels. "You rolled your dough and filling to make a perfect pinwheel design, the exact ratio of filling to dough. Did you hand-make the individual crusts for the pizza?"

"Yes, I find it easier to pinch up the edges to hold the sauce and filling." Michael tried to stick his hands into his pockets. His apron prohibited the gesture, so he moved them behind his back, showing off the frilly bride's dress screen printed on the apron. A comical contrast to his gray-bearded face.

"Well, you made them all the same shape and size, which is quite a feat by hand. I like your presentation of the buffalo chicken resting on French bread rounds and topped with a spear of celery. Very nice. Very colorful. Very eye-pleasing. Let's see how they taste." Harrison started with a sausage pinwheel. Shannon followed his lead.

I noted the small, almost miniscule, bites Shannon took, obviously trying to safeguard herself from contracting a virus or food poisoning. Harrison seemed brave in comparison. He popped the entire bite-size appetizer in his mouth. Both of them liked all three of the offerings, but suggested Michael toast the French bread in the future to avoid the base soaking up so much sauce, which created too much heat. Both needed more celery to crunch on after their tasting.

I pinched off a piece of a pinwheel and gave it a taste. Delicious. I took the rest and moved to the next kitchen station behind Harrison and Shannon.

Lynne wowed us with roasted golden beet and goat cheese crostini, egg and bacon canapés, and grilled eggplant and tomato stacks until, that is, Harrison and Shannon tried them.

"They're visually aesthetic." Harrison pointed to the colorful arrangement on a large rectangular silver serving platter. "And we do eat with our eyes; however, your eggplant isn't done." He put the appetizer he tried on a napkin on the counter.

"My eggplant is done." Shannon finished her sample. "It lacks seasoning, though. You need much more salt on the tomato. Pepper, oregano or basil would season this well too."

"The problem is your slices of eggplant aren't consistent. Mine was thicker and required more grilling time. Shannon is correct on the lack of seasoning. It's mandatory a cook test their food for the proper seasoning before serving." Harrison waggled a scolding finger.

"Your other appetizers taste good. You definitely have an eye for a colorful plate," Shannon said, and received a tentative smile and thoughtful nod from Lynne.

We breezed through the next eight contestants. Donna, Alex and Jeremiah received a chiding for making common appetizers that could be found on any franchise restaurant menu. Harrison then challenged them to stretch their culinary muscles with new ingredients. Afton drew praise for a roasted butternut squash, cranberry and soft herb cheese served in a slice of endive. Diego and the Smiths made excellent appetizers that reflected their ethnicity, which both judges and I appreciated and, sadly, had expected from Marco.

"This is disappointing." Harrison slid the plain ceramic tray on which Marco displayed his fare back away from the counter.

Shannon drew her brows together. "Everything has

run together. Did you put too much filling in your spaghetti cups, or not drain the pasta properly?" She lifted a corner of the tray and the watery liquid flowed downward.

"None of this can be eaten with your fingers. Your sauce soaked into the bottoms of your antipasto sandwich and your crostini base on your eggplant parmigiana. Not to mention, the spaghetti cup can't hold its shape." Harrison lifted the appetizer. The bottom gave way and the meatball in the center fell out. Harrison turned around. "We'll need a plate and utensils to try this food."

A crew member scurried to provide the requested table setting. Both Shannon and Harrison tasted a bite of each appetizer.

"Your sauce is lovely, but not on everything." Shannon placed the fork back on the plate.

Harrison shook his head while drawing his lips into a thin line. "I really would have liked to have tasted your appetizers before you plated them. I was intrigued by the spaghetti and meatball cups. It's a unique idea for an appetizer."

"I'm sorry," Marco said. Neither his tone nor his expression were apologetic. Both leaned toward anger.

Brenden cut the segment before anyone could say anything else. He released us all for lunch. The contestants, minus Nadine and Carla, were hurried out the side exit to wherever it was they ate their meals at the resort. The crew descended upon the catering tables while Shannon and I quick changed our clothes so we could join Eric on the set of *Cooking with the Farmer's Daughter*. He said he'd order takeout from the steak house.

We chose to walk since the breeze created by the UTVs would mess up our fancy hair. The late-September temperature was a perfect seventy degrees. A few of the leaves on the trees teased us with splotches of red and gold, a promise of the variety of color soon to dot the valley of the Pocono Mountains range. I hoped to leaf-peek toward the end of our filming schedule, which ran into the first week of October. The airing of the wedding edition of the baking competition was planned for January to coincide with the dates of many bridal fairs and wedding expos.

"Believe it or not, I'm starving," Shannon said. "Let's pick up our pace."

I laughed and did as instructed. "I'm not surprised. You nibbled today."

"Well, I'm trying to stay healthy. I can't believe as finicky as Harrison is about eating with his fingers and getting germs, he ate such large samples of the food."

We stopped conversing and concentrated on speed walking. The sunshine warmed our faces, the pace our bodies. I hoped our activity didn't mess up our hair. My feet loved the comfort of my athletic shoes, yet still stinging under the stiletto morning abuse, a slower pace would have made them and my French twist happier. Once we entered the building, we made a straight line for the conference room suite that housed my set.

"I'm famished." Shannon puffed out the words on a heavy breath from our fast pace.

"You should have eaten bigger bites of the appetizers," I chuckled while using my key card to unlock the door. The light flashed green and I turned the knob.

Eric and Pamela sat side by side on the front row of the audience chairs. They perused Eric's tablet, heads together and laughing.

"Hi." My greeting silenced what I'd call flirty banter.

"Courtney! Shannon!" Eric's welcome held a high level of surprise. Pamela nodded with a smile stretching from ear to ear.

My mouth puckered, I looked around the room. "Where's lunch?"

"Well, um . . . we." Eric looked at Pamela and smiled. "We lost track of time." He stood, tucking his tablet under his arm. "I didn't get lunch ordered."

"What?" Shannon's tone, raised and snappy, verified she was hangry.

My disgruntlement had little to do with food and a lot to do with the green-eyed monster living inside me. Our set wasn't that big. We limit the studio audience to fifty. What were they doing to lose track of time? And what were those guilty smiles all about? And why was his sports coat off? He always wore it when he was working with someone, other than me, to project professionalism. He'd rolled up the long sleeves of his green button-up shirt, too.

"We can go to Castle Grounds. They have a soup and sandwich special today," Eric said. He walked toward my counter area and retrieved his sports coat from where he'd draped it. Then he remembered his sleeves, laid it back down and began unrolling the fabric.

"How do you know that?" He didn't bring me a hazelnut latte from the coffee shop this morning before I left for the set.

"I saw it on the menu board when Pam and I went for coffee."

What? The green-eyed monster inside me roared. I felt cheated on. *I* was his morning cup of coffee partner.

"Courtney?" Eric asked.

"Sure, let's go." My words were clipped. I'd tried to tamp down my emotions. I failed.

Eric turned to Pamela. "You are welcome to join us."

"Thank you." Pamela stood. "I'd love to." She smoothed her hand over her slacks, then her hair.

Why did he do that? For some reason I wanted to slap the happy smile off of both of their faces. I had to get a grip on the monster within. Shannon flashing a what's-up-with-them look in my direction didn't help me rein those negative emotions to a stop.

Silence ensued on the short walk to Castle Grounds. Eric led the way while Pamela trailed behind. Since fewer reservations were made at the resort, we sped through the ordering and pickup line and had our choice of tables. We chose to sit beside the stone fireplace that ran up the length of one wall. It would be a cozy spot in the winter beside a crackling fire.

Eric, gentleman that he is, waited for us to unload our trays, and carried the empties back to the counter to give us more room. Shannon dug right into her chicken salad on wheat, pushing her broccoli cheddar soup to the side. Pamela and I both chose minestrone with a half of a gourmet grilled cheese, brie and apricot on brioche. Eric went with tomato bisque and a classic grilled cheese, American on white bread.

When we were settled and tucked into our lunch, Pamela smiled at me. "Eric showed me the layout of your set. Other than disabling the door so people can enter from the staff hallway, I think we have your set secured."

Henry Cole had built a secret passage into his home for his use to get back and forth to his workshop. The resort uses it as a staff hallway to aid with keeping the guest hallways uncluttered with catering and housekeeping carts. Last season, the thought hadn't really occurred to me as to why Henry Cole would have a secret passageway in his home. Did he need it to elude robbers? Or were his business dealings unscrupulous? A bit of trivia worth researching in my spare time.

"Courtney."

I turned to Eric and read his warning expression. He wanted me to reply.

"That's great. Although I doubt we'll have the same trouble as last time." I mean, what were the chances of another murder? I forced a smile.

Pamela shot me a reassuring look. "Better safe than sorry. Drake insisted I keep an eye on you."

No, Sheriff Perry did. I almost wished something would happen at the resort so I could have a little talk with the sheriff about me and trouble. I'd be lying if I didn't admit it hurt my feelings a little bit. I wanted to lash out at Pamela. Not because Sheriff Perry considered me trouble, more because Eric kept looking at her with a silly grin on his face.

Shannon, always astute to the situation, except with her observation of Eric having a romantic interest in me, interceded the conversation before I could make a snide comment. "Tell us about yourself, Pamela."

"I grew up in a farming community."

Of course, she did.

"My mother was in law enforcement, county sheriff. I wanted to follow in her footsteps, except in a city."

My ears perked up. This was not how I guessed the conversation would go. "So, it didn't work out for you to get on a force somewhere?"

Pamela finished chewing. "It did. I was a beat cop in

Chicago before I applied for a position with the FBI. That's where I met Drake."

"A beat cop in Chicago? That's where I grew up."

She smiled. "I know. I love it there. The food, the culture." Her tone turned wistful.

The same reasons I enjoyed living in the heart of my hometown. "You still live in Chicago?"

"Yes, I have a condo downtown."

"You have a lot in common." Eric broke into the conversation. Even though he was talking to me, he was looking at Pamela.

"So I'm learning." I smiled at Pamela and my newfound knowledge of her background was making it difficult to dislike her. "So, did you get a position with the FBI?"

"Yes, I worked on Drake's team until I was shot."

"What?" Shannon exclaimed.

"Took a bullet in the leg and decided I was done."

"I'm impressed." The awe in my voice was sincere.

"Thanks." Pamela shrugged off the compliment. "This soup was delicious."

"I agree." I turned to Shannon. "Do you think Skylar would appreciate some soup since he wasn't feeling well? We'd have time to take it to him."

She nodded.

I whipped out my phone and sent him a text. "Do you think he was acting funny?"

"Most people do when they don't feel well."

"I meant before. Did he seem nervous or on edge to you?"

She didn't have time to answer. My phone started to ring. I looked down. "It's Skylar. I bet he wants to know the flavors of the day. Hello?"

"Courtney? Horrible. Something. You come?"

"Skylar? What's wrong?"

"Help. I need help."

The line went dead.

"Something is wrong with Skylar. He's incoherent." I stood while slipping my phone into my jacket pocket.

"Let's go." Shannon jumped up.

We left our lunch mess with Eric and Pamela at the table and hurried to the elevators. Riding up to the fourth floor, we hoped he was housed in the same suite as last time like we were. We rounded a corner from the elevator shaft.

Skylar sat on the floor, slumped over a wastebasket. The door of his room stood ajar.

"I think we need to call the front desk and see about getting him to the nearest clinic," I called over my shoulder as Shannon and I ran toward him.

"Skylar!"

When Shannon called his name, it took effort, but he lifted his head. Blood covered the left side of his face and was matted in his hair. Crimson stained his clothing all down one side. Eyes wide and full of fear, he stared at me. He shook his head slowly. "I don't know . . . need help . . ." His words came on huffed breaths.

Had he fallen and cracked his head? It would explain the blood and disorientation.

Skylar lifted a finger and pointed at the door to his room. A wave of nausea must have come over him. He buried his face in the wastebasket and retched.

My heart sank. Once we reached him, we saw the blood covering him looked dried or at least not flowing. What had happened in his room? Walking around Skylar, I toed open the door. Peeking around the door, I saw a pool of blood on the carpet and smears of blood across the floor where Skylar crawled to the door. I lifted my gaze to a five-tier wedding cake sitting on the coffee table.

The round tiers, smashed and broken, leaned to one side because the cake topper was too heavy. Push-in pillars littered the floor. Instead of an ornate or thematic decoration sitting atop the smallest layer, someone placed a bride across the cake.

Decked out in a gorgeous wedding gown, the young woman lay faceup askew in the confection like she'd fallen asleep in a bed of buttercream. Judging from the pool of blood on the floor and the knife stabbed into her chest, she wasn't snoozing.

She was dead.

Chapter Six

I heard Shannon murmuring words of comfort to Skylar. "Shannon, don't touch him." I shouted louder than necessary as I backed away from the door.

"Okay." She drawled out the word. "What's wrong?"

Slipping my phone from my pocket, my eyes met hers.

"I recognize that look, Courtney. He didn't fall and crack his head against a piece of furniture, did he?" She stood from her squatted position in front of Skylar.

I shook my head. I'd learned my lesson last season when I dialed 911 before alerting Drake. Hand shaking, I texted Drake. I kept my message brief by saying there was a serious situation in Skylar's room.

"Bad, bad, bad." Skylar's eyes beseeched me, then Shannon. "I didn't . . ."

"I know." I hoped my tone didn't reflect my shock or

the panic gnawing at my insides. Seeing another dead body wasn't in my itinerary for the day. "Drake will be here soon. He'll know what to do."

The slide of the elevator doors opening pulled Shannon and my attention to the hallway. Pamela rounded the corner on a run, gun pulled. She stopped short in front of Skylar. After a quick perusal of his condition, she jerked her head toward the opposite wall. "Back away from him."

"But," Shannon started to protest. I grabbed her arm and stepped us both back against the opposite wall, then down a foot or so to keep the pathway open.

We watched Pamela peek around the door of the room in almost the same manner I had. Still, except for the movement of her head, she checked out Skylar's room, then backed out into the hallway.

I wasn't sure if Skylar had fallen asleep, blacked out or was too weak to hold his head upright. He slumped even farther down the wall. Limp-necked, his head hung over his right shoulder.

Holstering her gun, Pamela replaced it with her cell phone and dialed. "Drake, it's a crime scene. Bring yellow tape and gather enough staff to head off anyone else staying on the fourth floor." She ended the call, slipped her phone into its holder and squatted down beside Skylar.

"Mr. Daily? Mr. Daily, can you hear me?"

Lifting his head, Skylar looked at Pamela through heavy-lidded eyes. "I don't feel good. I need to change clothes. My room." He didn't finish his sentence. He couldn't finish his sentence. It was all he could do to lift the wastebasket before his stomach turned over again.

The slide of the elevator door alerted us that someone arrived. I turned to see Drake jogging down the hall. His gaze roved the area, resting on Skylar. "What do we have?"

"Possible homicide." Pamela jerked her head toward the cracked-open door. She stood back to allow Drake to take in the gruesome scene.

He stood in the doorway several minutes before turning around. "How long have you been here?" His gaze went from me to Shannon.

"Maybe five minutes."

I backed Shannon's answer with several nods of my head.

"Why are you here?"

My turn to answer. "Skylar called me asking for help." I held up my cell phone. "Do you need to check the time of our calls and the time now?" I'd made this recipe once before and knew the ingredients needed to check an alibi.

Drake's eyes moved to Shannon.

"I was with her. We were both worried since he didn't feel well and left the set earlier."

Before Drake could ask another question, Pamela cleared her throat. "The call came in while the four of us were having lunch in the coffee shop."

Drake turned to Pamela. "Four?"

"Eric Iverson, Shannon, Courtney and me."

"Okay, good. Pamela, take these two down to our offices and get their statements. I'm going to call Sheriff Perry. I'll keep the area secure until he arrives."

I stepped forward. "What about Skylar?"

"He stays put."

"But he's sick. I think he needs to see a doctor."

Drake shot me an are-you-kidding-me look before saying, “Procedure.”

“Let’s go, ladies.” Pamela sounded more like we were going to have a girl’s night out than give her an official statement.

A fellow security officer allowed us access to the elevator. The last thing we heard as the doors closed was Skylar retching. The situation started to sink in during the short ride to the first floor. A woman, in a bridal gown, had been murdered in Skylar’s room. Had Skylar committed the murder? He was covered with blood. Yet, could Skylar murder anyone? He was squeamish. More than squeamish, blood or the smell of it made him physically ill, as evidenced in the hallway. I tried to come up with a logical scenario of what took place in the resort suite, but instead a million questions popped into my mind. Had he opened the door and found the scene? Did he slip in the blood trying to get to the wastebasket to retch in? How long had he sat in the hall vomiting before he made the plea for help? How did the woman get into his room?

I continued to run through a list of questions on the short walk down the hallway to the suites where Drake headquartered his offices. Pamela motioned for us to sit down. She clicked on a recording device and took the chair across the table from us. “I’m going to ask a question. Shannon, you respond first, Courtney, second. Okay?”

We nodded.

“You both need to agree verbally.” She pointed toward the microphone.

“Okay,” we said in unison, which I’m sure was all right since we had distinctly different-sounding voices.

"Tell me what happened."

"Well." Shannon cleared her throat. "We finished lunch at Castle Grounds. Courtney wondered if Skylar would like soup. She texted him. He called her. She said he was sick and asked for help. We ran up to his room and found him in the hallway."

"I texted Skylar to see if he wanted some soup. He called me back. He was incoherent, not making any sense. When he finally said the word "help," I ended the call. I told Shannon, Eric and *you*." I stressed the last word because it seemed redundant to me to be telling Pamela something she already knew. "We hurried to Skylar's suite and found him sitting in the hallway, vomiting in a wastebasket and partially covered in blood. It was so odd that only one side of him was covered in blood. Do you think he slipped and fell into the puddle on the floor?"

"Ewww." Shannon sniffled. "That would be horrible to fall into blood. Good catch, Courtney."

"She didn't catch anything," Pamela said with a dry tone, then pointed. "I don't want your questions or theories. I need your statement of events leading up to and after you reached Skylar's room. What happened after you arrived in the hallway?"

"We both ran to Skylar. When he turned, I saw the blood on his clothes. He still didn't make sense to me, but Courtney figured out something was wrong in his room and looked."

I took my turn. "I didn't notice the blood until I was closer to Skylar. I was at a different angle than Shannon. I knew something was wrong. At first, I thought he'd fallen and maybe knocked his head on something since he really made no sense when he spoke. When he uttered the word 'room,' I peeked inside the door and saw the dead bride on top of a wedding cake. There was an odd squiggle, like a half-coiled snake, on the bottom layer of the smashed cake, which appeared to be white with raspberry filling. It wasn't any type of cake decoration patterns that I'm familiar with and it didn't match the other piping on the cake, which struck me as odd on a cake covered in smooth fondant with buttercream flowers and no other frosting designs."

Pamela covered the microphone. "I know you make your living from cooking and notice details in cooking and baking, but we don't need a description of the cake, just the facts about what you saw. Got it?" Annoyance edged her tone. She lifted her hand.

I crossed my arms over my chest. "I saw a woman wearing a bridal gown laying on a five-tier wedding cake who I presumed was dead because she had a serrated cake knife stuck through her heart and a huge puddle of blood on the floor." If she wanted facts, there they were in a nutshell.

"Oh my God."

Whoops! I forgot Shannon had no idea what lay behind Skylar's door. Never once did she ask what was inside his room. She probably didn't want to know. I turned to my friend. The color had drained from her face, turning the blusher on her cheeks into red blotches. She'd placed a hand over her heart. When her eyes met mine, a sheen of moisture hazed her baby blues.

Sorry. I mouthed the words since we were being recorded.

"So, you didn't look into the room?" Pamela directed her question at Shannon.

"No." Shannon sniffled a little. "If you think Skylar murdered her, think again. He can't handle gore." She covered her mouth with her fingers and appeared to be on the verge of tears.

"I agree. Skylar has a weak stomach. Sheriff Perry and Drake can vouch for that." He'd found bloody evidence last season and didn't handle it well.

"Okay." Pamela looked at us. "Last question, did either of you notice anything strange about Skylar today or yesterday? Other than being ill, anything out of character?"

"No." Shannon choked out the word on a sob.

My stomach flipped, then flopped. I did notice and what I noticed could be incriminating. Although I hated to, I had to tell the truth. "Skylar seemed nervous, always looking over his shoulder. He didn't do that last season."

"So, you think something was troubling him?"

I nodded. Pamela pointed to the microphone. "Yes."

"Anything else?"

I sighed loud enough it'd be caught on tape. There was something else. I knew if I told the truth, I wouldn't be helping Skylar. Instead, I'd be giving the authorities possible incriminating evidence against him. Did I really want to do that?

Pamela stared at me waiting for me to continue.

I caved. "Yes, he seemed to have an aversion to the wedding-themed show."

"Can you elaborate?"

I could. Again, I didn't really want to. I wasn't helping Skylar. I knew from experience none of this looked good for him. In my heart, I knew Skylar wasn't a killer, yet the evidence seemed to point right at him.

"Courtney, please elaborate?" Pamela showed no signs of irritation or urgency now. I glanced at Shannon before I looked at Pamela. "He said that women get too wrapped up in wedding planning and it was just one day."

After a moment of silence, Pamela asked, "Anything else?" Her facial expression was unchanged.

"No." I knew better than to elaborate on my theory of why Skylar disliked weddings, a broken heart. My stomach knotted. Brokenhearted people sometimes did crazy things. It's where the term "crime of passion" originated. Since I only speculated, I didn't share my thoughts with her.

Pamela turned off the recording device. "Someone will type this up and you'll need to sign it."

"Can we go now?" Shannon asked.

"Not until Drake arrives and gives me the okay. Would you like anything to drink? We have bad coffee, water and a couple of different kinds of soda." Pamela smiled at us. "Good job on the statements. I'll add a line that you were dining with me at the time the call came through. In addition, once we know the time of death, we can check your whereabouts. There is no reason to worry. I doubt either of you will be added to the persons of interest list."

"Good to know." Shannon flashed me a look conveying her astonishment of why we'd even be considered.

Before either of us could respond, our phones jingled in unison, my alert a birdsong, Shannon's wind chimes. Pulling them from our jacket pockets, we read the message.

"We need to go." Shannon started to push away from the table.

I held my phone up for Pamela to see. "Kinzy is texting wondering where we are. We were supposed to report back to set ten minutes ago."

Pamela shrugged her shoulders. "You can't leave until Drake gets here."

"Drake is here." Drake walked through the door, followed by Skylar, still in blood-covered clothes, with another Nolan Security staff member bringing up the rear. "What's the problem?"

"We're supposed to be on set." Shannon stood. "Are we free to leave?"

"You can sit over there." Drake pointed out a chair to Skylar, then looked at us. "You aren't free to leave."

"Can we text Kinzy back?" I asked.

"I'll call Brenden." Drake pulled his phone from the case on his belt. His conversation seemed one-sided while he basically told Brenden there was a situation concerning Skylar and he needed to postpone filming for at least one hour. As an afterthought, he added that Shannon and I were with him. He listened for about thirty seconds, gave a short snort and said, "I don't care what he wants to do, postpone your filming for an hour." Brenden was still speaking when Drake ended the call.

Poor Brenden now had to deal with Quintin.

"Courtney." Skylar croaked out my name.

I walked over to where he sat. "Do you need some water or ginger ale?"

He nodded. To my surprise, Pamela stood, then walked over to a small refrigerator and retrieved a water. She walked to Skylar and handed it over. Looking at me, she said, "Don't touch him."

"I won't." After I gave Pamela my assurance, she went

over to where Drake sat behind a long table with a computer and printer setup.

"Is it all right if I take a call from my husband?" Shannon asked. She slipped back onto the chair where we'd given our statements.

"Yes," Drake said. "Don't discuss the current situation."

While Skylar quenched his thirst with about half the bottle of water, I wondered how long it'd stay down. Still covered in blood, although dryer and darker than before, he did have an unpleasant odor. I'm sure they needed to photograph him and bag his clothes. Maybe saying blood-covered clothes was an overstatement. There were no splatters of blood on him or his clothes. Instead, it mostly covered his left side, like it'd been poured over him.

I flashed back to the scene. Had I seen any blood splatters?

"How do you do it?"

I turned my attention back to Skylar just in time to see him scrunch his face and hold his stomach. I looked around, spotted a kitchen garbage can and ran for it. I got it to Skylar in time for his stomach to relieve itself of the water he'd just drank.

Trying to give him as much privacy as I could, I looked around the coffeepot for napkins. When it sounded safe, I rejoined Skylar, giving him a napkin to wipe his mouth. "What did you ask me?"

"I can't un-see the horrific scene in my room. It's there when my eyes are open or closed." He shivered. "It's horrible. Who did that to her?" Again, his eyes beseeched me.

"I don't know." I knew he was in shock. He didn't realize the authorities would think he did it.

"How do you do it? Look at dead bodies and not feel ill?"

First, I wanted to tell Skylar I'd looked at only two dead bodies in my life and not by choice. I'd been looking for my cherry cobbler when I found Bernard Stone murdered by blunt force trauma. Occasionally, I still saw his vacant staring eye in my dreams. I'd been trying to help Skylar, when I got a glimpse of my second. Hmm. I closed my eyes to think hard. I don't think the victim's eyes were open. In my mind I retraced my steps. I toed open the door and peered around it. Blood and smashed bits of cake littered the floor. The woman laid on top of the cake, arms limp and hanging down each side. The serrated knife protruded from her chest, and blood soaked the bodice of the dress. Her head rested on a tier of the cake, her eyes were closed and her face placid, like she was sleeping. Could that be right?

"Courtney."

My name jarred me from my thoughts. I looked at Skylar.

"I'm sorry if I brought up bad memories."

I realized my expression might have shown my puzzlement and Skylar mistook it for me being upset.

"Can you go to my room and get me a change of clothes?"

"Your room is a crime scene." Drake walked over and stood beside me. "Mr. Daily, we'll contact wardrobe to have them bring your clothing. I'm assuming the tux is a costume for the show. Shannon and Courtney, I listened to your statements. You are free to go. I am sure Sheriff Perry is going to want to talk to you."

With a hand to the small of my back, Drake guided me away from Skylar and motioned for Shannon, who was still on the phone, to head out. By the time she joined us beside the door, she'd ended her call.

"Sheriff Perry's people are on the scene. If your phone rings, answer it. Want one of my staff to give you a ride back to the set?"

"No, thank you. I don't know about Courtney, but I need to walk."

"Walking is a great idea. Bye." I waved at Drake, and once he closed the door, I pulled my phone from my pocket and immediately texted Eric to meet us by the coffee shop exit. For one thing, I thought he might be worried, although he hadn't texted me. Second, Eric was the first person I wanted to talk to in times of trouble or celebration.

He waited at a table by the door when we reached Castle Grounds. Three coffees sat in front of him. He lifted a cup and handed it off to Shannon. "Plain latte with skim milk. And for you, hazelnut."

I sipped the rich brew. "This is just what I needed." The smooth nutty java comforted my frazzled nerves.

Eric pinned me with a look. "Did I forget to tell you to stay out of trouble?"

"We'll tell you about it on the way to the set." Shannon pushed through the door. Eric and I followed.

Shannon and I relayed what we knew. Silence ensued while Eric digested the information. He sipped his own coffee, then said, "What are the odds of two murders happening in the same location while filming the same television show?"

"Slim to none?" Shannon asked.

Both of their questions raised more in my mind. Was this a copycat killer? Someone who saw the news coverage last time and wanted in on the action? If that was the case, how did the person know about the show's wedding theme? Was the murderer employed by the show? Had the murderer chosen a random room or targeted Skylar?

I swallowed hard when a thought popped into my mind. It seemed too coincidental that Skylar hated weddings and a bride was murdered in his room. As much as I wanted to deny it, somehow, someway, Skylar factored into this murder.

Chapter Seven

"I am just so glad this 'incident'"—Brenden air-quoted the word and cast a nervous glance at Quintin—"didn't happen on the set this time."

Shannon and I had bid Eric goodbye and changed back into our wedding finery with assistance from our stylist, who also gave our updos a quick smooth and spritz. Now, we stood under the arch on set, toes on appropriate colored tape, waiting for Brenden to cue us to start the next challenge. He'd rescripted the challenge opening, giving me all of the cohost lines.

"Why are we calling illness an incident? And it did happen on set." Harrison knitted his brows in confusion. Shannon and I exchanged a look behind him. Had no one told him what had happened in the resort? Namely, Skylar's room?

"What's the holdup?" Quintin's voice boomed from the wings of the set. Hands stuffed into his trouser pockets, he paced back and forth.

Brenden jerked his head toward Quintin. "Almost ready." He turned back to us, lips drawn into a perturbed line. "We aren't that far behind schedule. Everyone understand their lines?" Brenden addressed all of us, but he was talking to me because I had the only part that had changed. I nodded.

"Great." Brenden hurried out of the camera shot. "Action."

"The second challenge of the day was chosen by our judges." I smiled. It was clearly a lie because I knew the challenge and there was no way Harrison would choose this type of food. "So, I'll let them issue it."

Harrison smiled my way, then back into the camera. "Your second challenge is to prepare a finger food main—"

"Cut!" Brenden hollered. "You grimaced on the words 'finger food.' We'll pick up from your line. Action."

Harrison started again. Brenden cut again for the same reason two more times. Quintin headed toward Brenden on the fourth cut. "What is the problem?"

"I don't believe in finger food for the main entrée." Harrison wrinkled his nose. "We are dressed formal, and who wants to eat their wedding dinner with their fingers?"

Quintin frowned.

Before he could respond, Harrison added, "You should check with us before issuing a challenge that you say the judges chose."

The corners of Quintin's lips drew down farther, deepening his frown. Anger blazed in his eyes.

Before he could say anything, Brenden injected, "We'll flop the lines. Shannon, you take Harrison's. Harrison, you read hers. Pick it up from the top."

Quintin remained beside Brenden. Brenden cued up the action. Shannon read the line flawlessly with a bright smile. Harrison explained the nutritional value and that the entrée must be larger than an appetizer. When they both looked at me, I said, "The baking begins now."

"Cut, great." Brenden smiled our way. Quintin rolled his eyes behind Brenden's back, letting the talent know his true feelings.

Harrison huffed. He stepped off his mark. "This is nonsense." He stared at Quintin, who'd turned to watch the contestants hustle to make their entrée in the allotted time. "Did the nurse practitioner check out Skylar? The two contestants received medical care and made it back to the set." Harrison indicated their presence with a wave of his arm. "I'm concerned."

"You obviously haven't heard." Shannon made no attempt to lower her voice. Instead it seemed to amplify through the high-ceilinged building. "A woman was found dead in Skylar's room."

All noise on the set ceased. Wide-eyed, the crew and some of the contestants stared our way. Finally, a male voice broke the silence. "Did you say there was another murder?"

My gaze followed the voice and landed on Marco, who wore a lopsided grin.

"Keep cooking." Quintin, jaw clenched, growled out the order to the group. A few of the contestants shrugged and fidgeted with the items in front of them. The crew looked to Brenden.

"No, everyone stop working and listen." Brenden stepped away from Quintin and closer to the kitchenettes. "We are going to take a minute and tell everyone what we know." He cast a hard look over his shoulder. Quintin closed his gaping mouth and took a step back.

"A situation has happened at Coal Castle Resort. We don't know all of the details, but we have been told there was a loss of life."

A loud bang sounded through the silent room, startling most of us with a jerk of our bodies. All eyes turned to the door and Sheriff Milton Perry, who'd thrown it open. "If you are filming, stop. I need Shannon and Courtney to come with me." His barked-out order echoed through the large room.

Brenden held up his hands. "We aren't filming. We were just alerting everyone to what is happening."

Sheriff Perry stopped beside me and tugged the waist of his uniform pants up a few inches on the paunch of his belly. He wore his signature cap with the County Law Enforcement emblem emblazoned on it. He'd had a haircut since the last time I'd seen him because it no longer curled over his cap band. He looked over his plastic framed glasses at me and quirked a brow. "Even when I assign someone to watch you, you still find trouble."

Annoyance stirred inside of me. "Nice to see you again too, Sheriff Perry." I flavored my tone with sarcasm.

He gave me a wan smile and turned to Brenden. "You need to postpone filming until tomorrow unless you can do it minus three of your stars. They will be tied up the rest of the day giving my team statements."

"Would you address our group, so we all know what is happening?" Brenden asked.

"Sure." Sheriff Perry hitched the waist of his uniform pants again. "A female was found dead in the resort." Sheriff Perry went on despite a collection of gasps. "There is an active homicide investigation. Parts of the resort are off-limits to guests. I doubt it will affect most of you since you are not housed with the network stars."

Lynne held up her hand.

"I'm not taking any questions." Sheriff Perry turned to Brenden. "Close it down for a day."

Quintin didn't allow Brenden to answer or give an order. He stepped toe-to-toe with Sheriff Perry. "That is unacceptable. We have altered our filming day in consideration of Mr. Daily and the incident. They can make their statements after we've ended our work for the day."

"Who are you?" Sheriff Perry puckered his lips to the side.

"Quintin Shepherd, the producer of this show." Quintin made no motion to hold out his hand for a shake.

With a slight nod of his head, Sheriff Perry appeared to be considering Quintin's position or request. I wasn't sure which. "I see." He pinned Quintin with a hard stare. "Shut it down. We need their statements now."

Brenden looked at the contestants and crew. "It's a wrap. Report to the set tomorrow morning at the normal hour."

Kinzy corralled the group to the door the contestants used. There were hushed whispers and stolen glances our way. Except for Marco. He trailed behind and intently watched our group. When his eyes met mine, he flashed me a smug smile.

What is that all about?

"You have no authority to stop our filming," Quintin declared, drawing my attention away from Marco. Incensed, Quintin pointed a finger in Sheriff Perry's face. Used to giving orders, Quintin was having trouble taking them. Surely, he understood the gravity of the situation. And that Sheriff Perry was the law.

Sheriff Perry didn't flinch. He fixed his stare on Quintin. "I can arrest you for obstructing justice, you know." Threat edged his tone.

In a huff, Quintin pushed past us and stalked out the workshop door.

I heard a muffled chuckle before Sheriff Perry turned to Shannon and me. "I need a formal statement from both of you." He looked us up and down. "Not that formal, though. I suggest you change into something more comfortable. You have five minutes."

A deputy transported Sheriff Perry, Shannon and me from the set to the resort in a UTV; the sheriff rode shotgun while Shannon and I bumped along on a back-bench seat. All of this felt too familiar.

Sheriff Perry had commandeered the same set of conference suites he and his deputies used for their offices last time. He escorted us through the door. Skylar sat on a chair beside a table. His head rested on his bent arms with a half-full plastic cup of ginger ale beside him. Someone had wardrobe bring his clothes from the set—jeans and a plaid shirt. He'd also been allowed to shower.

"Have a seat while I get set up." Sheriff Perry nodded toward a conference table.

"Skylar." Shannon sat on the opposite side of the table, reached across and squeezed his hand. I took the chair beside her.

Skylar lifted his head and looked up at us. Pale and drawn, his chiseled features showed the stress of illness and the situation.

"Would anyone like something to drink?" Sheriff Perry asked while pouring himself a cup of coffee from a catering carafe.

"Water?" I asked since he offered no choices and I saw several plastic pitchers filled with ice and water.

"Me too," Shannon said.

Sheriff Perry poured waters and brought them to the table. He retrieved his coffee and entered an adjoining room. I assumed he needed recording equipment for our statement.

"What do you remember?" I asked Skylar before taking a sip of water.

"I wasn't feeling well. I went to find Drake to warn him."

"Warn him?" Shannon and I looked at him. "About what?" I asked.

"Yeah, I found Drake to warn him. He didn't take me seriously, which made me angry. He should have listened to me." Skylar stopped and shivered.

Did he notice he didn't answer my question? Had he avoided it on purpose?

"I came back to the set and I felt so sick, dizzy, tired and nauseous." Skylar's demeanor brightened like a turned-on lightbulb. He looked at me. "You and Brenden put me in a vehicle to come back to the resort. Thank you."

I nodded and hoped my expression would encourage him to continue since this is the part of the story that was missing for Shannon and me.

"He dropped me by the coffee shop entrance. I stumbled through the area. I think I might have bumped into a woman. No, a man, or was it a table on my way through." Skylar focused his eyes on the ceiling while rubbing his left temple.

"What happened then?" I hoped my question urged him to continue before Sheriff Perry came back. It was obvious his shock hadn't worn off.

"I got into the elevator, pressed the button and got out at my floor. I struggled to stay upright, so I leaned against the hallway wall as I walked. I knew if I could just lay down, I'd feel better."

"Did you?" Shannon asked.

Skylar scrunched his features in confusion. He didn't understand her simple question.

"Lay down," I added.

He shrugged. "The next thing I remember, my phone rang. I fished the phone from my pocket. It was Kinzy." His eyes widened. "Do you know what she wanted?"

I checked my urge to grimace. If Skylar gave his official statement in the same manner, it wouldn't look good for him. "To call you back to the set."

"Oh. I never returned her call. The sheriff took my phone."

"It's okay. They know where you are." Shannon squeezed his hand again. Distress marred her features at his inability to concentrate.

"Where were you when Kinzy called?" I asked, trying to prompt him again.

Skylar gagged. "Laying on the floor by the coffee table in my suite. When I realized I was on the edge of a pool of blood, I jumped up. Then I saw the body." Skylar gagged again and looked around the room.

I spotted a wastebasket and ran for it. By the time I brought it back to the table, Skylar seemed to have regained control of his squeamish tummy. "How do you do it?"

My shoulders sagged. He'd asked me this before, so I knew what he meant. "I have a stronger stomach, I guess. What happened after you saw the body?" I gentled my tone.

"I tried to run from the room, but slipped. I crawled then and collapsed where you found me."

"How long were you there?"

"I don't know. She had . . ." He swallowed hard. "A knife. So much blood." His eyes widened. "Bathroom!" He ran and exited the conference room.

"I don't think he should have left."

"He has permission to use the restroom down the hall. The deputy at the door will watch him." Sheriff Perry had entered the room. I don't know when; I never heard the door open and close. Perhaps he'd left it open a crack and eavesdropped on us.

I pressed my luck. "Did Skylar tell us the same thing he told you?"

In a rare moment, Sheriff Perry smiled. "He did. Touché, Miss Archer. Now, I'd like to hear from both of you." Shannon and I recanted the same information we gave Pamela a couple of hours ago. Time had not diminished or added to our memory of the events. We'd wrapped up the statement when Skylar reentered the room, a fresh can of ginger ale in his hand.

"He took me to the bar." He threw his thumb over his shoulder to point at the door.

Sheriff Perry nodded. "Anything to stop your incessant vomiting."

"I can't help it." Skylar slipped onto a chair. "The scene in my room was beyond gross. You're used to it. I am not." Skylar seasoned his words with a dash of indignance.

He earned a deep frown from Sheriff Perry. "Do you want to be taken into town and locked up until I figure this out?"

Skylar turned his focus to his can of soda.

"What is it with everyone here questioning my authority?" Sheriff Perry leveled me with a look. "Do you have anything to do with that?"

"No!" I held my hands up in an "I surrender" fashion.

Before Sheriff Perry or I could spar on the subject, a deputy came in and handed him a slip of paper. He opened it and read. His mouth drew into a deep frown.

"What is it?"

Looking over the edge of the paper, he sighed. "We've identified the woman."

"Already? It took quite a while the last time." I got my zinger in for his earlier accusation. I gave him a sweet smile so he knew it.

"Her prints were in the system." He rubbed his fingers over his mouth and chin all the while looking at Skylar.

Skylar pulled his gaze away from the open soda can. "You didn't need to go to all that trouble. I could have told you who she was."

"You know her?" Astonishment raised my voice.

"I wouldn't say know her. She wasn't my friend or

anything." He turned to Sheriff Perry. "To be honest, it's a relief." Skylar huffed a laugh. His features relaxed and his lips curled into a lopsided grin. He must have seen the question on Shannon's and my faces. "The woman's name is Lisa Mackliner. I had her imprisoned for stalking me."

Chapter Eight

Dazed by Skylar's admission, Shannon and I walked to the suite that housed my home-away-from-home set. After Skylar dropped the bomb about the dead woman being his stalker, Sheriff Perry wasted no time shooing us out the door.

Swiping my key card, Shannon and I stumbled across the threshold. Eric, who sat on a stool by the counter working on his laptop, looked up. "Hey!" he said at first glance. Then he pushed his laptop aside and slipped off the stool. He met us halfway across the room. "Are you two okay?"

"I don't know." Shannon lifted a hand to her forehead and rubbed between her eyes. "What does this mean?" She turned toward me. Her eyes searched my face. By her expression, I could tell her thoughts went the same direction as mine.

Had Skylar had enough and killed his stalker?

"Let's sit down." Eric led us over to the studio audience chairs. "You're both pale and look, well, stunned." He arranged three chairs in a triangular pattern. Shannon and I obeyed his hand indication and sat down.

Once seated, Eric took my right hand in his and squeezed. In an instant, his warmth and strength filled me and calmed the conflicting emotions mixing together inside of me since Skylar identified the murder victim.

"What's going on?" His gentle tone encouraged me.

Before I answered, I looked around the room. The door leading to the adjoining room was closed. "Are we alone?" I jerked my head toward the entry. I didn't want Pamela to hear our conversation.

"We are. If you were talking about Pamela, I haven't seen her since you called Drake for help."

Good. Although it wasn't the time, my jealousy sent a small victory message to my brain. Thankfully, I managed to keep the comment internal because it wasn't fair for me to have interest in Drake and not expect Eric to appreciate another woman.

"Courtney?"

My name jolted me from my thoughts and back to the present conversation. Eric expected an answer. "Skylar knew the murdered woman."

"She was his stalker." Shannon drawled out the last word with more than her usual Southern accent.

"What?" Eric looked from her to me. His expression matched the daze I'd felt earlier.

I sighed. "He told Sheriff Perry her name was Lisa Mackliner. He'd imprisoned her for stalking him."

"Did she break out of prison?" Eric asked.

"I don't know." I shrugged. "Sheriff Perry practically pushed us out the door at Skylar's admission."

"Oh boy." Eric whooshed out the words on a long breath. "This doesn't look good for Skylar. His stalker murdered in his room."

"I agree." Shannon blinked rapidly.

I grabbed her hand and squeezed. Moisture burned my eyes too.

Eric regained his normal posture. "Let's call it a day. I'll order pizza and wine from room service. We can head up to Courtney's suite and have dinner together. How does that sound?" Not waiting for a response, he stood and walked to the counter. He grabbed his cell phone and woke up the screen with a swipe of his finger.

"Great." I wiped the wetness from my eyes with my fingers, glad the show used waterproof mascara.

Standing, we watched Eric pack up his laptop and tablet after he put in a call to room service. "Let's go." He led us out the door, to the elevator and my room.

I entered my suite first. Shannon came next and whispered, "He takes such good care of you," as she walked past me. Shannon, always a romantic. I looked at Eric and tried to get a read on his actions. Right now, they seemed personal and not professional. Although compared to Quintin, all of his actions felt personal.

Shannon took a seat in an overstuffed chair, leaving the sofa for Eric and me to share. I collapsed on a cushion close to the armrest. Eric dropped his bag on the desk and cleared the centerpiece off the coffee table before he sat down just inches from me. "How do you think this woman got to the resort if she was imprisoned?"

"Her name is Lisa." She was a person, not just a victim. We needed to treat her as such. "I thought I heard Skylar mention parole as we were being pushed from the room." I looked to Shannon.

She nodded. "I just don't think Skylar is the killer type."

"Me either." I sent a questioning expression Eric's way.

He shrugged his shoulders. "Some murderers appear to be nice guys in public. What about Sheriff Perry? Could you get a read on his thoughts?" Eric ping-ponged his gaze between the two of us. "Could it have been self-defense?"

I sighed. "By the grim look on his face, he thinks Skylar killed her. As for self-defense?" I closed my eyes and called up the scene I'd witnessed. Opening my eyes, I said, "The scene didn't show a sign of struggle, other than the crushed cake where Lisa's body rested."

Shannon sniffled at my statement.

"Sheriff Perry seems fair. And Skylar is innocent until proven guilty," Eric said. His reminder brought out a weak smile from Shannon. "It's a strange coincidence another murder happened here during the filming of *The American Baking Battle*. If I were the county sheriff, I wouldn't be happy."

I considered what Eric had said, even though Sheriff Perry thought I was trouble, he was a fair law enforcer. "I agree. Sheriff Perry will do a thorough investigation. Do you think it could be a copycat?"

Eric shrugged, then pinned me with a pointed look. "That is for Sheriff Perry to determine."

I noted his subliminal message. He didn't want me to get involved with the murder investigation. I dropped my gaze to my lap. I could make no promises.

"I feel so badly for Skylar. He has such a weak stomach and it didn't help that he was ill when he found the body." Shannon missed Eric's passive-aggressive warning to me.

I smiled. There was no doubt in Shannon's mind that Skylar was innocent. "True. Do you think he has a stomach bug or got food poisoning from something he ate? Two contestants didn't feel well either."

"They were back on set, though." Shannon lifted her eyes to meet mine, her expression thoughtful.

"Maybe they were powering through." Eric checked his watch. He must have thought it was taking room service too long. "The prize is a lot of money, and the exposure could land them a cooking show."

"Right. Or maybe they powered through because Quintin is on set. He's quite intimidating." I wrinkled my nose. Not to mention dark and brooding.

"He also points out the cost of the loss of time for the show in front of the contestants." Shannon slipped off her shoes and tucked her feet under her legs. "I find him cold."

A knock sounded on the door followed by an announcement of room service. Eric opened the door and a young woman pushed a two-shelf cart through the door. The upper shelf held a bottle of wine chilling in an ice bucket with three crystal glasses, plates and silverware wrapped in pristine white napkins. Two oblong platters with domed covers sat on the bottom shelf.

In seconds, the food had been transferred from the cart to the coffee table. While Eric tipped the server and sent her on her way, Shannon opened the wine and poured us each a tall glass of red. I lifted the dome covers and set them on the desk, moving Eric's bag to the chair so any of the built-up steam on the cover didn't leak onto his electronics.

"The power struggle between Quintin and Brenden is intense." Shannon picked up the conversation where we'd left off.

"It's creating quite a bit of dissension." I passed a plate to Shannon.

"Do you think Lisa is the reason Skylar was arguing with Drake." Eric slid two pieces of pizza onto his plate.

I'd lifted a slice of veggie flatbread pizza to my lips. I set it back on my plate. "Maybe. If he knew she'd been paroled, he might have wanted extra security." I didn't add that Drake could reassign Pamela. "Skylar mentioned paroled. Would he have been alerted she was freed? Or had he seen her lurking around the resort?"

Neither Eric nor Shannon had a response to my questions. I made a mental note to do a little Internet research to see if stalkers' obsessions were notified when a stalker was released from prison.

"You know." Shannon slid a piece of the all-meat flatbread onto her plate. "The chef could make this a gourmet meat pizza by using three types of sausage, pork, chicken and turkey, on a pesto sauce, sprinkled with sage instead of traditional pizza spices and topped with feta."

"That sounds delicious." Eric snatched another piece of each pizza.

"I think they need more family-friendly types of flatbread pizzas. Most are so gourmet that typical children wouldn't eat the ingredients. For a family, you could take your basic idea, the three sausage types, use a mild marinara sauce, ground oregano and a mix of mozzarella and cheddar." I popped the last bite of my veggie pizza in my mouth and lifted my glass for a sip.

Eric flashed a broad smile in our direction.

"What?" I asked after I swallowed the fruity vintage.

"This is your show! It comes natural to you. Shannon is used to preparing gourmet recipes and you"—Eric rested his gaze on me—"family fare."

"What do you think?" Shannon untucked from the chair. She set her plate on the coffee table and scooted to the end of the overstuffed cushion. Excitement pushed the sadness from her features.

My mood brightened too. "I like the idea. After the first few episodes where we choose a recipe to alter, maybe viewers could text, e-mail or tweet recipes they'd like to see revised and prepared one way, giving us a segue to make the recipe both ways." I looked at Eric, then Shannon.

"Yes!" Shannon clapped her hands. "Everyone is into interactive nowadays."

Eric stood and retrieved his tablet from his bag. He booted it up and started to make notes. "I know you both have network cooking shows and appear on the competition together, but you have good chemistry, feeding off of each other's suggestions. You should consider submitting a sample segment working side by side to show your chemistry when we pitch the show."

"Maybe Shannon should cohost one of my live tapings. Of course, we wouldn't be preparing the same recipe in a different way, but the network could see how well we interact together." Creative excitement folded through me.

Looking up from his tablet, Eric wore his professional expression. "I'll consider all angles of the guest hosting idea. I'll have to run it past the network. Shannon, you should clear it with your people."

Shannon laughed and flipped her hand through the air. "My people is my husband. I'll talk to him about it tonight when we Skype." She picked up her wineglass and held it up for a toast. Eric and I obliged.

Shannon smiled. "To a good ending of a very bad day."

The next morning, instead of Eric bringing my hazelnut latte to my suite, he met Shannon and me at Castle Grounds, Pamela by his side.

I fought the snarl my lips wanted to curl into at the sight of them standing too close together in my opinion. I admit human emotions are sometimes ridiculous. Neither of them indicated they were a couple or had interest in becoming a couple.

"Good morning." Pamela smiled at us as we approached the table. Her bright smile a complete contrast to what should be the sorrowful mood of a murder.

I had to stop those kinds of thoughts. Pamela had every right to be happy unless that happiness came from standing close to Eric. Again, I had to rein in those green-eyed monster thoughts. "Good morning," I mumbled, and reached for one of the cups of coffee Eric held.

"Hazelnut latte." Pamela held her right hand out to offer me a cup.

"Thank you." I snatched the coffee from her hand and took a sip. Over the plastic lid, my eyes met Eric's. He gave me a narrow-eyed stare and slight frown before smiling at Shannon and handing her a cup of coffee that she seemed more grateful than me to receive.

I turned to Pamela and Eric. "Thank you." I held up my cup. "It was just what I needed." The smile I flashed them was genuine. As soon as the rich, nutty brew hit my tongue, it awakened all of my senses, including my common sense, which chided me to stop harboring jealous feelings toward Pamela.

"You're welcome." Eric smiled. "We hope you have a better day today." He pushed through the exit door and held it open.

Pamela indicated with her hand for Shannon and me to follow. She brought up the rear. "In light of the recent incident, Drake wants you escorted to work in the morning since you report so early. We can take a vehicle or walk. Your call."

I stopped and turned. "Drake wants or Sheriff Perry ordered?" I'd gotten my hopes up one too many times thinking Drake worried for my safety. Guilt poked into my heart. He is why I needed to get a grip on my emotions. If I could be interested in Drake, Eric could be interested in Pamela, and since Eric and I had never expressed romantic interest in each other, my envious feelings were uncalled for.

Pamela looked at me, dumbfounded. "I take my orders from Drake."

Of course, she did. I'm sure he didn't tell her Sheriff Perry issued the order. It still bothered me that Sheriff Perry thought I needed a security detail assigned to me.

"We'll take a ride. I'm hungry and want to eat my

breakfast before our stylists need us in the chair." Shannon made the decision for us.

She and I rode on the backseat bench of a UTV in silence. Mostly because I was sipping my coffee and wondering if Skylar would be on set today. Dare I ask Pamela? Would she know? Drake might be gun-shy in sharing information with his second-in-command. I took a chance. "Will Skylar be on set today? Will there be extra security?"

Pamela tilted her head to her right shoulder while she kept her eyes on the path since she was driving, and raised her voice, "I don't know."

Some help she was. My shoulders sagged.

Except for the purr of the engine, silence descended on our group. Once we arrived at the workshop, Shannon and I slipped from the vehicle, expressed our thanks and headed toward the door. Pamela watched until we were entering the building; then I heard the UTV retreat.

"Was that weird?" Shannon hitched her thumb toward the path.

"That she watched us walk into the building? Yes, unless . . ." I stopped talking until we passed Kinzy at her post inside the door. On the phone, she waved a greeting. We started our climb up the stairway, and I continued. "Skylar isn't a suspect and they think the killer is still on the resort premises."

Shannon stopped stepping. She put a hand to her heart. "I never thought of that. They wouldn't know if this was a serial thing or not. I am so glad Drake saw to our safety this morning."

I nodded my agreement, but wondered again if Drake or Sheriff Perry had made the order. Either way, Shannon was right, it felt good to be protected. "Shannon," I laughed. "We are so preoccupied, we forgot to grab breakfast."

Her giggles tinkled through the rafters. We skipped down the stairs to the catering table. Full light illuminated the set. A few crew members shuffled down the sides, making their selections. A hearty breakfast was something I didn't partake in until I met Shannon, now I couldn't live without a protein-enriched start of my day. I scooped scrambled eggs onto my plate and rounded it off with turkey sausage and a small bran muffin. I'd drained my latte dry, so I hit the beverage station for another cup of java.

Justin smiled at me while he added more fruit to a large bowl. Shannon chose a breakfast of oatmeal topped with blueberries and a glass of orange juice. We stepped up to the wardrobe room and entered.

Harrison sat in his makeup chair reading something on his tablet. He looked up and smiled. "Good morning, ladies." His eyes twinkled. "Courtney, you no longer have to drink the tasteless coffee from the catering table." He pointed over my shoulder.

I laughed out loud. "I forgot. I'll do better tomorrow."

"Here." He took the cup from my hands. "I'll get rid of this and make you a fresh *gourmet* cup. Shannon, would you like one too?"

"No, thank you." She leaned close to my ear. "So very different from last season. I like this version of him much better."

"Me too," I whispered.

Since they'd eliminated our table, we sat in our makeup chairs to eat our first meal of the day. I didn't like not having the table and wondered who authorized the remodel. Quintin?

"Has Skylar come in yet?" Shannon twisted her chair to face Harrison.

"Haven't seen him." Harrison carried two coffees our way, his and mine.

As if on cue, the door banged open. Skylar staggered into the room. Although his walk and look, haggard and tired, might scream hangover, I knew he still didn't feel well. Had anyone taken him to a doctor, or at least had the nurse practitioner examine him?

Harrison jumped from his chair and ran over to Skylar. Taking him by the arm, he led him to the vacated chair. Skylar sat and scooted into a slumped position.

"Would you like some coffee or tea?" Shannon started to rise.

He shook his head.

"How did you get here?" I set my empty breakfast plate on the countertop by the mirror and swiveled my chair toward Skylar.

"Drake dropped me off." His tone held a touch of snarl.

Harrison, who now stood behind Skylar, pulled his features into a yikes expression.

"Sorry. My tone sounded mean. I didn't mean it to. I'm just . . ." Skylar stopped talking and drew a few raspy breaths. "I'm tired, hungry and confused. There is no reason to eat. I'll just lose it and they still won't let me in my room."

"Where are you sleeping?" Shannon cleared my breakfast garbage and took it to the waste can with hers.

"I've been moved to a room on the floor where the Nolan Security team stays. Drake is my neighbor. The room is small." Skylar wrinkled his nose. "They did bring me my things. Drake explained the move was for my protection. . . .” Skylar’s voice trailed off like he didn’t believe it.

Had he realized he was the prime person of interest in this case? Although no one had officially made that statement, I knew enough from the murder last season to know it was true. I believed Drake moved Skylar to a room near him to keep Skylar under surveillance.

“Anyway, he is dropping me off and picking me up every day until the sheriff closes the case.” He shrugged. “The sheriff. What’s his name?”

“Sheriff Perry.” I decided I’d have a word with Brenden about Skylar’s condition. He needed to see a doctor. He knew Sheriff Perry’s name. This memory lapse might have more to do with shock than illness, but a medical professional needed to make that call.

“Yeah, Perry. He made me take a drug test.”

Our stylists entered the room and halted our conversation, which was okay with me. I needed to think through Skylar’s situation. Was a drug test standard procedure? Or had Sheriff Perry noticed the not-so-subtle difference in Skylar’s personality? Did they suspect Skylar murdered Lisa, or was he moved for his own protection? Had they found some type of evidence on the scene and knew a murderer walked among us? It would explain Security providing taxi service. Harrison never mentioned a ride to work; I’d have to strike up a conversation during our downtime today.

Kinzy popped in to tell us to come down as soon as we were finished in makeup and wardrobe. Her announcement kicked our stylists into a higher gear and in no time, we were comely, coiffed and costumed.

Today, we celebrated the early seventies with our wardrobe.

"I don't know why I agreed to costume participation this season," Harrison huffed, and exited the room.

He looked something other than dapper in the evergreen leisure suit with a polyester shirt swirled with orange, brown and green.

Shannon complemented him in an orange gown. The designer emphasized the Empire waist with a daisy appliquéd ribbon. A dotted Swiss overlay covered the dress and created the puff sleeves. Her stylist pulled her blond hair into a knot and placed a lacy, floppy hat over it, making sure most of her face was visible, then pinned it to her head. The ribbon around the brim of the hat matched the ribbon under her bust.

"I can't believe people dressed like this." She rolled her eyes.

My gown, a pale-pink eyelet, boasted a scooped elasticized neckline with a ruffle that created a mock-capped sleeve. The fitted bodice ended at a V in the front. A gathered skirt with a twelve-inch flounce completed the formal. My stylist French-braided my dark hair in a halo around the crown of my head, then attached a wreath of white and pink baby's breath over the braid.

"My shoes beat yesterday's stilettos." I lifted my gown to reveal pink platform Mary Janes. The three-inch heel and a two-inch platform provided much more comfort.

"True." Shannon lifted her skirt and pointed her toe. Her shoes, a deep shade of orange, twinned mine in style.

Shannon and I started to head downstairs when we heard Skylar arguing with his wardrobe person through the paper-thin wall. The door to the dressing room opened and Skylar stalked out. He wore a beige leisure suit with brown embroidered wagon wheels on the yoke.

The shirt was a shade darker beige. Even in makeup, the ensemble washed him out. Which was a problem for Skylar. He worried about it often on set. Yet, I did have to wonder if the outfit was the sole contributor to his ashen appearance. Lack of sleep and illness could do that to a person.

Then again, so could a guilty conscience.

Chapter Nine

"Places." Brenden clapped his hands.

Skylar and I stood, not quite centered, under the arch. Skylar thought the bright-pink peonies helped add color to his skin, so he stood close to the side of the lattice form. They didn't, but I wasn't telling him. I was just relieved he felt well enough to stand on his own. Following our cue, we kicked off the second challenge of the day.

"Your next challenge is to create an entrée for an engagement party." Skylar smiled into the camera, a faint hint of weariness in his voice.

"It requires two things. You must prepare individual servings and use a surprise gift ingredient chosen by our judges." I paused while Harrison and Shannon waved to the contestants, cheesy grins plastered on their faces. "You can reveal your surprises now."

We watched the contestants whip off the cloth napkin

covering the gift on their counter. A few smiled, a few grimaced and a few just stared at the item.

"You have two hours to complete twelve entrées."

Skylar's voice drew the contestants' attention to us. Together, we said, "The baking begins now."

The contestants flew around their work, pantry and refrigerated areas.

Brenden hollered, "Cut."

"I need to sit down." Skylar headed toward his chair on the set.

I followed him, taking mine beside Shannon.

"Mr. Daily." Justin walked into the group. He carried a cup of coffee and a cinnamon roll. "I noticed you didn't have breakfast."

"Thank you." Skylar took the coffee and eyed the cinnamon roll. "And remember, it's Skylar." Skylar smiled.

"I hope you are feeling better." Justin held out the roll.

"A little better. I'm going to pass on the roll, but I would try a slice of toast if there is any on the catering table." He started to stand.

"No, no. I'll get it." Justin hurried away and returned with two slices of toast. "I do hope you feel better."

"Thanks, pal." Skylar patted Justin on the shoulder and took the plate of toast.

Justin nodded and walked away.

"He's a good kid," Skylar said before he took a nibble of toast.

I watched Skylar sip and nibble for a few minutes; then Brenden approached our group. "Shannon and Harrison, you will interview the contestants while they cook. Skylar and Courtney, are you ready to shoot the opening scene?"

Skylar leveled Brenden with a look. "Really, with the

way I look and feel, you think I can pull off funny today?" He shook his head.

"Well, we lost time yesterday. . . ." Brenden glanced over his shoulder to check Quintin's whereabouts.

"Because of me." Skylar drained the coffee cup and placed it on the floor beside the plate with a half of piece of uneaten toast.

"I didn't say that." Brenden held up his hands. "I'm just trying to keep us on track."

Turning to Brenden, I said, "Skylar looks ill. I'm sorry to say this, but there is only so much makeup and lighting can do. Can't we postpone it another day?"

"Postpone what?"

I cringed. Quintin had walked up behind me.

Turning, I said, "The opening sequence. Skylar is ill and doesn't think he can pull off funny."

Quintin moved his unemotional eyes from me to Skylar, giving him a once-over. His lips drew into a deep frown. "I have to agree. We can wait a day. Why are they in different costumes and hairstyles than yesterday?"

"The opening scene involves smearing cake icing on their faces and would require a change of clothing."

Quintin turned to Brenden. "Yet, they opened the first challenge in the other clothing." He snorted. "That doesn't make sense. Didn't someone change wardrobe's notes?" He threw his hands in the air. "Harrison and Shannon will have to change their clothes and hairstyles. This is a nightmare." He stalked off while bellowing, "Kinzy."

She jumped and ran with her tablet tucked under her arm.

"Sorry."

Brenden looked at Skylar. "Don't be. A change of clothes and hair doesn't take that long, especially for Harrison. And we have to reshoot everything we did yesterday due to you and two contestants not feeling well. We should have canceled filming." He shot a look in the direction Quintin had stalked off. "Skylar, you get some rest. Courtney, I don't need you until we call time, and then you can accompany the judges."

After Brenden left us, Skylar sighed. "I'm beat. I just don't know what is wrong. I feel so tired again. I'm going upstairs to rest."

"Okay." I walked as far as the catering table with Skylar and watched as he ascended the stairs.

"Do you think he's okay?"

I looked in the direction of the voice. Justin.

"I don't know. I think he needs to see a doctor." My eyes roved over the catering table.

"Is there something I could get you before I start cleaning up?"

"Is there hot water for tea?"

"Yes." Justin picked up a cup and walked to a large silver decanter. "Tea bags are in the basket."

I chose orange pekoe. Justin took the package from me, opened it and dunked the bag in the hot water. Then handed me the cup.

"I'm worried about Mr. Daily." Justin gave his head a firm shake. "I mean Skylar. He's so kind to us. Treats us like we're equals. You know what I mean?"

I smiled. "I do." I bet Justin had no idea of the social status held by Skylar's mother. Justin didn't look the type to read the society news, he looked like the boy next door. Young, I'd guess in his early twenties judging by his slender frame and boyish face. He hadn't grown quite into manhood yet. In my heels, we were eye level, so he measured at least five feet five. He wore his brown hair cropped short on the side. The longer hair on his crown, he gelled into a peak. Although the style was fashionable, to me it was reminiscent of a Kewpie doll's hair.

"I consider Skylar a friend. I don't believe he killed that woman."

My face must have shown my shock at his statement. Justin took a step back and fumbled with the tea wrapper.

It didn't surprise me that employees of the resort knew about the murder. My alarm came from Justin making that statement to someone he barely knew. The matter-of-fact way Justin stated his belief in Skylar told me gossip and conjecture about Skylar was circulating through the resort.

"Sorry, I didn't mean to offend you. I wanted people to know I support Skylar. I don't believe the rumors. Would you tell him that?" His eyes searched my face.

"No, you tell him the next time you see him. It will mean more. I'm sure he'll be around at lunchtime. And it's okay to support your friend." I followed my words with a wide smile. A little bit because I'd made him feel uncomfortable, a lot because I wanted to hear the gossip. "May I ask about the rumors?"

It was Justin's turn to wear a surprised expression. "S-s-sure." He turned away from me and began to combine trays, mixing muffins, donuts and bagels.

I sipped my tea and waited. After a minute or so, I asked, "What are they?"

"Oh, you know." Justin stopped working a minute and looked at me before looking both ways and behind him. "He killed his stalker," he whispered.

Two kitchen staff members came through the side door pushing a cart filled with fresh beverages.

Justin glanced their way, and whispered, "I need to get this stuff back to the resort. Nice talking to you."

I walked back to my chair and watched Justin and his coworkers tear down the breakfast buffet and set out new warming trays for lunch. Once they were packed up, they headed out the side door.

It was too bad I hadn't learned more of the rumors about Skylar from Justin, yet I understood he probably didn't want to get caught gossiping by his coworkers. I'd try again later. I sipped my tea and wondered if Sheriff Perry and his team found any evidence in Skylar's room or anything pertinent out about the murder or the victim, Lisa Mackliner. The question Eric posed earlier popped back into my mind. Had Skylar have been notified of her parole? I'd find a way to work that question into my next conversation with Skylar.

Lisa Mackliner seemed like an uncommon name, so I felt confident I'd find out about her with a quick Internet search. Especially if I added felony to the search it would help. Why would anyone who was sent to prison for stalking get out and then repeat the same depraved behavior? Of course, anyone who was a stalker must suffer with some mental illness, delusions or something. Was it possible she set Skylar up? Could she have taken her own life in his room? Was I grasping at straws trying to eliminate Skylar from the mix? I hated to admit it, but he did have a lot of motive to want Lisa out of his life.

"I lost what I ate again." Skylar swayed toward me. I grabbed the side of the arch for support.

"Are you still seeing the murder scene?" I wrapped an arm around his waist to help my balance.

"No, I actually went to sleep in the chair. My upset stomach woke me up. Now, I can hardly keep my eyes open."

Our camera light blinked to green.

"Smile," I said to Skylar through my own. We were calling time together, so I hoped we could get this in one shot. If not, the bakers would stop and we'd repeat it until Brenden found it acceptable.

Brenden stood, fingers counting down the seconds. On his fist we said, "Time's up. Stop baking."

The activity in the kitchenettes stopped.

"Try it again. Skylar came in too slow." Brenden stuffed his hands in his pockets and glanced over his shoulder.

My eyes searched the set for Quintin. Preoccupied with Kinzy and a tablet, I knew we were safe for a redo. "Skylar, we need to get it this time to keep Quintin off Brenden and your cases. Okay?"

I turned to find his eyes half-lidded.

"Skylar! Did you hear me?"

"Yeah, yeah." His body perked up a little. "I'll get it this time. Ready?"

I nodded and smiled into the camera. Together, we repeated our lines. Brenden sucked in the corner of his lips, cast a glance over his shoulder. "One more time. Quickly."

Skylar swayed. I pushed him with my shoulder to keep him more vertical. "Ready?"

He nodded. This time I spoke slower and our words were in unison.

"Great." Brenden started to walk toward us, well me. Skylar had headed for his chair.

"Thanks for holding him up."

"I think he needs to see a doctor. It's been two days

since he's kept anything down." I hitched a thumb in the direction of Skylar. He'd sat and slid down until his head rested on the back.

"I'll talk to Drake. Right now, I need you to get over to the kitchen area and be a part of the judging with Harrison and Shannon."

I nodded and took a step.

Brenden reached out and touched my arm. "Thank you again. You are always such a trooper during filming. You put up with a crazy contestant last time and now a sick cohost. I sure hope your fans stay loyal to you once your admission and apology airs."

Apprehension twisted through me. With all that had happened with Skylar, I'd completely forgotten about this possible detriment to my career. Eric didn't even remind me when we'd discussed the new show last night.

Knowing Brenden meant well, I mumbled thanks and headed over to where Shannon and Harrison stood, hoping I could concentrate on my cohosting job. Which, to be honest, I hadn't been doing while holding Skylar vertical. I noticed the contestants still wore the aprons from yesterday.

"We're starting from front to back." Harrison gave the cameraman a nod.

Once we had the green light, Harrison smiled at Mike. "Tell us what you made."

Mike wiped his hands down his apron. A habit, I guessed, by the smears of food discoloring the white frilly bridal gown design. His offering sat in pristine rows of three down and four across on a silver serving platter lined with a white paper doily. "I tenderized turkey breasts, smeared them with sausage and mushroom stuffing, and rolled it together. Once it was baked, I sliced it and placed it on a homemade biscuit. I drizzled it with a thick orange cranberry sauce before adding the biscuit top."

Shannon lifted the top of a biscuit. "Very nice presentation. It looks pretty and smells wonderful."

With a knife and fork, Harrison cut them each a sample. I couldn't get a good read on his expression while he tasted Mike's fare. As he swallowed, he lifted the top of the biscuit with the fork and perused the food once again.

Looking up at Mike, he said, "These biscuits are excellent. Light and fluffy. You took a simple dish and made it elegant and edible by hand."

"I agree. The stuffing is seasoned to perfection. And this dish could be served hot, room temperature or cold."

"Well done." Harrison smiled.

Mike exhaled. All the tension in his face released with his breath. "Thank you."

We stepped over to Carla.

"What have you prepared for us today?" Shannon perused four taco racks sitting on the end of her counter, clearly not holding traditional tacos.

"I made fish tacos. Following my Norwegian heritage, I used lefse as the soft shell and cod with special salt seasoning to mock a Norwegian favorite, lutefisk. The topping is mashed green peas drizzled with melted salted butter."

Shannon tried lifting one from the rack. The lefse, soft and pliable, threatened to spill the contents. Harrison slid a plate underneath and handed Shannon a fork.

"It sounds like quite a bit of sodium in this recipe." Harrison lifted his bite eye level. "It's colorful and smells good."

"Yes, traditional lutefisk is dried salted whitefish and

lye. The lye makes it gelatinous in texture. My recipe has the flavor of traditional lutefisk without the gummy feel." Worry lined Carla's sober expression.

Shannon and Harrison tried the dish at the same time. Harrison forked a bite of the mashed peas only, then gave a small nod of the head. "No salt in your peas." He smiled. "It complements the salty fish well. This is a dish I've never tasted before and perhaps it's traditionally high in sodium, but I'd dial the liberal use of salt back a little."

I watched Shannon swallow hard to get her bite down. "I agree. It's too salty. For me it needed some crunch, everything is soft in this dish. It needed more texture. However, you nailed a main course in an individual serving, but it can't be eaten with your hands." Shannon turned and called to Brenden, "We need some water over here."

During the wait for the water and Shannon and Harrison to quench their thirst and clear their palette, I decided to find out how Carla was feeling.

"Are you feeling better?" I inflected concern in my tone.

Carla looked at me. Her lips rested in a thin line. She stepped closer to the counter and glanced from side to side. She leaned across the counter. "Yes, thank you," she whispered.

"Did the nurse think you had a touch of food poisoning or a stomach bug?" I kept my voice at a whisper level, although I wasn't sure why we were talking in such a covert fashion.

"No, nothing like that." She rolled her eyes. "I have severe acid reflux. The quiches I chose had onion and garlic in them, which are a huge trigger for me even on a daily medicine. I didn't want to be rude and throw them away, so I ate them. I knew better. It was my fault. I had to take another pill for relief. I feel so silly. Please don't tell anyone."

"Your secret is safe with me." I reached out and patted her arm. I filed a mental note to talk to Eric about doing a show for people like Carla who suffered from acid reflux or food allergies. Something along the lines of how to make the food tasty without disrupting their sensitive digestive track.

Carla smiled and stepped away from the counter.

I flicked my gaze to Nadine. In the order we were going, she'd be second to the last for judging, which would work fine for posing my question as to her health. What were the odds she suffered from acid reflux too? Slim, just like two murders happening in the same resort during filming of the same show. I'd wait to see what Nadine reported, but I had a feeling Skylar wasn't suffering from food poisoning or the aftereffects of seeing a murdered body. If Nadine had a simple explanation for her nausea, I was insisting Skylar see a doctor.

"Courtney, we're ready." Shannon used her hand to beckon me to follow. I complied.

Next up was Marco. I wondered if he'd fare any better than yesterday. Harrison and Shannon had been nice but firm in their judging of his dish. He'd failed the challenge.

Unlike the apron Mike used to its full advantage, Marco's was pristine. His screen-printed bridal gown had a lacy bodice with long, curly blond hair spilling down the shoulders, a fun contrast to his dark black hair.

Before either of them could ask, Marco spoke. "I used items from a traditional antipasto platter to make individual entrées. I breaded the eggplant with a panko and Parmesan coating and crisped it in olive oil, then topped it with salami, added an artichoke-and-olive remoulade, pastrami, a slice of Roma tomato, fresh mozzarella and a crisped piece of prosciutto."

He'd placed his food on a bright-colored platter with each serving on a small paper doily, so it'd be easy to lift from the serving dish. It looked and smelled great. When Harrison sliced one into bites, I grabbed a piece too.

"I wasn't sure your base would hold, but you did a very good job with the eggplant. The texture on the inside and outside is perfect." Shannon lifted another one from the tray and held it up. "There is no grease or moisture on the doily either."

A wide smile broke on his face. Palms together as if in prayer, Marco made a slight bow in Shannon's direction.

"This has every flavor from an antipasto tray. Your seasoning is spot-on." Harrison nodded his approval. "My only suggestion is a better serving display. Maybe an antipasto board; you have a variety of color in your food, so you didn't need to add more color."

Marco frowned and brought his hands around behind him.

"I liked your presentation. Good job." Shannon smiled at Marco, while Harrison raised his brows at her contradiction. They started toward the next contestant.

"Oh my gravy!" Sometimes my catchphrase from my show slips out in my real-life situations. "If my opinion counts, I love it." I snatched another small bite. "A little ground pepper on top of the tomato slice would be nice."

"Thank you. I'll incorporate your suggestion next time. Miss Archer, when the competition started, I'd hoped for screen time with Skylar to impress my girlfriend, Lisa. Now I'm glad you are accompanying the judges." His lips drew into a deep frown. "I don't like her being such a fan since he's suspected of murder." He shivered. "A knife to the heart. What a way to go."

Nothing about Marco's appearance looked like a Goth, yet his conversations bordered on the macabre. Could Lisa Mackliner be his Lisa? It would explain how she managed to get into Coal Castle Resort. But how did Marco know the murder weapon? Sheriff Perry had an uncanny way of keeping murders in his county out of the public eye, so I couldn't believe the details of the murder had been released. Perhaps Marco heard the rumors circulating through the resort. Or was his conversation a cover-up? Had he killed Lisa and slipped up by talking about the murder weapon?

"Cut!" Harrison shouted, and jerked me from my thoughts. I looked around and everyone else had jumped to attention. Brenden, Quintin and Kinzy stood. Our cameraman took several steps back and lowered the camera. Harrison turned as he spoke in order to address all of the contestants. "You are here to bake. If you want to win this competition, you need to keep your mind in your work, not on what is happening in the resort."

"It's hard to work when a murder's taken place and you're working with the main suspect." Marco stepped away from the counter; his face remained sober, but his eyes held a chilling emotion.

Harrison turned to him. "People are innocent until proven guilty."

"That's right," Donna piped in. "Courtney is a perfect example. She was the main suspect in a murder on the set last year and she was innocent. Just because all the evidence points to Skylar doesn't mean he murdered the woman."

I opened my mouth to correct her because I'd never been a suspect, just a person of interest, but heavy footsteps stopped my speech.

"I'll have you all know, I didn't murder Lisa." Skylar stopped beside Harrison.

Movement drew my attention to Marco, who stumbled backward at the mention of her name. He grabbed the countertop for support and kept his head hung so I couldn't see his face. Was Lisa Mackliner his girlfriend? Was he trying to hide his face because he murdered her? Or was he feeling guilty he started this subject?

"Enough." Quintin's command echoed off the high ceilings of the workshop.

Quintin and Brenden moved toward us. Skylar turned. He must have leveled them with a look because they stopped in their tracks. Brenden's face remained expressionless. Quintin narrowed his eyes and glared at Skylar like he could kill him.

It didn't seem to faze Skylar. He turned back to the contestants and continued. "So everyone is clear on this. Lisa Mackliner made my life a living nightmare for months. She vandalized my house, my cars and part of the studio where my show, *Grocery Store Gambit*, filmed." For a man who staggered and swaggered so badly earlier that I'd had to hold him up, Skylar stood erect. His face blazed red. His voice strong and firm. I guess anger is a great fortifier. He continued. "She mailed me racy photos and letters. She showed up at my studio dressing room wearing a bridal gown and wielding a knife. She threatened to stab me if I didn't marry her."

My eyes widened. My knees weakened. My thoughts swirled. I grabbed the countertop for support. The crime scene in Skylar's room resembled what he'd just described. Only Lisa was stabbed, not Skylar. Did Skylar realize that? He needed to be quiet. Once the details got out about the murder, it could incriminate him. I had to do something, say something to stop him.

Mike beat me to it. "Guess you had a really good motive to kill her then," he said.

The room went silent.

Chapter Ten

Dawning morphed on Skylar's features. Had he finally realized he could be in trouble? Turning on his heel, he ran from the room. He threw the heavy door open and disappeared into the glare of natural sunlight.

The bang of the door closing echoed through the room and started a buzz of hushed and not-so-hushed voices. It seemed like Marco shouted above the din, saying, "Wow, that was a guilty move."

I hoped Shannon, Harrison or Brenden came to his defense because I didn't have time. I, of all people, knew how it felt to be a person of interest in a murder investigation. I also knew how evidence and opinions changed during the course of an investigation. Because of my experience, I'd be the best person to talk to Skylar. I lifted my skirt and ran after him. My clunky platform shoes beat a rhythm across the wooden floor. Slipping out a crack in the door, I shielded my eyes against the bright sunshine, a stark contrast to the lighting inside. I looked both ways and spotted Skylar on the path that would head to the lake on the resort grounds. The same lake where he hooked evidence last time.

I turned, intent on running after him, when a strong hand grasped my arm and stopped my motion. The abrupt halt knocked me off balance. I wobbled in my platforms. Another strong hand to my shoulder steadied me. I turned and stared into the dark, cold eyes of Quintin.

"Where are you going?" He barked out the question. His grip tightened.

My heart drum-soloed against my ribs. "After Skylar." I tried to jerk my arm from his grasp.

He held tight. "No, you're going back into the building and finishing filming for the day."

His tone begged no argument.

I argued anyway. "Skylar needs to talk to someone. I'm the best person because I've been through something similar."

"I'll handle this." Quintin's stare bore into me.

With my free hand, I slapped his grip from my shoulder. "I'm the best person to talk him down, if that's what is needed. Besides, I'm worried about him. I believe in addition to the shock from seeing a murder victim, he's ill." My plan had been to corner Brenden about this subject. Quintin seemed handier at the moment. "Did any kind of medical professional check him out?"

Pursing his lips, Quintin stared into the horizon in the direction Skylar walked. A few more steps and Skylar would be out of our sight. "Not that I'm aware of. Now go back inside. I'll tell Skylar you're worried."

"I'm going with you."

"Security!"

I knew the look I shot at Quintin was incredulous because it's how I felt. I didn't trust Quintin.

"Take Miss Archer inside and don't allow her to wander outside until I get back."

The guard gave his head a nod and motioned with his hand for me to walk back toward the building. Quintin started to walk after Skylar.

Huffing, I stomped to the door of the workshop and entered. Once my eyes adjusted, I found Shannon relaxing in her chair. I marched over and flopped into mine.

"Couldn't find him?"

"Wasn't allowed." I recounted my confrontation with Quintin, ending it with, "I don't trust him."

"I think he's a bully," Shannon drawled. "He uses intimidation to get people to see things his way. Brenden almost cowers around him. The only one who doesn't is Kinzy."

"Agreed." I huffed out the word, my heart rate still erratic from how Quintin had treated me. "He treated me like he was the boss and I was his employee." I crossed my arms over my chest.

"Well." In a meek tone, Shannon said, "When you point it out, as the producer, he is our boss, so we are his employees."

My shoulders sagged. "True."

Shannon giggled. "We are spoiled with good producers. Men who listen to our ideas and opinions."

I smiled. "And if we disagree, they make a fair case or compromise."

"That is because they love us."

"Your husband loves you. Eric is"—I paused, trying to find the correct word—"fond of me."

"Eric is more than fond of you." Shannon snorted a laugh.

I knew Shannon believed Eric had romantic feelings for me. She'd been telling me since the taping of the last season. Eric and I had been professional partners and friends for over five years. Nothing in our relationship seemed out of the ordinary or romantic in any way until Shannon planted the idea in my brain. Now I was constantly looking for signs. After seeing him interact with Pamela, I was sure Shannon was wrong. Eric and I had never sat with our heads together whispering and then acted guilty when caught, like he and Pamela had yesterday. I heard their happy laughter as they drove away this morning. Sure Eric and I shared laughter and inside jokes, yet our laughter didn't have quite the same lilt.

My thoughts caused my stomach to ball and knead with resentment toward Pamela. I couldn't feel this way. I didn't hide my attraction to Drake. Tall, dark and hunky were traits I considered my type. I thought Drake and I shared a spark, yet our dinner date last season had been all business, an interrogation of sorts. Of course, with Drake being the Head of Security and me a person of interest in a murder, we couldn't explore a more in-depth relationship at the time. He'd promised we'd date after our show wrapped for the first season. Our schedules never meshed for the date to happen and now we were back to where we started, a murder investigation. Even though he'd mentioned a dinner date, I was skeptical it would happen.

And should it? Eric showed signs of hostility toward Drake when I was around. Was he experiencing the same feelings of jealousy and envy like I was around Pamela? I sighed. I needed to talk to Eric before I went on a date with Drake. I sighed again, realizing "I need to talk to Eric" was becoming my mantra.

"Wow, those were loud sighs. What's on your mind?" Shannon asked.

I looked at my friend. I knew if I shared my thoughts, she'd lobby on the side of Eric.

She reached out and squeezed my hand. "I'm worried about Skylar too."

Before I could correct her assumption, Brenden clapped his hands together. I looked out over the set. The kitchenettes were stocked with cleaned appliances, and the contestants moved into place.

"Did you and Harrison finish judging while I was outside?"

Shannon nodded.

I stood in preparation for Brenden's direction while Shannon remained seated. She wouldn't be needed until time to judge or if they took her and Harrison to the set with the bistro table and baker's rack to talk about the contestants, the challenges and the food.

Standing in front of the first counter, Brenden addressed the contestants. "I want no more gossip or speculating about the murder or Skylar while you are on set. Understand?" His question was answered with affirmative nods. Most of the contestants looked serious and contrite. Not Marco, he rolled his eyes while he nodded.

What was going on with him? His expressions whenever anyone mentioned Skylar or the murder were, in my opinion, an inappropriate response. He seemed happy Skylar felt ill and could be arrested for murder. Was he jealous of Skylar because of his girlfriend's interest? Or was his girlfriend Lisa Mackliner? He'd only called his girlfriend by her first name. Was there a way for me to ask him her last name during the interview segment that didn't sound awkward or nosy, or if he was the murderer alert him to the fact I was onto him?

Brenden interrupted my thoughts when he turned and called, "Skylar and Courtney to your tape."

"Skylar isn't here," I said.

Brenden swiveled his head from side to side.

"Neither is Quintin." My statement stopped his neck craning.

He walked toward me. With a lower voice, he said, "They haven't come back?"

Pursing my lips, I shook my head. For a man who insisted we stick to a shooting schedule, I figured they'd be back by now.

Again, Brenden looked around. "Kinzy?"

She looked up from a tablet.

"Go upstairs and get Harrison."

Taking her time, Kinzy finished what she'd been doing and headed toward the stairs. Brenden sighed. I understood why. Last season Kinzy jumped as high as she could to make Brenden happy. This season it appeared her loyalty was with Quintin.

In a few minutes, she and Harrison joined us.

"You need to stand in for Skylar to kick off the next challenge." Brenden pointed toward the arch. "He and Quintin left the set and haven't returned."

Harrison nodded and accompanied me to our places. With our toes on the tape marks, Brenden took a minute to check camera angles and proper lighting. Harrison stood an inch or two shorter than Skylar. Once Brenden was happy, he hollered, "Action."

"For your third challenge today, we'll wrap up the engagement party with a decadent dessert. Not only does the dessert have to taste spectacular, it must be in the shape of something that symbolizes a wedding."

"That's right, bells, rings, dresses, bow ties, to name a few." With perfect timing, Harrison hit his line.

"All in individual portions." I stifled a giggle. Some of the contestants' reactions were priceless. I hoped a cameraman caught the panic on Afton's and Nadine's faces, as well as the confidence on Marcos's.

"But wait, there's more." Harrison inflected excitement in his tone.

Several contestants' eyes widened. I'm sure they expected a surprise ingredient.

Harrison continued. "You must create a signature drink to serve with the dessert."

Smiles broke out all around.

"But wait, there's more." This time I didn't suppress the giggle. "The beverage must be able to be served with or without alcohol."

A few of the contestants' smiles faded and stress etched their features.

"You have two hours to complete this challenge," Harrison said.

We briefly looked at each other as instructed by the monitor before we turned our eyes back to the green light on the camera and said, "The baking begins now."

"Cut, perfect." Brenden walked toward us. "Harrison and Shannon, we'll film your conversation scene now about the judges' challenge. Courtney, you'll interview the contestants while they prepare their food." He turned to our cameraman. "Give them about fifteen minutes to get a good start on their baking."

Released for a few minutes, I took my chair. Had something happened to Skylar, Quintin or both? I couldn't imagine a pep talk by time-rigid Quintin taking much longer than a minute. Perhaps Quintin listened to me and took Skylar back to the resort for a health assessment. Skylar had showed signs of illness before Lisa was murdered. A sudden thought sent a chill shivering down my spine. Unless he killed her before he reported for work. I didn't know the time of death. Maybe guilt and remorse caused his nausea. If she came after him with a knife again, could he have killed her in self-defense?

I wondered how long Lisa had stalked Skylar. I left my phone in the dressing room today so I couldn't try to do an Internet search. I thought about Skylar's appearance. Off screen, he wore jeans and plaid shirts with longish hair that framed his face. The first time I saw him in this natural state, I didn't even recognize him. Was his television image a camouflage to his normal appearance? Was it done on purpose to keep anonymity from overzealous or obsessed fans?

A bright sliver of light pulled me from my thoughts about Skylar and the murder. Someone entered the workshop. I turned toward the door, hoping to see Skylar and Quintin had returned. Two men had entered the set, Drake and Sheriff Perry. Both twisted their necks in a perusal of the room.

With Quintin outside somewhere and Brenden and Kinzy filming the judges' discussion, I stood and walked over to them. "Are you looking for someone?"

Sheriff Perry pursed his lips. "Not you."

I returned the expression, then smiled at Drake.

"We're looking for Skylar. Do you know where he is?" Drake smiled and winked.

Happiness lifted my heart and widened my smile. "He's not here." I sighed. "The contestants were gossiping about the murder. He overheard and left in a huff of anger. Quintin followed him. I know which way they went. I'll go look for them." I started to walk toward the door.

Sheriff Perry caught my arm. "Just point us in the right direction. I told you, you are not getting involved in this investigation."

The sternness of his tone deflated my happiness, replacing it with a huff of anger.

"I was only trying to help." My gaze went from Sheriff Perry to Drake.

Drake now wore a sober expression, although I thought I saw a hint of amusement in his eyes, which fanned my flames of anger. Did he think Sheriff Perry's treatment of me was funny?

"Of course, you were." Sheriff Perry didn't hide his annoyance. "You'd have thought almost getting killed a few months ago would have made you more conscious of your safety."

I fought an audible huff. He had a point and Quintin *had* banished me to the set. Allowing my annoyance at both men to season my tone, I clipped out, "They headed in the direction of the lake."

I didn't have time to nurse my deflated and defeated feelings. My cameraman called my name and I reported to the kitchenette area of the set. We started on stage left with Miller Smith.

"What are you making?" I asked while watching him pour a peach-colored liquid into a freezer container.

A bright smile lit his face. "This is the base for the drink. It's a citrus punch." He snapped the lid on tight.

"I'll stick it in the freezer and hope it turns solid." He stopped working for a moment. "When vodka or lemon-lime soda is added to the frozen base, it becomes a slushy beverage." He lifted up the container, waved into the camera and headed toward the refrigerator.

I laughed and panned to the camera. "I guess that interview is over. Let's see what Miller's better half, Mary, is doing?" We moved to the kitchenette behind Miller.

Mary stirred a steaming pot on her stovetop. When she looked up at me, her face glistened with moisture. "I have to get this done. It's supposed to set overnight for the flavors to meld. I'm hoping two hours are enough." She picked the pan up from the heat and dumped green leaves into the pot.

"Are those tea leaves?" I stretched my neck to see what was in the pot.

"No." Mary said. Not looking up, she poured her concoction into a jar. "It's kaffir. I'm making a Philippe Khallins."

"I don't know that I've ever had one of those. What's in it?"

"Coconut milk, pineapple and lime juice, ginger, lemongrass, Chinese red chilies, sugar and salt. For the non-virgin version, I'll add gin." Mary glanced at the refrigerator, then back at me.

"Go on." I waved her off, not wanting to intrude on her time. Every minute counted for the contestants while preparing their challenge.

The cameraman filmed her hurrying away from her kitchenette. I walked over to where Alex stood by his mixer. He added flour to the whirring paddle a tablespoon at a time.

"I smell maple."

He smiled. "I'm making a maple and walnut cookie dough." He stopped the mixer, removed the bowl and dumped ground walnuts into it. He stirred his mixture with a spatula. "I'll roll it out and use a round cookie cutter, then pipe frosting in the shape of rosettes. Cookies are individual and easily eaten with your fingers."

I didn't recall the dessert needed to be finger food, just an individual serving. "Can you tell us what beverage you plan to serve with them?"

"Sure." Alex took a minute to look up at me. "I'm keeping the drink simple. I'm making a tea tini. I'm brewing decaffeinated tea and adding lemon, which is the non-alcoholic version. The adult beverage has lemon-infused vodka in it. Both are served chilled in a martini glass with a slice of lemon."

Although I wished Alex would refrain from using maple in his recipes, I had to admit his dessert and beverage sounded good. "I can't wait to sample it."

"Thanks." Alex glanced up when he grabbed his rolling pin.

I found Alex hard to interview. He kept his focus on his cooking, seeming not to care for camera time. I moved on.

Up next was Jeremiah. He'd worked fast. He'd cut piecrust into heart shapes using a cookie cutter. On a parchment paper–lined baking sheet lay six solid hearts. The six remaining on the counter had a small heart cut in the center.

"Are you making hand pies?" I thought of the apple finger pies I'd made on one of my live tapings of *Cooking with the Farmer's Daughter*.

"Sort of." He held up a Popsicle stick. "I'll put a strawberry rhubarb filling in each one and add the stick.

I'll crimp the top to the base and stick. It will make eating it with your fingers easier."

"Great idea!" Again, eating the dessert with your fingers wasn't in the instructions. Had the guidelines from the earlier challenges stuck with the contestants?

Jeremiah dumped chopped fresh strawberries into a saucepan. "I'll serve it with strawberry lemonade or vodka-spiked strawberry lemonade."

"Good choice having an underlying theme of strawberries."

Giving me a thumbs-up, Jeremiah headed to the pantry area.

"Vodka is popular today." I turned to the cameraman. "I hope we don't run out."

We moved to the last kitchenette in the row and the person who could answer a question for me, Nadine. Of course, we'd talk about what she was baking, but first I planned to ask how she was feeling and what the nurse practitioner diagnosed as her problem.

"Nadine, I am so happy to see you healthy and working with vigor." For her age, she was moving faster in the kitchen than the other four I'd interviewed. "You must be feeling better?"

Nadine stopped working. Her face flushed and she threw me a sheepish look. "I feel so silly. I caused everyone so much worry." She gave her head a small shake.

"It's nothing to feel bad about. Everyone gets sick." I seasoned my tone with a pinch of comfort.

She rolled her eyes. "I wasn't sick. I mean, yes, I was nauseous, but it wasn't from a bug or food poisoning."

"What do you mean?"

"I had a case of stage fright. Nerves, you might say. When I got onto the set and saw everything. I had no idea how many lights and cameras are used to film a television show. Then when all the stars walked onto the set." She threw her hands in the air. "Well, it hit me. The butterflies in my stomach decided they didn't want to stay there."

Whoa. Too much information. I knew this footage would hit the cutting room floor.

"I considered quitting. Carla talked me out of it. I took some medicine to calm my nervous tummy, and here I am making individual lemon meringue pies." Nadine waved her hand over her creation, giving me a perfect segue into talking about her baking.

Looking down, I saw she'd pressed graham cracker crust into gold foil cupcake liners. "How are you going to make this into a wedding symbol?" I wanted to make sure she'd heard all the rules for this challenge.

"That is where the meringue comes in. I'm going to pipe linked wedding bands and dust them with gold sanding sugar. Those will be baked separately, then placed on top of the lemon curd."

"Nice twist on the symbol. What drink are you planning to serve with it?" I loved the creativity of all of our contestants.

"I don't know." Eyes wide, she lifted her hands, palms out with her fingers splayed in a back-off fashion.

I took my cue. "I'll let you get back to your baking."

The remainder of the interviews were short, a few words and glances at the camera while they baked or created their beverage. We learned Mike, like Nadine, had no idea what to serve as his beverage. He stuck a pan of brownies in the oven with no concrete plan on what to do with them either. Afton, Donna and Carla worked on varying cheesecakes; however, their drink choices differed and revolved around punch, coffee and a flavored tea. While Diego and Marco promised their dessert and drink would reflect their heritage.

Lynne surprised me with an ice-cream-based dessert she planned to dip into dark chocolate and decorate with marzipan doves. Keeping with her theme, she planned to serve virgin and spiked grasshoppers made with ice cream as her beverages. Although her choice sounded good, I wondered how feasible serving an ice-cream-based dessert and beverage would go over with the judges. Then again, if the engagement party was a small, intimate affair, it would work perfect. I hoped she conveyed that idea, or Shannon and Harrison considered it during their critiquing.

With the interviews finished, I went to my chair to relax. I mused about the varied ideas our contestants came up with, even with three contestants making cheesecake, I knew there'd be no duplicates.

I drew in a deep breath and looked around the set for Skylar and Quintin. They were still nowhere to be found. My concern, once a low simmer, began to grow into a full boil of worry. Where could they be? I knew Quintin had heard me, but had he *listened* to me and taken Skylar to a medical professional to be checked out? I now knew something other than food poisoning or the flu caused his tummy trouble since Carla's and Nadine's illnesses were contained to them individually.

Did Sheriff Perry and Drake find them? Or had I sent them on a wild-goose chase? I caught my breath. Had Sheriff Perry and Drake needed to find Skylar to arrest him? The thought hadn't occurred to me earlier when I'd pointed the way. Maybe Quintin went along to post bail.

The bang of the heavy wooden door being thrown open startled me from my thoughts. I turned and squinted my eyes against the sunlight filtering into the darker wings of the set. Quintin stormed into the room, stopping beside my chair.

His lips were drawn into a thin line, grimmer than usual. "Where is Brenden?" His hard stare and hovering body made panic boil inside me.

I stood. "They're shooting the judges' conversation . . ." I stopped talking as three more figures walked through the door. Sheriff Perry and Drake flanked Skylar. Certain they'd arrest him, I ran over to them.

"What is going on?" My demanding tone earned me a stern look from Sheriff Perry. I took a closer look and realized Skylar was swaying between the two men, his chin bobbed down to his chest.

"What happened out there?" I spun toward Quintin, and my eyes searched his face. He answered my question with a cold, hard stare and slight smirk.

"I don't feel good."

I cringed at what was becoming an all-too-familiar sentence coming out of Skylar's mouth and turned just in time to see him collapse and fall to the floor.

Chapter Eleven

"Skylar!"

Drake and Sheriff Perry grabbed his shirt to break a hard fall, then eased him to the floor.

I ran to Skylar, dropped to my knees and cradled his head.

His closed eyes opened to slits. "So tired."

Looking up, I saw all three men staring down at Skylar. "He needs to see a doctor. He seemed better and now he's relapsed. Something is wrong." I shouted the last word.

"I agree." Sheriff Perry hunched down beside me. "Do you think you can stand?"

"Yeah." Skylar made no attempt to move.

Drake held a hand out to me. I grasped it and allowed him to leverage me back to a standing position while Sheriff Perry helped Skylar sit up.

"Can this wait?"

Horror widened my eyes. Had I heard Quintin right?

"No!" Sheriff Perry's voice boomed and drew the attention of a small group of crew members in the wings. Drake and Sheriff Perry gripped Skylar under the arms and lifted him to a standing position. "We're taking him to a clinic."

I watched the two men half guide, half drag Skylar through the exit door. I turned on Quintin. "What happened out there?"

"Nothing you need to worry about." Quintin cold-shouldered me and messed with his cell phone.

I marched around and planted myself in front of him. "Aren't you concerned one of the stars of your show could be very ill?"

Quintin's head shot up. His features twisted into an expression that let me know he didn't appreciate my tone or my question. Glancing back down at his phone, he finished what he was doing when I'd interrupted. "What I'm concerned or unconcerned about is no business of yours." He gave a disgusted harrumph and stalked off toward the door leading to the bistro table set.

Anger fisted my hands. Quintin clearly didn't care about Skylar's health. How could someone only care about the bottom line and not the people involved in the show? I slumped down into my chair. Skylar had seemed to be getting better, drinking some water and trying some food. Had Quintin said or done something to put Skylar under more stress, causing him to relapse? Or was Skylar becoming severely dehydrated from the inability to keep something in his stomach? Lack of food or water would cause him to collapse.

I sighed and released a little of my anger with it. At least he was finally getting medical care. If nothing else, a doctor could prescribe anti-nausea pills and hook him up to an IV for liquids. I flexed my fingers. I needed my phone to send Drake a text asking him to keep me posted on Skylar's condition. I stood, planning to head upstairs and retrieve it, when Quintin led Brenden, Shannon and Harrison back onto the main set. No one looked happy.

Shannon and Harrison trudged over to me. Brenden and Kinzy continued to follow Quintin.

"What's going on?"

"Quintin is making Carla and Nadine stay when we break for lunch so Shannon and I can sample their appetizers from yesterday morning. I told him it was ridiculous because the food wouldn't be fresh." Harrison huffed. "Not to mention the four of us will have to change clothes and change them back. Why not judge the current challenge first? The man simply will not listen to reason."

Shannon lifted her dress and sat. "We should have just redone the entire appetizer segment so there'd be no change of clothes for anyone."

Harrison dropped his body into a chair and then his voice tone to just above a whisper. "I don't want to give Marco a second chance at those appetizers." He grimaced. "Something about him rubs me the wrong way."

"I guess that is true. It wouldn't be fair after we critiqued and gave suggestions to some of the cooks. They could implement them on the second time around." Shannon sighed.

"Right." Harrison nodded; then he stood in an aggressive stance. "I've had enough. I'm going to go throw my celebrity around."

Shannon and I watched Harrison march over to Brenden and Quintin.

"Think it will work?" Shannon leaned forward in her chair.

I couldn't have been prouder of Harrison. "It just might. If Harrison would threaten to walk, Quintin might concede. And what difference does it make if we break for lunch now or in an hour. It seldom takes you and Harrison very long to judge their food."

Brenden interrupted our gripe session. "Courtney, you are calling time alone. Shannon and Harrison no longer need to change clothes." He tried to fight a smile and lost the battle. He even chuckled.

"What did Harrison threat?" I smiled.

"To call his attorney. Sadly"—Brenden turned to Shannon—"you will need to work through part of your lunch."

She flipped a hand through the air. "No problem."

"Here is the change of schedule." Kinzy pushed a piece of paper at Brenden.

Harrison joined us, a smug smile on his face. I mouthed *good job* to Harrison.

"We'll call time and judge the challenge. Everyone will break for lunch except Shannon, Harrison, Nadine and Carla." Brenden sighed. "Courtney, later you will need to do a voice-over explaining there was an illness on the first day so viewers know why Harrison and Shannon are in different clothing." He sent me an apologetic look.

"No problem," I said.

Brenden continued, "Courtney, to avoid any further wardrobe explanations, and since Skylar is incapacitated, the judges will announce the winner and loser of the first challenge without you." Brenden looked up from the paper.

I knew he wanted an answer. "Okay."

"After lunch, it's business as usual. We'll award the winner of the episode and send someone home." Brenden nodded.

"What about Skylar?"

Brenden shot me another apologetic look. "We'll have to shoot around him if he is not back."

"Where is he?" Worry peppered Shannon's question.

Holding up a hand to Brenden, I said, "I'll fill them in on what happened to Skylar."

He nodded. "After you call time, though."

"Courtney, take your place." Kinzy issued my orders.

Once under the arch, my cameraman and I waited for Brenden to count down time. A few of the contestants scrambled. With just a few minutes left, Lynne needed to add the doves to her dessert, Alex shook a martini shaker, while Miller ladled his very runny slush into his glasses and still had to pour in vodka or soda. None of them seemed aware the end time was near.

"Bakers, you have one minute to complete this challenge."

Mike wiped the edges of his plate clean; Jeremiah rearranged his desserts on his display tray. Afton and Donna were adding garnishes to their glasses. Marco stood arms crossed over his chest leaning against his counter. A confident smile stretched across his face while both his challenges rested on the edge of his counter and looked quite appetizing.

My gaze dropped to Brenden's finger countdown. At his fist, I said, "Time's up. Stop baking."

The bakers stepped away from their creations. Crew members buzzed around them, removing dirty pans and dishes and wiping the counters until they sparkled. Harrison and Shannon huddled around me.

"Skylar seems to have had a relapse. Drake and Sheriff Perry took him to a medical clinic. I don't have my phone with me or I'd text Drake for an update." I glanced at the state of the set, wondering if I'd have time to pop upstairs and grab my phone.

Kinzy made final adjustments to their offerings at the end of the counter. A crew member brought in the last two stools for the contestants to be seated on during their judging. "We're ready," Kinzy called over a low din of conversation.

I'd have to wait and text when we broke for lunch.

Brenden beckoned us over with his hand. "I want you to go back and forth in a right, left, left, right fashion. We should have separated Miller and Mary, although it makes for good television when they hackle or support each other while baking. I don't think it films well in the judging, though."

The contestants made two offerings of each item. We headed toward Miller as instructed. Two heart-shaped desserts awaited us.

"We'll start with the dessert, then move to the beverage." Shannon smiled at Miller. "Your offering is very pretty and color-coordinated."

Harrison lifted a plate. "What is it?"

"A meringue tart with a peach filling. I added gold sugar into the egg whites for a little sparkle. I'm serving it with a slushy citrus punch." Miller fisted his hands and rolled his shoulders in a sitting dance move.

The meringue crunched when Shannon and Harrison cut the fork through. "It's a little too crisp." Harrison popped a bite into his mouth. Shannon followed his lead.

After swallowing, Shannon licked her lips. "And too sweet."

Miller's dancing shoulders stopped.

"I agree. The bottom of the meringue is soggy. Did you put a layer of jam or something as sealant down before you added your peach filling?" Harrison laid his fork on the table.

Miller shook his head.

"I think your filling is too loose and needs more peaches. Sorry, Miller, all I taste is sugar." Shannon frowned.

"We'll try the nonalcoholic version of the drink first. Which is it?" Harrison looked at the identical glasses.

"The one with the mint leaf is nonalcoholic."

"Okay. Just a note to everyone." Shannon encompassed the group with her gaze. "A mint leaf is easy to lift from a nonalcoholic version to a drink with alcohol. You should give your beverages more distinction than a simple garnish or different-colored straw." She lifted the glass and sipped. "I like the flavor, but where is the slush?" Shannon peered down into her glass and back at Miller.

"There wasn't enough time for it to freeze properly."

Harrison and Shannon both sampled the spiked version. "Not enough alcohol." Harrison set the glass down. "Overall, you had a nice idea, but both your drink and dessert are sweet."

"I agree. They didn't pair well together."

Disappointment crept onto Miller's face. He hung his head.

Moving on to Afton, we found baked cheesecake in ramekins. The topping was traditional cherry. She'd piped a solid heart out of pink whipped cream into the center. Her beverage had a tea base.

"Obviously, you have made a cherry cheesecake." Harrison smiled. "It looks festive. Let's see how it tastes."

Shannon and Harrison dug into it. Shannon moaned in pleasure. "This is everything anyone would want in a cheesecake."

Harrison nodded. I lifted a spoon and scooped into the creamy mixture.

"Perfectly baked with just the right amount of crust-to-filling ratio. What are your beverages?" Harrison smiled.

"I made cherry tea by adding maraschino cherry juice." She pointed to a glass with a clear stem. "And cherry liquor." She pointed to a glass with a red stem.

"This is an excellent example of a distinction between an alcoholic and nonalcoholic beverage. Good job." Shannon smiled and took a sip from each glass.

"Perfect." Harrison threw his hands in the air. "The traditional dessert adorned with a traditional symbol of love is accentuated with a drink that adds a hint of cherry to keep the theme, yet isn't too sweet. Well done."

A wide smile eased all the apprehension from Afton's face.

The cheesecake Donna prepared didn't firm up, but

her fruit punch, which included Jell-O as an ingredient, was a hit in both versions.

"You used the right amount of vodka to punch up your drink." Harrison did a cocky head swagger at his joke, which drew laughter and smiles from the contestants.

This version of Harrison was such an upgrade to last season.

"And you made a great distinction by using a traditional punch cup for the nonalcoholic version and a high ball glass for the vodka-laced punch."

Donna nodded her thanks while rapidly blinking emotion from her eyes. I hoped she took the praise to heart for the beverage and didn't focus on the cheesecake critique.

Mary's beverage failed, not enough time for the flavors to steep. Her brownies cut into heart shapes and dipped into melting chocolate tasted great but were messy, with not all the side surface covered, and the flakes of crumbs made a bumpy not smooth finish.

Alex and Marco earned high marks from the judges. Harrison did suggest Alex stray away from his go-to ingredient, maple syrup. Internally, I did a fist pump. I wanted to see Alex succeed. I didn't want him to use the show as a commercial for their family-owned business. We had a barbeque sauce manufacturer on the show last season, and although his team tried to convince Shannon to use and plug his product on her show, he never used it as a main ingredient in any of his challenge recipes.

Marco prepared cannoli. He dusted powdered sugar over a stencil to create an image of a tiered wedding cake on the top of the pastry and served it with Italian roast coffee, plain and spiked with amaretto. The cannoli tasted delicious, as did the coffee. Shannon suggested bolder decorations, but Harrison felt the powdered sugar decoration was understated and a good finish to the dessert. I wondered why he chose a cake instead of another wedding symbol. Was it a twisted psychological clue, like when serial killers keep an item of their victims'?

Shannon and Harrison moved on, so I filed my thought about Marco away for later. The remaining contestants made passable desserts and drinks with the exception of Mike. He blew the judges away with a mocha brownie cut and frosted to look like a ring box with a silhouette of a diamond ring made from white molding chocolate. The band dusted with gold sugar, the diamond, silver. He served homemade peppermint hot chocolate in a silver mug and peppermint schnapps–laced hot chocolate in a gold mug.

Harrison took the gold mug with him when he left the station, Shannon the brownie and me the hot chocolate. His offering satisfied the chocoholic in all of us.

I followed Shannon and Harrison to the bottom of the staircase where they would wait until the crew reset Nadine's and Carla's kitchen and appetizers for judging. I ignored their whispers. I knew they were conferring on the last judging and contemplating who'd stood out and who failed the engagement party challenge.

Hurrying up the stairs to the wardrobe room, I snatched my phone from my purse, I noticed I'd missed a text from Eric asking Shannon and I to meet him for dinner at the steak house. I RSVP'd for both of us telling him Shannon might run late for filming. I received a thumbs-up from him while I composed my text to Drake inquiring on Skylar's health. With nowhere to carry my phone, I tucked it back into my purse. I planned to get my lunch from the catering table and come back. That should give Drake plenty of time to respond.

I stepped back down to the main floor. Harrison and Shannon stood by the commissary table munching on celery. Justin and crew had set out a full-blown salad bar with two soup choices. I passed on the cream-based soups and heaped a plate with mixed greens, a variety of veggies, chickpeas and grilled chicken cut into bite-size pieces. I snagged the small container of salad dressing with my name on the label. It was my only food preference in my contract, a salad dressing made with extra virgin olive oil, lemon juice and pepper. A bottle of sparkling water rounded out my lunch; then I carefully headed toward the stairs.

Harrison snagged a cucumber from my salad plate as I passed by.

"It's a good thing we get to taste food on this show, we aren't going to get much of a lunch." He glanced at Shannon, who looked ready to head to the set.

"I know." She perused my plate and slipped off a slice of hard-boiled egg.

"Eric invited us to dinner at the steak house. I took the liberty to RSVP for you since we were planning on having dinner anyway." I moved my community plate out of their reach.

"I agree to dinner." Shannon giggled as she and Harrison walked to a kitchenette.

I climbed up to the wardrobe room, looked around, and then sighed. "We need a table," I said to no one. I set my plate on the counter by the mirror. Grabbing my phone from my purse, I settled into one of the swivel makeup chairs to eat my lunch and see what Drake had to say. Disappointment sagged my shoulders; obviously Drake had nothing to say. I'd received no reply to my text. Dare I text Sheriff Perry? I had his number. My poised thumbs hovered over the number; then I decided I wasn't up for a lecture whether in person or text about staying out of his investigation. Drake may be driving; I needed to give him more time to respond. I also needed to believe that no news was good news for Skylar.

I enjoyed a few bites of my salad before pulling up a search engine. I tried a search to see if a victim was told when the convicted person was released from prison. I had my answer in a second. Yes, according to the Crime Victims' Rights Act. I forked another bite of salad.

Was that why Skylar had acted so nervous? Could it explain the reason he'd called private meetings with Brenden and argued with Drake? Had he insisted on extra security? Or an assigned security detail? I'd have had no objections for a reassignment for Pamela. As far as I knew, I wasn't in any possible danger. Of course, I hadn't realized I was a few months ago either. I still didn't understand why Sheriff Perry insisted on extra security for my show. Pamela was guarding Eric and two conference rooms turned into my set, not me. If he really thought I was trouble, wouldn't it be best to have Security on the same premises as me?

I gave my head a slight shake. I'd gotten off course. I had more questions to plug into the search engine. My thumbs tapped out "Lisa Mackliner" and "felony" before I tapped the search icon. The first item was a national news report about her sentencing in the stalking of Skylar Daily. I clicked the headline and read the article. It outlined everything Skylar had hollered at the group earlier this morning. The article quoted Skylar as saying he hoped she received counseling and help for her delusions while incarcerated.

I also learned she grew up smack dab in the middle of a flyover state. She'd moved to the West Coast but for some reason kept her permanent residence in Iowa. The last job she held before being arrested was a clerk at Under the Covers, a local bookstore in the neighborhood where Skylar lived. The article listed no prior arrests for anything.

Drumming my fingers on the armrest of the chair, I tried to remember if Marco had said where he was from. He'd mentioned a family-owned bakery, but had he said where it was located? I tapped his name into the search engine and found the publicity page of *The American Baking Battle* listing him as a contestant, every social media site and then a bakery. I accessed the bakery link and the browser opened to an About Us page on a website.

The Martino family business had been established by his great-grandfather and passed down for generations. Currently, Marco's father ran the business with the help of Marco and his sister. I scanned the rest of the page, looking for an address and found it at the very bottom along with a link for directions. I tapped the link and the bakery's storefront popped up in a strip mall. The sign used the colors of Italy's flag. On a large plate glass window, bold black letters said, "Martino's Italian Bakery."

Beside the close-up picture was one showing the entire strip mall, which consisted of six businesses. Placing my finger on the screen, I scrolled left to see the rest of the picture. I found an eclectic group: a manicure shop, a

Chinese takeout, the Martino family bakery, an insurance company, a cell phone business. I enlarged the picture to get a better look at the large end store.

My breath caught in my throat.

Two doors down from the Martino family bakery was a bookstore.

Under the Covers.

Chapter Twelve

Before I had time to do any other searching, Shannon and Harrison had blown back into the dressing room to eat a quick lunch before we filmed the end shot for the first episode of season two and told me Quintin wanted me on set immediately.

I'd reported to the set and now stood under hot lights in front of the kitchenettes between crew members who matched Shannon and Harrison in height so the camera angles and lights could be adjusted for the final shot of the episode. I tried to stand still, but nervous energy coursed through me from the information I'd found online. I shifted from one foot to the other while my mind stirred the information trying to complete the recipe, which was impossible because I was missing key ingredients about Lisa's life. I'd found information to link Lisa with Marco. But how sturdy was that link? They worked in the same strip mall. They had to know each other, right? Was Lisa Mackliner not only Skylar's stalker, but Marco's girlfriend, Lisa? It would explain why Lisa was on the premises of Coal Castle Resort. Or was the name Lisa and workplace locations a coincidence?

I contemplated my many questions. I wanted to get filming wrapped up so I could delve deeper into my research and maybe run a few theories by Shannon and Eric at dinner. The bakery, a longtime established business according to their website, stood at the current location for fifteen years. How long had the bookstore rented a space in the strip mall? How long had Lisa Mackliner worked at the bookstore? Did strip mall employees patronize Martino's Italian Bakery? Another thing to consider was how long Lisa had been incarcerated. The article I'd read, dated eighteen months ago, said the most recent job she'd had was at the bookstore. That didn't mean Lisa had worked there right up until the time of her arrest. She may have been unemployed or employed elsewhere. Would Skylar know that information? Was there another way for me to find out?

One thing I knew for certain. I'd keep my eye on Marco. His conversations bordered on troubling. His expressions seemed inappropriate for the circumstances.

"Whew." Shannon pulled up beside me, breath heavy from hurrying. I'd been so lost in thought, I hadn't realized the crew members no longer flanked me.

"I'll say." Harrison sneaked a baby carrot into his mouth. "I'm going to talk to my agent so he can deal with Quintin. This wardrobe snafu and working through lunch should never have happened," Harrison said, his tone indignant.

He was right. The wardrobe staff should have been notified to dress us the same as yesterday.

"The shot is ready. Bring in the contestants!" Brenden hollered over the noise of the crew.

Quintin paced on the sidelines while Kinzy escorted the contestants onto the set and lined them up in front of the first set of counters. The contestants had shed their comical aprons. Once everyone was in place, Brenden walked over to our trio.

"Courtney, read all the lines. I'd thought Skylar might be back for filming, so I didn't change anything on the script." Brenden shrugged and walked back to the side-lines of the set.

Drake had never answered my text. I'd left my cell phone in my on-set chair seat when I'd taken my place. Perhaps Skylar had been admitted to the hospital. Could his illness have been caused by something else, maybe a ruptured appendix?

Brenden counted down my cue.

Pushing my thoughts and worry aside, I smiled. "Bakers, your appetizers, main courses and desserts for an engagement party were varied. Some offerings surprised the judges while others disappointed them." I paused so I could sweep my gaze across the bakers. "Like the judges, one of you will be surprised when you are awarded the baker of the day, while another will leave the kitchen and experience disappointment."

Marco puffed out his chest when I mentioned baker of the day, a satisfied look covered his face. With his failed appetizers, did he think he'd cinched the title? Donna dropped her gaze down and wrung her hands at my reminder one baker would be sent home. Most of the contestants faced forward, stoic with nerves.

"The baker of the day is Mike."

Shock dropped his jaw. He watched as his peers clapped.

"Mike, the judges loved your appetizers and liked your main course, but it was your dessert that put you over the top today. The brownies and beverages appealed to both adults and children, and could easily serve a large number or small, intimate group. The judges"—pausing, I smiled and looked first at Harrison and then at Shannon before continuing—"do suggest if it was a summer wedding serving chocolate milk and spiked iced mochas rather than a hot beverage. Congratulations on a job well done."

Again, his peers clapped. Mike finally let out a breath and smiled.

I waited for the applause to stop. I sobered my expression. "Now for the hardest part of the day, sending someone home. Although the judges, and the cohosts, enjoy eating ethnic food or recipes handed down throughout your families . . ." I locked my gaze on Marco, whose expression never changed even though he'd presented recipes that reflected his heritage. However, when I moved my eyes to Carla, she knew her name would be called. She buried her face into her hands. "They sometimes miss the mark. Carla your lefse and mock lutefisk entrée left the judges thirsty and confused on how to eat them. Your dessert and beverage were not a good paring. Carla, you are the contestant leaving the kitchen today."

By the time I'd made my announcement, tears rolled down her cheeks. She swiped at them with the backs of her hand while nodding her head. The other contestants circled her. Nadine wrapped Carla in a side hug.

Brenden cut our camera, and the three of us went to congratulate the winner and extend condolences to Carla. After a few minutes, Brenden hollered, "Cut."

Shannon, Harrison and I stepped back. The contestants stayed in a tight group, chatting and sharing how they thought they would be the one to go home. Brenden joined our group.

"Look, Brenden, this time you achieved what you wanted, a big, happy family." I jerked my head in the direction of the tight-knit group.

He smiled. "I did."

Kinzy escorted Carla away from the fray to shoot her exit interview while the other contestants headed for their exit door.

"Any word on Skylar?" Harrison addressed his question to Brenden.

"No." Quintin clipped out the word as he stalked past us. He stopped and turned toward the group. "I wish you'd all stop worrying about him and his whereabouts, and do the job you were hired to do." He flicked a narrow-eyed stare toward Brenden. "You are coworkers, not family." He tromped toward the door.

"How can someone be so uncaring?" Shannon harrumphed after her question.

I shared her disgust, yet I also wondered about Quintin. He was cold and unemotional, just like some killers.

I checked my phone before Shannon and I changed. No message from Drake. I texted Eric we'd be at the resort in about twenty minutes. He told me to meet him at Fit for a King. I sent Drake another text and turned to the business of disrobing out of the wedding-themed attire.

It felt good to be back in my street clothes, black leggings with a pink long-sleeved tunic. The cowl neckline on the tunic helped frame my face and show off my onyx dangle earrings. My feet loved my pink flats with memory foam. My stylist offered to comb out my hair, but I liked the French braid, so I declined the offer. He did remove the wreath of flowers.

Shannon requested her stylist remove the bun and add some curl to her blond locks. She wore jeans with flat ankle boots and a soft cotton sweater in peach. She fluffed through her hair with her fingers. "This feels so much better than all of those pins poking into my head."

"Beauty hurts." I laughed.

"Don't I know it! Between the last two days, my feet are killing me. Let's get a ride back to the resort." Shannon slung her purse over her shoulder.

I checked my phone one more time and found no reply. I stuffed it into my purse, and together we stepped down to the now-darkened set and out of the heavy wooden door.

We caught a lift with Brenden and Harrison back to the resort.

Saying our goodbyes, Shannon and I hurried to the steak house, gave them our names, then followed the hostess when she told us part of our party was seated.

I wasn't surprised to be led to the more secluded booth in the back of the restaurant. I decided to lovingly call it my booth since it seemed to be where I was always seated when eating at the establishment.

The closer we walked to the booth the more it looked like two people occupied it. I furrowed my brow. When we rounded the corner, I saw Pamela seated across from Eric. What was she doing here?

"Hi, y'all." Shannon's smile extended to her tone.

Pamela looked up from the menu and smiled. Eric looked from Pamela to us with the same dazed smile he wore while looking at Pamela.

"Bad day?" Concern replaced his smile. Eric scooted over in the booth, leaving ample room for both of us.

"Oh, excuse me." Pamela inched over toward the solid wall of the booth.

Shannon slid into the padded seat beside Pamela.

What a romantic! Even when there was no need to be. Didn't she see the smitten look on Eric's face when we approached? I slipped into his side of the booth.

"I'm serious." Eric patted my shoulder. "Everything okay?"

"Yes. Well, no." I looked at him before I pulled my phone from my bag. "Skylar collapsed on set today. Sheriff Perry and Drake took him to a medical clinic."

"And no one knows what is happening. Not even Brenden or Quintin." Shannon got in on the conversation.

"I texted Drake three times. No answer." I held up my phone for proof. I don't know why.

"Let me give it a try."

Concern edged Pamela's tone, which chased away a tinge of my annoyance at her presence here. I really wanted to talk about the murder. Share the information I'd found with Eric and Shannon, and run some of my theories past them even though I knew I'd get a verbal warning from Eric to stay out of the murder investigation.

Pamela, still dressed in a fuchsia Nolan Security polo and jeans, pulled her cell phone from the carrying case on her belt. Her thumbs tapped out a rhythm; then she laid the phone on the table. "Hopefully, he'll answer me." She smiled my way. "In the meantime, I'd like to talk about your upcoming filming."

"She has some good ideas."

An enchanted look shone on Eric's face. I fought my external eye roll.

"I'm sure Courtney would love to hear them." Shannon's foot nudged my foot under the table. I looked up to see her pursed-lipped expression.

"Yes, I'd love to hear them," I said, although my tone lacked sincerity.

The waitress interrupted us, setting down water and asking for our beverage order. I ordered a vodka gimlet. Shannon decided on a dirty martini, while Eric asked for imported beer. Still on duty, Pamela went with iced tea.

I wondered how long their shifts were. Twelve hours?

"After studying your perimeter."

I looked at Pamela. My expression must have been blank.

"Of the suites where your show is filmed," she added for clarity.

"Right."

"I am requesting that during filming the door to the employee hallway is locked so only security personnel assigned to the show can unlock it with their pass key, which leaves one entrance or exit to eliminate unauthorized persons on your set. Especially in light of the new development here at Coal Castle Resort."

"You mean the murder." My tone was direct.

"Yes. Now, we don't think you are in any way threatened, but we aren't taking any chances. As a matter of fact, due to emergency evacuation rules, a guard will be posted by the locked door to unlock it if need be. There will also be personnel outside of the main door to the suite during filming. Of course, Drake and I'll be present in your audience." Pamela stopped talking and leaned back while the waitress distributed the beverages and took our food order.

Which gave me time to remember a few terrifying moments I'd managed to live through last season when the murderer accessed my set through the employee entrance, which was once a secret passageway in the castle. "That is a good idea."

Pamela smiled, then took a sip of her iced tea. "Also, during the meet and greet, I'll only be a few feet away at all times, whether you are sitting signing an autograph or standing for a picture."

"Is that necessary?" I set my glass on the table after sampling my drink.

"I need to be close enough to cover your body with mine if there is a threat of danger."

I sat back in the booth. She was willing to throw her body over mine if there was danger? I knew it was her job and she was being professional, but still, it touched me. I needed to be nicer to her. "Thank you."

"It's the least I can do for my favorite cooking star." Pamela blushed a little at her admission.

Before I could respond, Drake appeared at the end of the table. "Room for one more?"

He jerked his head toward Eric in a slide motion. Eric pretended he didn't notice. I know he had to because he was looking right at Drake and frowning.

"Sure, we've got plenty of room over here. Don't we, Pamela?" Shannon plastered a smug smile to her lips.

"Yes." Pamela scooted closer to the walled part of the booth while Shannon slid to the middle, leaving plenty of seating space for Drake in the booth designed for a party of six.

His features fell as he took a seat across from me instead of beside me. My heart danced a little bit in my chest. *That* was a sign I couldn't misread.

Pamela leaned over Shannon. "I was telling Courtney about our security plans for the live filming of her show."

"She has good ideas. Things that should have been implemented last time."

My gaze flew to Eric. It seemed he'd stretched his spine and threw back his shoulders to appear taller and broader. He lifted his beer and took a long swallow.

Again, Shannon bumped my foot under the table. I glanced her way to find a sly smile on her lips and a twinkle in her eye.

"Well." Drake motioned the waitress over and placed a drink and food order. He was obviously off duty because he ordered scotch and water. "I told Brenden to ax the live shows when he hired Nolan Security." Drake zoned his line of vision on Eric. His tone dripped with challenge.

Eric's beer bottle bottom met the table, hard.

Pamela's eyes widened and her face morphed into a what-is-happening expression.

"Maybe Brenden should have hired—"

"Drake." Shannon cut off Eric. She turned to face Drake while laying a hand to his forearm.

Once his attention was focused on Shannon, I turned to Eric and shot my hands out in front of me, palms out, and mouthed, *What are you doing?*

He answered my question with a deadpan look.

"We were wondering." Shannon's drawl was soft, soothing and filled with concern. "How Skylar is feeling?"

Thank goodness for her Southern charm to defuse the impromptu macho situation.

The waitress dropped off Drake's drink, inquired on refills and received a nod from Eric.

"I texted you several times inquiring after Skylar. Did you receive them?" I lifted my glass and took a sip. Although I was annoyed Drake hadn't answered my texts, I kept my tone light.

"I did. I was driving when the first two came through. The third I thought I'd answer in person after my shift ended. I was cleaning up when Pamela texted and let me know to meet you in the steak house."

For priding myself on noticing things, I'd totally missed Drake wore a plaid flannel shirt with jeans versus a shirt with the company logo.

"So," I prompted. "How is he?"

"He is fine. Or will be." Drake took a drink of his scotch.

"That means?" I crossed my arms. I didn't want to do an information dance. I wanted to know if my cohost was ill.

"The doctor tested Skylar's blood again today and diagnosed his nausea, too much Ambien in his system. He had high doses the day of the murder and lower doses today."

The next morning while getting ready to head to the set, I received a text from Eric asking me to meet him in the coffee shop. My shoulders sagged. I'd hoped he'd deliver it to my suite. He and I needed to talk. I asked for fifteen minutes to finish up and received a blue thumbs-up symbol.

After the tense dinner last night where Shannon, bless her heart, deflected their snide remarks, I decided it was time for he and I to clear this matter up. I also decided my snarky actions toward Pamela weren't any more becoming than the machoism we'd all experienced last night.

The sad part was, I still didn't know if Drake and Eric were interested in me or Pamela or simply didn't like each other. Shannon was the only person who could speak and obtain a civil answer from either man where the other man didn't have an uncivil, for lack of a better word, commentary.

At least we knew Skylar's illness wasn't life-threatening. However, his illness and connection with Lisa Mackliner kept me up most of the night researching. I had no concrete answers on anything except the side effects of Ambien on some people. Had his doctor overprescribed the sleep aid? Had Skylar not read the side effects warning or reported them to his doctor? Those were easy answers to obtain. I'd ask Skylar today when he showed up for work. Tight-lipped, all Drake would tell us to alleviate our concern was that Skylar should feel better once the drug was out of his system. Anything else about the investigation he said would have to come from Sheriff Perry.

I gave myself a once-over in the mirror. With no plans after work, I slipped into black yoga pants with a matching jacket and a turquoise long-sleeve T-shirt. Certain my outfit held protection from the crisp September morning, I draped my wallet purse over my head and arm. I tucked my long hair behind my ears. I knew with a wedding theme, my hair would be twisted into some type of formal do. I hoped not another French twist. Although the style was timeless and stunning, my scalp still hurt from the hairpins two days ago.

I hurried from my room, grabbed the elevator and stepped out into the lobby. With our sunrise makeup and wardrobe call, getting an elevator took only seconds. Today, due to lack of sleep or too much research, I envied people who could sleep in. Stifling a yawn, I walked directly to Castle Grounds.

Eric, dressed in navy dress pants and a cashmere sweater, waited by the sign indicating pickup. "Good morning." He smiled and gave his head a sideways nod toward a table where a bowl of oatmeal and large cinnamon roll sat.

"Morning." I took a seat at the table. In a minute, Eric joined me.

I took the cup from his hand and sipped. The warm coffee-laced milk infused with hazelnut flavoring woke up my taste buds and senses. "I needed this."

Eric spooned into his oatmeal. "I'll share." He slid the plate with the roll closer to me.

"I shouldn't. I can eat on set." I pinched off a piece and popped it into my mouth.

"I meant to tell you and Shannon I'm working on the proposal for your show. When I get it where I'd like it, we'll have a meeting to go over the details. I've e-mailed about Shannon cohosting with your next live taping. I've yet to receive an answer." He ate some of his breakfast.

"Okay." I drew a deep breath. With the murder and Skylar being so ill, I'd pushed my problems to the back burner. With Eric talking about my career, it seemed like a good time to discuss it. "Have you heard anything from the network about my apology?" I took a long drink of my coffee so I could have one last sip that tasted good in case Eric had bad news to deliver.

"Actually"—Eric pulled at the cinnamon roll until a piece broke free—"no. Nothing more than they felt you handled the apology well." He looked at me with an encouraging glint in his eyes. "No news is good news."

I sighed. "I hope so." I fiddled with pinching off another piece of the roll. "If you want to put feelers out for another show to produce . . ." I stopped talking when my voice cracked.

"I don't." Eric's tone made it clear he was done discussing the subject.

After enjoying another bite of cinnamon roll, I approached another topic. "I did some research on Ambien last night. One side effect is nausea. It can also cause nervousness and confusion, which are all the symptoms Skylar had. Do you think he had to take Ambien because of his stalker? Do you think his doctor overprescribed the drug, or he just took too much?" I hated to think of Skylar abusing any type of drug even prescription.

Wide-eyed, Eric stared at me. I braced for a lecture to stay out of the murder investigation.

"Stop speculating."

Surprise bugged my eyes. I hadn't braced for Sheriff Perry to be standing behind me. Before I turned around, he moved to the end of the table, where he was visible. "And stay out of my investigation."

"I am not investigating anything. I am concerned about my colleague and friend's health, both physical and mental."

Sheriff Perry didn't care for my reaction by the look he pinned on me. "Need I remind you that you were almost a second murder victim last time?"

"Seriously, Courtney, stay out of this. Skylar's medical problems aren't any of your business."

I could not believe Eric had sided with Sheriff Perry.

Well, I could because he did last time too. I just didn't want him to. I stood so Sheriff Perry wasn't looking down on me. "Skylar is incapacitated right now. I'm not even sure he knows how serious of a situation he is in because he's been so ill. He needs an advocate and I'm it." I thumbed my chest and jutted out my chin.

Sheriff Perry puckered his lips to the side and blew out a breath. He started to walk away, then turned around and said, "You are right about one thing. Skylar is in serious trouble. All of the evidence points to him. He's our main, and only, suspect in the murder of Lisa Mackliner." Then he turned and strode away.

Chapter Thirteen

I watched Sheriff Perry walk away from me, mouth agape. I closed my mouth and drew my lips into a perturbed line. How could he drop information like that and just walk away without waiting for questions from me? Or had he told me because he needed my help to figure out who murdered Lisa Mackliner? Last season Sheriff Perry told me he'd ruled Skylar out as a person of interest in the murder because Skylar didn't have the stomach for murder. Had he hit a dead end and needed a fresh perspective on the case?

My lips stopped being perturbed and curled into a smile, certain the brief conversation was the sheriff's passive-aggressive plea for my assistance. I mean, I'm not a police officer or even a licensed private detective, so he wouldn't outright ask for my help.

"I know that look." Eric stood. "Don't get involved

with the murder investigation." He lifted his cup and breakfast garbage.

I grabbed my coffee and followed him to the door, where he pitched the trash in the waste can before pushing through the exit onto the back path to the workshop.

"I think Sheriff Perry's information dump was a cry for help."

His loud sigh echoed through the morning stillness. "I think he was alerting you to the fact Skylar may be arrested."

Eric and I had fallen into step, shoulders a few inches apart. Eric laid a hand on my arm and stopped our pace. His blue eyes stared into mine. Tone gentle, he said, "The side effects of Ambien can cause people to do things they don't remember."

I rolled my eyes. "Yes, I know, like binge eating."

"Courtney, stop. Some people actually get behind the wheel and drive and never remember doing it. It's possible Skylar needed sleep, took the medicine and killed Lisa." His eyes implored me to agree.

I sighed. "I know. I just don't think that is the case. Something has bothered me since I saw the crime scene: the cake. Where did the cake come from? They're expensive, so a local bakery wouldn't have one made and hope someone bought it. They're ordered and custom-made. Did Lisa order it? Did Skylar? Was it made on-site or delivered? A five-tiered cake isn't easily carried to a hotel room."

Eric shook his head and began to walk. I followed. "I assumed the cake served on the first day of filming was baked on-site by the bakery chef at the resort. Would he have time to make two? Why would he make two? Wedding cakes are costly not only in ingredients but time.

They're labor intensive." I wasn't sure Eric was listening to me. I bumped his arm with my elbow.

"Those are good questions, Courtney. Have you expressed them to Sheriff Perry or Drake so they can follow up?"

I let silence be my answer.

"Share those concerns with Sheriff Perry, then stay out of it."

I knew Eric cast a hard glance my way. I pretended not to notice by staring straight ahead.

"I mean it, Courtney. You need to think of your safety, your shows and your pitch for another show with Shannon. You can't put yourself in danger again by poking around asking people other than Drake and Sheriff Perry questions about the murder. If Skylar isn't the murderer, you don't know who is. You might inquire to the wrong person and find yourself on the wrong side of a knife blade." Eric spiced his words with anger, a little too much anger than the situation called for in my opinion. "It happened *before*."

Eric stressed the word "before" like I'd forgotten I'd almost become murder victim number two last season. "All right. All right. I'll be careful." We'd gotten to a fork in the path. One way led to a pond, the other through a small, dense forest.

"That is not at all what I said. I didn't say get involved but be careful. I said: Don't get involved." Eric cut in front of me. I stopped. He faced me. My breath caught in my chest. He looked so earnest, so ready to tell me something important. My heart pattered against my ribs.

"Courtney, people care about you. Think about them. Don't get involved in another murder investigation no matter how innocent or safe your questions seem to you.

No one wants to lose you." Eric grasped my forearms and tugged me closer to him until our faces were inches apart. "Not your family, not your colleagues." He tilted his head and leaned closer. His warm breath tickled my skin. "Especially not . . ."

The purr of a UTV engine cut off his words. His head snapped up. He looked past my shoulders and I turned my head in time to see a four-person vehicle pull up behind us.

My shoulders sagged.

Pamela smiled from behind the wheel. "Sorry I missed you this morning. Hop in and I'll give you a lift to the set."

My feet remained planted. "Thanks, I'll walk."

"Boss's orders."

Had Sheriff Perry found Drake and issued an order for Security to escort me to and from the set? Eric dropped one hand and slid the other down my arm until he grasped my elbow and tried to guide me toward the UTV.

"Didn't either of you hear me, I'd like to walk."

"Okay. Eric, you can take the UTV back to the resort. I'll walk with Courtney and meet you there in, oh"—she looked at her exercise tracker—"thirty minutes."

A walking escort wasn't my plan either. I sighed, long and loud. "I'll take the ride." Even though I'd said the words begrudgingly, Pamela still smiled. She seemed oblivious to the serious conversation she'd interrupted and my reluctance for a security chaperone. I marched over to the vehicle and crawled into the front seat. She'd have time enough alone with Eric the rest of the day. After strapping myself in, I crossed my arms and stared forward.

What was Eric about to say? That I meant a lot to him?

To the show? My gut told me by his expression, it was to him. Was Shannon right? Was he about to kiss me? My heart pattered again at the thought. Was Eric interested in me romantically? Or was he going to try to convince me to stay out of the murder investigation?

Questions spiraled around in my mind. I needed to talk to Eric in private. I had to get some answers, sort some things out. Focusing for a few minutes, I decided I'd take care of the Eric situation tonight. However, concerning the murder investigation, I'd ask Justin about the cake. Without fail, he always set up the breakfast buffet for the cast and crew. I felt confident he'd know the answer to my question.

Pamela stopped the vehicle in front of the workshop. "Have a nice day."

"Thanks." I gave Pamela a wry smile. I unbuckled and slipped from the vehicle. Eric had done the same and waited for me to vacate the shotgun position.

"Remember what I said." Eric wore a sober expression.

I gave a slight nod and headed toward the door. I would remember what he said, but I was asking Justin about the cake anyway. I wanted to have a few more facts before I presented a theory to Sheriff Perry.

Once inside, I nodded a greeting to Kinzy on her perch, then looked toward the catering table. It was set up with breakfast offerings. A girl busied herself making minor adjustments to the items on the table. Justin and another catering employee lit the chafing fuel wicks.

I walked over to the table. "Is the coffee ready?"

Justin looked up at me. "Everything is ready."

"Thank you." I set about making myself a cup of coffee with flavored creamer even though we now had a coffeemaker upstairs and I'd just finished a cup. The savory scents my nose breathed in caused my stomach to rumble. "What scrumptious food do you have for us today, Justin?" I'd purposely added his name because I didn't want either of the other catering staff to answer my question.

"Individual quiches, spinach and feta or bacon and cheddar." Justin pointed to the chafing pan while he spoke. "Corned beef hash and sausage burritos. Of course, like every day"—he rolled his eyes—"oatmeal with the standard fixings and fruit."

Was he not a fan of healthy food, or did he think we got tired of it?

"Help yourself." Justin smiled.

"I think I will . . ." I set my cup of coffee on the table, took a plate and lifted the lid on the chafing dish that held the corned beef hash. I scooped a generous spoonful, returned the lid and moved on to take a spinach and feta quiche. Both of the other catering staff had started moving the food transport carts away from the table to an out-of-the-way corner of the room. This was my chance.

Cutting a bite of food, I said, "The cake we had on the first day of filming tasted great. Do you know who baked it?"

Justin nodded. "Chef Hartsall. He is an excellent bakery chef." He laughed. "I guess you know that, cooking being your business and all."

"So it was made on-site by the resort's bakery chef?"

Justin pulled a face, but nodded.

"Did he happen to make two that day?" I popped a bite of quiche in my mouth and chewed while waiting for his answer.

He shrugged. "I don't know."

Not the answer I wanted. How could I rephrase the question without Justin being suspicious?

While I contemplated, Justin asked in a whisper, "Are you thinking about the cake in Skylar's room?" Justin narrowed his eyes to slits and glanced sideways to find his coworkers' whereabouts.

"I was." I lowered my voice. "Do you think the chef made two?"

Again, a shrug. Justin crinkled his features into a look of frustration, which seemed like an odd response to my simple question.

"It makes me so mad Skylar is going through this while not feeling well." Justin added fisted hands to his level of frustration.

I could relate. "Me too."

Justin sighed and relaxed his hands and features. "Is he feeling better?"

"I think so." I didn't really know, but I didn't want to add to Justin's concern. "Is it possible there is another event happening at Coal Castle Resort? A wedding event maybe, and that is where the cake came from."

Justin shook his head and shrugged. "I just deliver the food where I'm supposed to."

I worked on another bite of corned beef hash while I decided the best way to approach this. "What is the bakery chef's name, again? Maybe I can talk to him."

"Chef Hartsall." Justin's eyes grew wide. The corners of his mouth quirked into a grin. "Would you like me to poke around the kitchen and see if he baked two cakes that day?"

"Do you mind? It won't get you into trouble, will it?" I finished off my quiche.

"No, I'm chill with a couple of his assistants. I'll ask

them. I won't bother Chef Hartsall. He's really busy and really serious about his work here."

His tone indicated a pecking order of hierarchy in the kitchen. I knew it was true. "I don't want you to get into trouble. I can make an appointment with the chef."

"No!"

I drew back a little at Justin's abrupt, and loud, answer.

"I'll talk to the bakery staff or Chef Hartsall. You can count on me. I don't want to see Skylar go to jail." Justin dropped his gaze. "I know it probably sounds silly. I consider Skylar a friend."

I smiled. Before I could say anything, a couple of crew members approached the breakfast buffet. I snagged my cup of coffee off of the table. Walking past Justin, I whispered, "Thank you for doing this. Let me know what you find out."

Justin looked up. Relief washed his features. Had he thought I'd scoff at him for considering Skylar his friend?

"No problem. Let me take that for you." Justin reached for my empty plate, which I handed over.

Moving out of the way of the crew, I headed upstairs to wardrobe, where I'd dump this coffee and make a fresh cup. Mentally, I checked one thing off of my to-do list. Now I could focus on the next item, how Lisa Mackliner lived her life . . . besides stalking Skylar.

The minute I entered wardrobe, my stylist held out two fascinators that matched my cocktail dress for the day's filming with the instructions the choice was mine as to which one to wear. I ditched my coffee and took the hats. Both had a netting base set with rhinestones. The fascinator I held in my left hand had a smaller diameter of netting and not much height. Small white and turquoise feathers decorated the headdress. My right hand held a white hat with a large circumference of netting twisted into some sort of flower and appeared to give me about two inches of extra height.

I was attracted to the turquoise fascinator for a couple of reasons; the size and the feathers screamed fun to me. However, the white flower hat had a formal feel. I needed to see my dress before I made my decision. I entered my dressing room to find an A-line, sleeveless cocktail dress. The dress was white silk with a turquoise-and-white–pleated skirt. A wide turquoise belt accentuated the waistline.

Walking out to my stylist, who waited beside my chair, I told him my choice and asked if I could brew a cup of coffee before we started. He agreed and busied himself with preparation for my hair. I grabbed a coffee pod and disposable cup, and set the system to brew.

I heard Shannon consulting with her stylist in her dressing room. As my coffee gurgled to a finish, she came out holding a black large-flower fascinator. Black polka dots decorated her netting. She smiled. "I'm in a beautiful black cocktail dress. The bodice is lace and studded with rhinestone. This will look perfect."

We walked to our chairs. It didn't take long for our stylists to smooth our hair into low back buns and pin the fascinators into place. Makeup applied, we headed into our dressing room and met Harrison and Skylar, who still looked the worse for wear, heading to their chairs. Both were dressed in a basic suit. Skylar wore brown, while Harrison sported black. Thank goodness, Skylar wore a turquoise shirt so he had some color. He needed some color. The last few days shone all over his face.

We were all ready when Kinzy came to escort us to the set. Today we stood in line in front of the contestants' workstations. They wore smiles and aprons with embellishments of teacups, teapots or sweet desserts like pie or cupcakes for pockets.

Kinzy took her place beside Quintin. who sat with his arms crossed, a serious expression on his face. Brenden cued us, and Skylar read his lines with a strong voice. "It's time to prepare for the bridal tea."

I picked up the next line. "Your challenge today is to make a special dessert for the bridal tea."

"Although you will not be serving tea in cups today, you must infuse your creation with tea." Skylar smiled.

A few contestants took deep breaths while I added, "You have two hours for this challenge."

Together we said, "The baking begins now."

"Cut. Nailed it." Brenden's tone held surprise.

The talent retreated to their chairs on the wings of the set. "How are you feeling?" I looked at Skylar.

"Better. Not great." He eased into a chair.

Quintin and Brenden approached us and directed Shannon and Harrison to follow the cameraman to the bistro table to film their discussion on the secret ingredient in the next challenge.

"You two will be changing into the clothes you wore to issue the first challenge. You are going to have to film the season opening, which includes smearing wedding cake on each other. That is the only solution I can come up with to explain a wardrobe change."

"Is this really the best idea? We'll have to have a shower to get the cake and frosting out of our hair."

Quintin shrugged one shoulder. "Be careful of your hair. Aim for skin or clothes." He strode away.

Brenden held up his hands. "Go get changed and meet me in the back corner."

We did as we were told. Our stylists looked as happy as we did about this whole charade. Once changed with hair rearranged, we walked to a far corner in the workshop. The backdrop behind us looked like a stained glass window. A small, three-tiered cake sat on a table with a lace tablecloth. A catering crew member added a cake topper.

As I drew closer, I realized the cake was a miniature version of the one catering served to the cast and crew the first day of filming. I walked completely around the table to get a good look from every angle. In a corner on the bottom tier of the confection was a small heart. Just two piped lines with a curlicue at the bottom tip of the heart. I studied the cake, puzzled by the out-of-place decoration.

"Is something wrong?"

I flicked my eyes from the cake to the catering staff. "No, not really. I was just looking at the heart."

"Oh, that's how Chef Hartsall marks his creations. He puts it on all the confections he makes. You know, like an artist signs a painting. Only his symbol is a cute reflection of his name."

"Everything looks good." Brenden had approached the table. "We're ready to shoot." He pointed his statement at the catering staff, who hurried away from the table. "Courtney and Skylar, I need you with your backs to the window façade. You'll say your lines while you cut a large slice of the cake. Then you will strike the couples pose of feeding each other the cake. We'll hold for a moment, then I want you to gently smash it on each other's faces. Try to do the mouth down and clothes. Gently. We don't need any injuries, especially dental work."

Skylar snorted. "This is a stupid opening."

My eyes widened.

Brenden sighed. "Not my choice. The original opener was funny. This one is just messy." Leaving us, he moved behind the camera. After a few practice readings, he hollered, "Action."

I smiled into the camera. "Welcome to *The American Baking Battle: Wedding Edition*."

"Twelve bakers will compete, but only one will come out a winner." Skylar picked up the serrated knife on the table and whacked into the cake to cut large pieces.

I fought a visible cringe while I lifted a piece out as scripted. "Will they find the challenges a piece of cake?"

"Or will they get creamed." Skylar lifted a piece of cake with a large pink rose to my lips and pressed it into my face, then smeared down with his fingers. "Buttercreamed, that is, by the competition?"

On cue, I took the piece of cake I held and pushed. Icing smeared down Skylar's mouth and chin. Skylar, using a gentle hand, repeated my action. We both looked into the camera, lifted our brows and with hands in a who-knows fashion held a minute. Brenden hollered, "Cut."

A crew member brought us damp towels to wipe off the sticky frosting.

"That was humiliating." Skylar swiped off a glob of frosting. "It's one of those dumb wedding traditions." He huffed.

I wiped at my face with my towel. "Skylar, in light of the current situation, you should keep your negative opinions about weddings to yourself."

"What do you mean?" He frowned at me.

Did he still have no idea he was the main person of interest in the murder of Lisa Mackliner?

Brenden hurried our way. “Get cleaned up and head to wardrobe and change as fast as you can.”

“Why?” I asked over my shoulder. Brenden had drawn up behind us and was actually pushing on our backs to get us to move.

“Quintin called an emergency meeting.”

Chapter Fourteen

Skylar and I managed to get the frosting off our faces, out of the soiled clothing and back into the outfits for the day's filming. Skylar, who could take a prize for quick change, had his makeup touched up and hair restyled before I made it to the makeup chair. I entered the common area of the room to find Quintin, Brenden, Kinzy, Shannon and Harrison waiting for us.

Quintin waved the stylists out of the room, telling them to go to the first floor and wait. He'd let them know when they were to return.

"Take a seat." He gave a nod toward the chairs. Shannon and I obliged. Me because I'd need to anyway. Shannon because she wore four-inch heels today.

"I've watched all of the raw film of the first episode with the exception of what Skylar and Courtney just filmed. Something one of the contestants said, and Skylar's reaction to it, forced me to make a decision." Quintin settled a stern expression on Skylar.

I glanced at Skylar. Anger set into his features. I braced. We all knew Quintin was referring to his outburst after Marco made his comment. Was Quintin going to fire Skylar in front of the rest of us?

"In light of Lisa Mackliner's murder and Skylar's tie to it, I've decided Skylar will no longer interact with the contestants."

"What?" Skylar hollered.

Quintin seemed unphased by his indignation and continued. "Skylar will remain on set and can speak with cast, crew and catering." Quintin rolled his eyes on the last word, which told us a lot about his character. He continued. "Courtney will handle all of the hosting duties as well as accompanying the judges." Quintin took his eyes from Skylar and focused on me. "There will be no extra compensation for you since no one knows if your little admission is going to kill your career."

Quintin's lips drew into a deep, perturbed frown. So did mine while my anger started to simmer.

"Why are you doing this to me?" Skylar clipped out the words.

"It will make it easier to write you out of the show if or when you are arrested for the murder of Lisa Mackliner."

Shannon and I gasped. Now my anger turned into a full-fledged boil.

All of the color drained from Skylar's face. He looked at Brenden. "I can't believe what I'm hearing. You're going to let him do this?"

"I'm the producer. I make the decisions. It will cost the show a significant amount of money to reshoot any scenes you are in if you are arrested for murder. I can't air a show with a convicted felon. So far, it's the first episode and only three scenes, the opening you just filmed, the kickoff and the countdown," Quintin said with no emotion in his tone. "It's good business sense." Quintin turned and headed for the door.

In a quick move, Harrison blocked him. Although Quintin had height on Harrison, he didn't have breadth. "Our contracts lay out our specific duties as judges and cohosts. You are in breach of contract doing this to Skylar and Courtney."

Quintin harrumphed and stepped around Harrison.

"Everyone has two minutes to get back on set. With the exception of Courtney. I'll send the stylist up." Kinzy followed Quintin out of the room. Brenden looked at each of us and opened his mouth. No words came out. He hung his head and walked out the door.

The whole scene left me angry and dazed. Shannon and Skylar too. Not Harrison. He paced back and forth. "The audacity of that man." He shook his fist. "Skylar." He stopped in front of Skylar, who stared at the closed door probably in shock and disbelief. Placing his hands on Skylar's shoulders, he shook him until Skylar lifted his eyes to look at Harrison. "Call your people about your contract. Then lawyer up, because things aren't looking good for you, buddy, with this Lisa thing." He pointed at me. "Tell Eric about the extra duties right away. And don't worry about that admission and apology. You might lose some fans, but not all of them. Plus, you might gain new viewers since our society seems to thrive on drama."

He walked over to Shannon, took her hand and helped her from the chair. With his other hand on Skylar's back, he handled them like fragile ingredients and led them out the door.

My eyes moistened. Not from anger at Quintin or his unfair decision or fear about killing my career by admitting I wasn't the country girl all my fans thought I was. No, the tears forming in my eyes were actually happy tears. Somewhere between last season and this one, Harrison, Shannon, Skylar and I had become friends rather than coworkers. Harrison had just proved it.

My stylist must have sensed the tension still left in the room. He worked on my makeup and hair in silence, which left me ample time to think about the events that had transpired over the last three days.

With every reminder from Quintin, I was losing faith that my apology would be well received and not hurt my and Eric's careers. As angry as I was at his remark about not giving me more pay, it did make me realize the admission might not ruin my career but could reduce my earning potential. Although I'd enjoyed the grocery store job, I'd paid my dues in my career. Like everyone, I wanted my earnings to increase with my experience, and I'd have to start all over again on finding a company to help me develop a line of knives or resign to the fact a product endorsement wasn't in my future. The network supported my decision. I was certain they'd do everything in their power to field or prevent fallout. In the end, ratings would determine the fate of my show. With no fan support, *Cooking with the Farmer's Daughter* would end, and Shannon and my show would never begin.

As bad as that seemed, it was nothing compared to Skylar's situation. I know, I've been in his shoes. The thought of being a convicted felon and sent to prison for something you didn't do was desperation at its worst. At times proving your innocence seemed impossible.

Yet I'd already started asking questions that I thought could prove his innocence. I knew Justin, who took pride in knowing Skylar, wouldn't let me down about asking about the cake. In my free time, I planned to find out more about Lisa. Was she obsessive about other celebrities? Did she have a connection to Marco? Somehow, I needed to find out about Marco's macabre fixation with murder. Was it because he committed one? This question wasn't something I could pose during an interview or judging, like my inquiry to Nadine and Carla about their illnesses.

There was one thing I could take care of as soon as I returned to set, which wouldn't be long. My stylist had finished my hair and started to pin the fascinator onto my head. I remembered to grab my phone before I stepped down to the wings of the set.

Skylar leaned forward in his chair, elbows resting on his thighs with his face buried in his palmed hands. I walked over to him and looked to the set to get my bearings on where we were in the filming time. A large digital timer mounted on the wall read twenty-nine minutes and forty seconds. Harrison and Shannon visited with Diego while he lightly kneaded dough.

I pulled my chair close to Skylar and sat down. I don't know if he heard or felt the movement. He lifted his head. Sadness emanated from his eyes. "Sorry, Courtney."

I patted his back. "You have nothing to be sorry for."

"I'm sorry for this whole mess. I didn't kill her." His eyes searched mine.

"I believe you." I managed a smile. He returned it with a weak one. "Can I ask you a question?"

"Sure." Skylar sat up and leaned back into the chair.

"How long have you used Ambien, and what is your dosage?"

"I don't use the sleep aid."

"Not even during the time Lisa stalked you?"

He shook his head. "Never. The doctor said the drug hadn't been in my bloodstream long. He also thought it contributed to my severe nausea and confusion. Those are side effects for some people." Skylar stared over my head. Bewilderment scrubbed his features. "I have no idea how the drug got into my system. I ate and drank the same things everyone else did on the set."

He had. Would a drug test show exactly how long the sleep aid had been in his system? "What about the day before? What did you eat? Where did you go?"

"I ate breakfast at home, fast food in the airport. Harrison and I split an appetizer plate in the steak house after the taping of your show."

I bit at my lower lip. Had he forgotten something he ate? Was he lying about the drug? Or had someone broken into his home and tampered with his food? I ruled out my last question and the airport food. Skylar would have shown a reaction to the drug sooner. Wouldn't he?

Skylar stood. "Lunch is here. I'm heading over, want to come?"

"Not right now." I watched him go and Shannon approach.

"Harrison went to make a phone call. He is fired up. Not that he shouldn't be." Shannon added her last statement in haste. "I'm incensed. How are you holding up?"

"I'm angry at Quintin for his treatment of Skylar and crack about my career. However, I'm more bothered by Skylar's situation."

"Want to talk about it?" Shannon turned in her chair to face me.

"I do. I looked up the side effects of Ambien and I asked Skylar how long he'd taken it. Get this. He says he doesn't."

"How could it be in his system, then?"

"Exactly? He doesn't know either. Or so he says. You don't think this is the first time he used it and is embarrassed to admit it since it affected him and his job duties? If so, would one time cause the drug's severe side effects, nausea and confusion?" Excitement had started to raise my voice. I tempered it back to a whisper.

"Well, we can't contact his doctor. Would the nurse practitioner at the resort know?" Shannon asked.

"Great idea." I made a mental note to track her down. "Do you think someone set him up?"

"I never thought about it. Who would want to set him up?"

"I don't know. Maybe Marco, since his girlfriend is a fan." I refrained from sharing my suspicion with Shannon that Lisa Mackliner could possibly be Marco's girlfriend. Shannon hadn't been privy to that conversation, and I didn't feel like recanting the story. It was something I needed to tell Sheriff Perry, though. "Or Quintin, who singled Skylar out in private meetings and seems happy to remove him from the cast. Or . . ." My next thought seemed too ridiculous to share. I wasn't even certain it could be done.

"What?" Shannon urged me to continue.

"Could Lisa Mackliner have staged her own murder to put Skylar behind bars since he had her put in prison?"

Shannon had no time to answer my rumination. The workshop door opened, sending in a gust of cool fall air, natural sunlight and Sheriff Perry into the room. Drake pulled up the rear and closed the door.

It took only seconds for Quintin to rise from his chair and stomp across the room. He blocked their path to the set with his body. Sheriff Perry tried to step around him. Quintin countered the move.

Shannon and I stood to watch the scene. By the serious, and annoyed, expression Drake and Sheriff Perry wore, this was an official visit of some kind. The men kept their voices low, but their tone carried, which was tense with disagreement. Quintin lifted his left arm and pointed to his fitness band, then waved his right hand through the air.

Sheriff Perry rubbed over his mouth and down his chin with his hand and jerked a nod. He and Drake went and leaned against the entrance door.

"Are you ready to call time?"

My body jumped, and Shannon let out a startled sound.

"Sorry," Brenden said. "I didn't mean to scare you."

When Shannon and I turned, it created a gap and Brenden caught sight of the sentinels at the door. "What's going on there?" He whispered his question, then craned his neck to find Quintin, who'd gone back to his chair.

"I don't know. Quintin stopped them," I whispered.

"It seemed serious, though." Shannon glanced at Brenden, then looked back at the trio.

"We'll continue filming this segment like we don't notice they're here. Where is Skylar?" Brenden moved closer to me.

"He went over to the catering table." I pointed and Brenden followed my finger. Skylar worked on eating a taco while chatting with Justin.

I smiled at the normal scene and hoped Justin expressed his concern to Skylar.

"Okay, well, take your place under the arch and get ready to count down." Brenden left us. I watched to see if he approached Quintin. He didn't. Instead he conversed with two cameramen.

My heels clicked across the wood floor to the arch; I glanced at the food the contestants started to display on pretty trays. As I suspected, there appeared to be several offerings of scones, which was not very original but would pair well with a tea-infused base.

Once under the archway, decorated today with peach-colored roses and white peonies, I put my toes to tape. The cameraman stood at the ready. Brenden approached and started his finger countdown. At his fist, I said, "Time's up, bakers."

The contestants stepped away from their creations.

Brenden hollered, "Cut." The cleaning staff rushed onto the set with shelved carts and started removing the dirty dishes from the challenge preparation, then wiped down the counters. While they worked their magic, I moved to where Shannon, Harrison and Brenden stood. I'd accompany the judges on this challenge round. Once Brenden was satisfied with the cleanliness of the kitchenettes and the offerings had been moved to the end of their counters, he cued the judges.

We started with Jeremiah.

"What have you made for us today?" Harrison asked.

"Earl Grey cupcakes with a honey and lemon buttercream." Jeremiah smiled wide.

I laughed. What else would the Cupcake King make?

He'd baked his confection in yellow cupcake papers.

The frosting, tinted to match, was piped on the cupcake in a flower design. Thin slivers of candied lemon rind sprung from the center of the cupcake in a festive fashion. He displayed the dozen cupcakes in a hexagon on a glass square tray.

"They're almost too pretty to eat." Shannon laughed. "Almost."

Harrison cut three pieces. The cake, light and airy, melted in my mouth. The honey and lemon in the frosting accentuated the Earl Grey flavor.

"This is very good." Harrison smiled. "I have no other comments."

"I agree. Good job," Shannon said.

We moved on to Diego. "I've prepared chamomile lavender scones with a chamomile-infused glaze."

His scones were round versus the traditional triangular shape.

Harrison cut into a scone and grimaced when the scone seemed to deflate, sticking to the knife. "I believe they should have baked longer."

Shannon popped a bite into her mouth. "They're very dense, but have a lovely and unique flavor."

"Yes, maybe five more minutes in the oven and you'd have served us perfection."

Diego nodded.

The next three contestants, Donna, Lynne and Alex, all prepared scones infused with green tea. Donna and Lynne had overbaked their offering, making them dry and crumbly. Alex drizzled a maple glaze over his and received a scolding from Harrison. Not only because they'd asked him to stop using maple, but the green tea and maple wasn't a good flavor combination.

We reached Afton's kitchenette. A quick look around showed me her offering hadn't been duplicated, cookies.

"Tell us what you made?" Shannon picked up a cookie and broke it into three pieces.

"They're chai snickerdoodles."

"They're very good," Shannon said.

"Yes." Harrison smiled. "And original."

Afton beamed as we moved on to the other contestants.

Marco, Nadine, Mary and Miller all made cheesecakes infused with various types of tea. Marco lost marks for the weak tea flavor; Mary's and Nadine's teas overpowered their confections. Miller had found the perfect balance.

Next up was Mike. Fancy dessert glasses held a scoop of green ice cream with a slender blond cookie spiked into it. "What have we here?" Shannon lifted the dish and raised her eyes.

"Green tea ice cream with a shortbread cookie."

Harrison used the cookie as a spoon and scooped a bite of the ice cream, as did Shannon.

"Yum." Shannon dipped the cookie into the frozen mixture for a second bite.

"My sentiments exactly. My only suggestion is to freeze your serving dish." Harrison smiled. "You surprise me every time. You really think out of the box with your creations."

"Thank you." Mike puffed out his chest and I noticed once again, his apron showed his hard work in the kitchen.

Brenden cut the cameras. It didn't take Harrison and Shannon long to decide the winner of the challenge. I felt certain it came down to Jeremiah, Afton or Mike. Not only were the creations perfectly prepared, they were unique compared to the other contestants, who'd played it safe with scones or cheesecakes.

Standing between Shannon and Harrison, I swept my gaze over the contestants who stood at the end of their counters beside their bridal tea dessert. "The winner of this challenge is Jeremiah."

He fist-pumped the air while the other contestants clapped. Brenden hollered, "Cut," and instructed contestants to head to lunch.

Skylar came over to our group. "I wish I hadn't been banned from filming. I hate watching from the wings."

"I know." I put my hand to his shoulder. "It will end soon."

"No one move." Quintin's voice boomed through the now-empty set.

I looked up to see him escorting Sheriff Perry and Drake toward us. During the judging, I'd forgotten about them being in the building.

"We've waited long enough." Sheriff Perry looked pointedly at Quintin. "Mr. Daily, I need you to come with me."

"Why?" Skylar took a step back.

I inwardly cringed. It may be a fight-or-flight response, but it certainly didn't look good for him.

"I have a few more questions for you."

Harrison cleared his throat.

Skylar received the message. "Not without my attorney."

"That is a wise decision, Mr. Daily. Although we can't find any Ambien in your room, preliminary forensics show the blood on your clothes belonged to the victim, your fingerprints are on the knife handle and her time of death is approximately five o'clock in the morning, when you told us you were in your room alone."

My stomach sank. If anyone ever needed an attorney, it was Skylar.

CHAPTER FIFTEEN

"Come on." Sheriff Perry grasped Skylar by the bicep.

Skylar roved a pleading gaze over the rest of us standing in the group.

"Go with them, but don't talk to them without your attorney present." I tried to inflect a confident tone into my words for Skylar's sake. Right now, I didn't feel confident at all about this situation. Sheriff Perry had some pretty weighty evidence against him in my estimation.

I watched the three men retreat toward the door, Skylar, head hung down, sandwiched between Drake and Sheriff Perry.

"We have to do something," Shannon drawled, and wrung her hands.

Her statement buoyed me and my belief Skylar was an

innocent man. "Yes, we do." I had a practice session tonight for my second on-location filming. I wouldn't be able to do any more Internet sleuthing on Lisa before then since Quintin kept our filming on a tight timetable. With two challenges left after lunch and me pulling double hosting duty, it left no free time for research. Thank goodness I had Justin working the cake angle. One less thing for me to do.

"I don't know what we can do except offer support to Skylar." Harrison ran a hand over his hair. A sincere expression covered his face. "I know I could have used some last season."

In an instant guilt whisked through me. "I'm so sorry."

Harrison reached for my hand. "Don't be. I was scared and acting, well, quite frankly, like a jerk. I know now I should have let my guard down, at least with the three of you, and told the truth." He squeezed my hand and flashed a smile at Shannon. "I'm going to go enjoy my lunch and send good thoughts into the universe for Skylar."

Shannon sniffled when Harrison walked away. "That is a good idea. Thinking good thoughts, and saying prayers, for Skylar."

"Are you free to join me on my set after work? While I create my practice dish, we can discuss how we can help Skylar."

A sly smile crept up on Shannon's face. "You have noticed something or have some ideas about his innocence, don't you?" She clapped her hands together. "I'm in."

"Great. Eric and I planned to eat what I prepare for our dinner. You can join us. There will be more than enough."

"Sounds great. Right now, we'd better grab our lunch since half of our time is gone."

Shannon and I had barely finished eating when Kinzy rapped on the door. "Quintin says it's time to film."

I rolled my eyes. I'd grown weary of hearing the phrase "Quintin says" right along with his coldhearted attitude.

"He is the boss, Courtney." Kinzy stood erect. Braced, I guessed, for confrontation. Had people complained about him to her?

"I know." I stood and so did Shannon. We'd eaten our lunch in our makeup chairs. Again. Although our stylists tried not to leave a mess, it wasn't the most appetizing place to eat our lunch. "Where did our table go?" I asked Kinzy while I pitched my trash in the wastebasket.

"How would I know?"

"Well, I am assuming Quintin gave the order for the redesign of our wardrobe room." A fleeting thought that the resort might have some control of this facility entered my mind as soon as the words dropped off my lips.

Kinzy didn't dignify my remark with an answer. Instead she turned and started down the stairs. Shannon and I followed.

Not one to give up easily, I asked, "Do you mind asking him? Or should I have Brenden ask?" I'd had more than one fleeting thought since the start of filming about Kinzy and her loyalty switch. I think she is a ladder climber. My last question should test that theory.

"I'll ask him." Her tone implied I'd come to the right person to do my bidding just as I thought she would. She'd briefly mentioned to me last season her career goal was to become a director. She'd made assistant director, so she just needed to climb one more rung.

I couldn't deny anyone the chance to meet their career goals. I knew how it felt to have something just out of reach, like my line of knives, when you'd worked so hard on a project. I wondered if she wanted to direct *The American Baking Battle* or she had something else in mind. If my fans remained loyal to me, Shannon and I would be in the market for a director. Would Kinzy be interested in the opportunity? It was an idea to discuss with Shannon and Eric.

The contestants stood behind their freshened countertops. Since the judges set the second challenge, I stood on the sidelines and watched the contestants' reactions to the twist on the challenge, three types of tea sandwiches. A traditional mayonnaise or salad dressing base or spread was a forbidden ingredient. Only Nadine and Miller looked appalled. The other contestants wore the usual expression, panic. With two hours for this challenge and the third, a salad, I was confident we'd wrap filming up early.

I was wrong. A stove stopped working, which halted filming until Afton could be moved to the kitchenette vacated by Carla to finish her tea sandwiches. We just kicked off the third challenge of the day when a crew member tripped on a cord and a light crashed to the floor. Thankfully, no one was hurt. It took a half hour to clean up the mess and replace the light. Finally, I stood ready to announce the winner of the day and to send another contestant home.

"Today, the contestant to win baker of the day wowed the judges in all three challenges. The avocado toast with sunflower seeds and kumquats looked pretty and tasted terrific. The sandwich paired well with your version of an Alba salad with truffles. Not to mention the scrumptious Earl Grey cupcake with lemon-and-honey buttercream frosting." I paused for just a moment before I said, "Jeremiah, you are baker of the day."

A pleased, wide smile stretched across his face while his fellow contestants patted his back and shook his hand.

"Now, for the sad portion of the show. The contestant going home today had trouble with all of their challenges." I saw fear settle onto Marco's features. And rightly so because overconfident, he'd not watched his time well for any of the challenges. However, it wasn't his name on the monitor. "You served the judges underdone scones, too much vinegar in your cole slaw dressing puckered the judges' mouths and your brisket bites wrapped in sweet bread dough were tough. Diego, you are leaving the kitchen today."

My camera cut while Brenden let the cameras roll on the contestants a few more minutes. Shannon and I did our obligatory congratulations and so sorry, then hurried up to the dressing room. I sent a quick text to Eric telling him Shannon and I were on our way and to get rid of Pamela, if she was still there. We had things to discuss that I didn't want anyone in an official capacity to hear.

In record time, Shannon and I changed back to our street clothes and walked to Coal Castle Resort. We used a front path that led to a side door closer to the suites that housed my show. Our small talk revolved around the growing spans of color dotting the Pocono Mountains and our plan to one day hike to the edge of the resort property or, at the very least, drive a UTV around the circumference of the property. We both agreed, it'd be after an arrest was made in the murder of Lisa Mackliner.

My thoughts went to Skylar, as I'm sure Shannon's did, because after that conversation we walked the remaining way in companionable silence. Once inside, I swiped the key card and poked my head into the room. Eric sat at the counter alone studying his tablet.

"Hi." Eric looked up from his work.

"Hello." We entered and walked to the counter. I found an apron and tied it on. Shannon slipped onto a stool next to Eric.

"What are you working on?" She glanced at his tablet.

He smiled. "The proposal for your show."

"Can I see?"

"It's still pretty rough. I do have good news, though. The network liked the idea of Shannon appearing on your show."

"Great!" I lifted my palm for a high five from Eric while Shannon clapped her hands together.

"Okay, I'm famished, so I want to get started with my preparations." I grabbed a whole chicken from the refrigerator and a package of chicken thighs. "Is this the show Shannon is going to cohost?"

Eric shook his head.

"What are you making for us?" Shannon asked.

"Well, this episode is more about using your knife to debone your meat and cut down your cooking time." I grabbed my knife and started with the chicken thighs, which would be our dinner.

Glancing up at Eric, I said, "Sheriff Perry and Drake came to the set today and took Skylar away."

"Wow." Wide-eyed, Eric continued. "Did they arrest him?"

"No, but they did say all the evidence points to him, fingerprints on the knife, time of death when he said he was in his room alone, the blood on his clothes belonged to Lisa." I sighed and grabbed another thigh. "I think Skylar is innocent, and I fear he'll be arrested soon unless new evidence is found."

"I agree." Shannon rose. "Let me help. What are you doing with these?"

"Putting them in the instant cooker with rice. The recipe is there." I pointed with the knife. Shannon set to work preparing the rest of the ingredients.

"There are some things that bother me." I ran my knife through a third thigh.

"Here we go." Eric sighed.

I stopped my work.

"I want to hear." Shannon urged me to continue.

"Here is what we know. Lisa Mackliner stalked Skylar and served prison time. Eerily, she was dressed and murdered in the same way as she threatened Skylar before her arrest." I stopped talking while I switched out to another piece of chicken.

"Which doesn't look good for Skylar, yet we know he's innocent because of his weak stomach around blood and dead bodies." Shannon finished adding all of the ingredients to the instant pot with the exception of the thigh I was working on.

"But," Eric said, "he had high doses of Ambien, which can cause some people to do strange things."

"I know. Although I asked Skylar and he says he doesn't take the sleep aid and has no idea how it got into his system. When Marco asked Skylar for an autograph for his girlfriend, he said her name was Lisa. Could it have been Lisa Mackliner? Marco seems to have a fixation with the macabre. He's asked me twice about finding a dead body."

"Have you told Sheriff Perry that?"

I avoided eye contact with Eric by giving Shannon the last piece of chicken.

"Courtney?" Eric moved so he was standing in front of me with the counter between us.

"No, I haven't. By your reaction, maybe I should."

"I think so." Shannon locked the lid, glanced at the recipe and set the cook time. "He should follow any lead."

"And what about the comment Mike made the day Skylar lost his temper. Was he just stating the obvious?"

Eric shot us a questioning look, so Shannon added, "He said that Skylar had a lot of motivation to kill Lisa."

"Oh. I'd say that was just a comment. If it bothers you"—he fixed a hard stare my way—"tell Sheriff Perry."

I almost hated to go on with my suspicions. I knew the only advice I'd get from Eric was to talk to the sheriff. I did have to admit once I'd repeated about Mike's statement out loud, it did just sound like a comment. Or a shocked reaction. I decided not to share my contemplations about the wedding cake since I had Justin working on it. I could bring that up later when I had more concrete information. "Then there is Quintin."

"He is pretty dark and brooding," Eric said, and sat back down.

I scrubbed my hands with antibacterial soap under warm water at the sink before I started spatchcocking the whole chicken. Using this boning method, you could roast a whole chicken in about thirty minutes in a regular oven.

"Yes, very unemotional and cold. It seems to me, he had singled Skylar out before the murder. After the murder it's more like freezing Skylar out of the show." Taking a deep breath, I looked at Eric. "Do you know anything about him or his background with the network?"

He shrugged his shoulders while shaking his head. "I don't."

I took another deep breath. This was probably a long shot since Eric felt the police should handle the investigative work. It was worth a try, though. "Do you think you could find out?"

The next morning, I gazed out the curved turret window of my suite, checking the weather. The vast landscape appeared to have changed color overnight, unless it was a reflection from the pink and yellows in the ascent of the sun. The view, glorious and pristine, was such an unbelievable contrast to the fatal events that happened during both of my stays here.

The jingle of my phone drew my attention inward to the suite. Eric texted Shannon and me to meet him in the coffee shop so we could talk about a game plan for our proposal. Last night, we failed to make any headway with our joint venture. We spent, or Eric would say, I spent the night talking about the murder and possible leads Sheriff Perry should follow up on. Eric also refused to poke around the network for information on Quintin.

I quickly pulled a hoodie sweatshirt over a pair of leggings and slipped into my favorite walking shoes. Hanging my purse over my head and shoulder, I left my suite and headed down the elevator to Castle Grounds. Shannon, dressed in a denim skirt, lightweight blue sweater and cowgirl boots, stood by Eric, who wore brown creased trousers, an olive-green long-sleeved button-down and loafers.

"Good morning." Eric handed off my hazelnut latte.

"Morning. No Pamela?" I looked all around and started to smile.

"She's waiting outside."

My smile and mood drooped. "We're going to talk business in front of her?"

"None of it's secret." Eric pushed through the door and held it open. "Besides, who is she going to tell?"

"Brenden or Quintin," I countered, my tone edged with snark.

"I call shotgun." Shannon giggled and walked as fast as she could toward the UTV.

Could she be more obvious? And how much more unromantic could riding in the back of a UTV be?

Eric and I slid onto the seat from opposite sides. After we shared greetings with Pamela, Eric said, "So, we know it's a go for Shannon to guest on your third on-location taping. What do you want to do?"

"I want Courtney to teach me how to carve a fruit or vegetable. Can that be the whole show? Food art?" Shannon angled in her seat, as much as the seat belt would allow, so she could see us.

Thinking for a moment, I said, "Maybe carve pieces of fruit and put on skewers to make a fruit bouquet as a gift? Or to take to a potluck or party? Those ideas would be useful to my viewers."

"Right," Shannon said. "I'm a beginner, as they would be, so if I could do it, then maybe they could too." She laughed. "I'll probably be the cautionary tale."

Eric chuckled. "The idea has merit. We could do something that shows three skill sets. Maybe, arranging fruit in an eye-appealing way without any carving, simple carving like pineapple rounds into flowers, then Courtney could showcase her in-depth carvings."

"I like it," I said. I'd wanted to showcase my fruit and vegetable carvings for a long time on my show, but it didn't really fit into the theme or my persona until now. I thought about my apology. Trepidation cut through me.

"Okay, I'll finesse it, show you two what I come up with before I submit it to the network since Shannon is involved," Eric said, drawing me back into the conversation and taking my mind off of my troubles.

"Great. I'll tell my hubby about it tonight on our Skype call."

"If he wants to see the proposal when I'm finished, I'll be happy to e-mail him a copy, or if he wants to call or Skype about it, I'm fine with that."

"This is exciting." Shannon smiled wide.

I smiled back, yet I wished my knife set had been developed. This would be the perfect showcase for them. There were many reasons I couldn't wait for the network to air that apology so I could move forward with my plans, or worst-case scenario, regroup for my career. Would my fans support or ditch me? The fear of the latter pounded my heart. My admission affected the careers of many people, not just Eric's and mine. We employed crew, a stylist and catering, just like *The American Bak-*

ing Battle, only on a smaller scale. As much as I wanted to come clean to my fans, and it was the right thing to do, this hanging in limbo was nerve-racking.

The not knowing made me think of Skylar and his current situation. I needed to ask Justin if he'd found anything out about the cake.

"Now on to the proposal. When you have some downtime, we could film you cooking together. We wouldn't script it, just see how it played out? What do you both think?"

I drained my latte and forced my thoughts to the current conversation instead of my doubts. "In a couple of days, when the contestant pool is smaller, we should have some free afternoons. What about doing a play on comfort food. Maybe meat loaf and mashed potatoes?"

"Great idea." Shannon took a sip of her coffee. "You could do a basic recipe to please a family. I could punch it up for a dinner party by doing a balsamic bacon-wrapped meat loaf with buttery roasted potato fingerlings."

"We could serve it with the same side, salad and dessert." I was getting excited about this model. "And we'll remind viewers no matter the geographic location, it's always fun to try new recipes."

Pamela glanced over her shoulder and smiled at me. "No one asked me for my opinion, but I'd watch that show. I like the concept."

"We do value your opinion."

Of course, Eric would say that to Pamela. I saw her glance in her rearview mirror and I was certain their eyes met because Eric smiled in a sappy way.

"Although, I think we should keep the audition shorter, maybe an appetizer or something. Deviled eggs maybe?

And"—Eric turned to me—"we should poll our next two studio audiences on this type of programming."

"What do you mean?" Shannon threw her question over her shoulder. She had straightened out in her seat.

"You know, questions like, are you interested in a recipe to feed your family that with a few ingredients would create an elegant dinner party or holiday entrée? Or, does your interest lie in time-saving cooking tips? If we take the most popular questions and create our show around them, we are sure to get viewers."

"You are a marketing genius!" Shannon clapped her hands together.

Pride filled my heart. My eyes found Eric's. I gave him a genuine smile. "He is very good at his job. I wouldn't be here if it weren't for him."

His gaze softened and his lips curled into an embarrassed grin. He reached out, captured my hand with his and squeezed. "Thank you. I wouldn't be here without you either."

Suddenly we both jerked forward, then snapped back against the seat. Eric let go of my hand while both of our gazes flew to Pamela.

"Oops, sorry. I didn't mean to hit the brakes so hard. This UTV is kind of touchy. We're here." She shrugged in an apologetic way, although I wasn't buying it was an accident. She'd watched Eric through the rearview mirror. I guess she didn't like what she saw. A small sense of satisfaction marbled through me and so did the realization that I needed to have a heart-to-heart talk with Eric before I went on a date with Drake.

Exiting the vehicle, Shannon waited for me to slide from the seat. Eric rounded the back to get into the passenger seat. "Stay out of trouble today, but talk to Sheriff Perry if you see him. Okay?"

"Okay."

Shannon and I waved goodbye as Pamela sped off. She didn't stay to see if we made it safely into the building today. Which confirmed my suspicion she saw the intimate moment Eric and I shared.

We greeted Kinzy in passing. Some of the crew were on-site so the overhead lights were on. Catering milled around the tables, readying the food for the hungry masses.

"Darn, the food's not ready. I guess I'll head upstairs and make a trip down for breakfast." Shannon started to step up to the second floor.

I'd spotted Justin readying the beverage table. "I'll be up in a minute." I watched Shannon enter the dressing room door, then walked over to where Justin worked.

"Good morning." I smiled.

He looked up. "Good morning, Miss Archer. I don't believe the coffee is ready. The hot water is if you'd like tea."

"Actually, I wanted to visit with you a minute. I was wondering if you'd had a chance to visit with Chef Hartsall or his staff about the cake."

Justin dropped a sleeve of disposable cups on the floor.

"Let me help you with that."

"No!" Justin bent down and quickly retrieved the few strays that escaped the sleeve. He placed the soiled cups back on his supply cart.

I was surprised by his curt answer.

"Sorry." He looked over both shoulders. "Unless you're part of the catering staff you can't touch this stuff."

I nodded my understanding. They wore latex gloves, after all. It made sense.

Justin moved around the table until he was a few inches from me and lowered his voice. "I actually had a chance to speak with Chef Hartsall. He didn't know anything about the cake in Skylar's room. It must have been baked off-site and brought in." He glanced over his shoulder again. "I'm not supposed to talk to you or any of the stars, including Skylar." An emotion flashed in his eyes. "Management's orders because of the situation happening again at the resort. It's not fair."

I was so taken aback by what Justin said my mouth gapped opened. Did the resort fear repercussions? Liability? Or were they trying to squelch rumors or keep their staff working instead of gossiping? I closed my mouth when another thought occurred. Quintin had said catering in a derogatory tone. Had he complained their conversations with cast, crew and contestants wasted our filming time?

"I heard the sheriff arrested Skylar." Justin kept his voice low. "Did he?" The corners of his mouth twitched like he wanted to smile.

The conversation and his body language left me confused and annoyed. I gave my head a few shakes. "No, I don't think so," I stammered, because I really didn't know and Justin seemed to keep fighting a smile. Was he the type of person who when upset had the inappropriate response?

"Oh!" Justin breathed the word on a sigh while an expression that looked like disappointment crept into his features. "I need to go." He turned before I could respond, and pushed his cart toward the staff exit.

I watched in stunned silence. He made it as far as the door; then I saw him slump over the handle of the cart, his shoulders shaking. In an instant I realized Justin had fought his feelings during our conversation. The poor kid was crying. Was it from relief Skylar hadn't been arrested, disappointment he could no longer interact with his friend on set, or sadness because Skylar was going through a difficult time?

Chapter Sixteen

The makeup area was empty when I arrived. I brewed a cup of coffee while half listening to Shannon and her stylist discuss her wardrobe choices for the day. My heart went out to Justin. Like the rest of us, it was hard seeing his friend going through such a difficult time. Then being told not to talk about the murder, the investigation or Skylar had to be hard on him. Many people dealt with stressful situations by talking them out. I also felt bad for talking to Justin. I didn't want to be the reason he was fired or reprimanded. His nervous behavior was understandable during the course of our conversation. There were security cameras on set. Did his boss review the tapes? Perhaps Quintin had nothing to do with this situation. Maybe another employee who didn't like Justin complained that he wasted time with the talent on the show out of spite or jealousy. We've all had coworkers ready to stab us in the back at some time in our life.

I winced at my poor choice of expression, although Lisa was stabbed through the chest. Closing my eyes, I pulled the crime scene from my memory. I'd only looked at the carnage for a few seconds, yet several things stuck with me: the cake, the funny icing design and her eyes were closed. Bernard died with open eyes. Movies showed victims with open eyes. Why would her eyes be closed? Did the killer close them? I shivered at the thought.

"Courtney."

I looked in the direction of the voice. Kinzy stood in the threshold. "Skylar is being detained and will not be on set today," she said in a matter-of-fact tone with a stoic expression.

"What does that mean? Did Sheriff Perry arrest him?" I forgot about my coffee and stepped toward Kinzy.

She shrugged. "All Quintin said is Skylar is being detained."

Of course, Quintin said. Would he tell us if Skylar had been arrested?

"Better get a move on." Kinzy looked me up and down. "You're in no position to be tardy either," she said with a smirk. I didn't appreciate her haughty tone and expression. I'm sure my face showed it. It didn't stop her, she continued. "Remember you are pulling double duty. You will interview all the contestants during every challenge. You don't have to accompany the judges during their tasting." Kinzy didn't allow any time for a rebuttal from me. She turned and strode away.

I grabbed my coffee, which had finished brewing. After my morning conversations, I needed the comfort it brought. The aroma wrapped around my senses like a warm hug. I didn't appreciate her tone or inference, but sadly, it gave me pause.

Even though I'd done the right thing by clearing up any confusion on my background, there was no guarantee the truth wouldn't tank my show. If Skylar was arrested and found guilty of murder, *The American Baking Battle* may be looking for two new cohosts. Quintin seemed to disregard our contracts. In light of both of our situations, my gut told me he'd make no hesitation to replace either of us with little provocation.

I sighed. A murder conviction was justifiable. Yet in my mind, there was no way Skylar could commit a murder. As Sheriff Perry told me last time, Skylar didn't have the stomach for it. Unless it was self-defense, Skylar didn't murder Lisa Mackliner. I'd seen the crime scene and other than the crushed cake, there appeared to be no struggle whatsoever. Skylar had looked disheveled, but not in a fighting-for-your-life kind of way. Had Sheriff Perry noticed that too?

As for me, it was possible Quintin might have justifiable reason to terminate my contract too. Misleading the public about my background for four years might kill my career. Time would tell. Eric and I needed to discuss an aftermath plan in case the public and media turned on me. I'd seen it done before. There wasn't much I could do about my circumstances until the apology aired. As for Skylar and the murder, I had some ideas. I just needed some free time to do some research, starting with the cake now that I knew it wasn't baked on-site.

"Good morning, Courtney." Shannon floated into the room in a summery sundress. The yellow background with bright-red Hawaiian lei flowers and strappy flat sandals gave her an island feel.

"Good morning. What is the theme today?"

"Bridal shower and by looking at my attire and yours, I think the recipes will have some sort of tropical ingredient." Shannon laughed, then winked because as a judge, she knew the challenges and surprise ingredients. She took her seat in front of the mirror.

I hurried into my dressing room and found a jade halter dress waiting for me. Palm fronds shadowed the background of the fabric. Pink and yellow lilies bordered the skirt that hit above my knee. Flat sandals with a beaded thong the color of the flowers in my dress pulled the ensemble together. My stylist showed me two sets of jewelry, and I chose the jade medallion necklace with matching earrings. We decided I'd wear my hair in a braid to show off the accessories.

Doing a quick change, I was relieved to find Shannon still in her chair so I wouldn't be the talent holding up filming. Her makeup had been applied, but her stylist had just started curling her hair into small ringlets. I knew my stylist could smooth and plait my hair in record time after my face had been made up. Harrison wandered in to the area wearing khaki cargo shorts, caramel-colored leather Huaraches and a brown button-down with palm fronds embroidered over pin tucks. He accessorized his ensemble with a deep frown.

"This theme is silly. Do bridal showers really happen in a tropical area?" He looked into the mirror and let out a disgusted snort before sitting down.

"Sometimes," Shannon drawled. "Mine didn't."

"Think of it this way, Harrison," I said. He gave me his attention. "It's just another day in paradise."

He pinned me with a look, then laughed. Shannon and I joined in on the merriment. My gloomy mood lifted with our giggles. The remaining few minutes we needed in hair and makeup went fast with good-humored teasing and grumbling, which continued as we stepped down to the floor of the set.

The tropical theme carried over to the contestants' aprons with varying prints of palm trees, beach balls, coconuts, exotic drinks, really anything tropical and not one was the same.

I took my place under the archway, where large orange hibiscus flowers were intertwined with palm fronds. Brenden counted down and I hit my cue. "Today we're cooking for a destination bridal shower! Your first challenge of the day is to create a tropical breakfast. Remember, during your preparations, the bride and her court must fit in their dresses on the big day. You have ninety minutes to complete this challenge. The baking begins now."

The puzzled expression on Mike's face was priceless. I hoped the cameraman got a shot. He'd done so well in all the other challenges, would this be the one to put him under? I knew what I'd create if I was faced with this challenge, homemade granola with large flaked coconut shavings and dried pineapple. I'd layer it into vanilla Greek yogurt and serve it with a banana smoothie made with almond milk. Tropical, healthy and waist friendly.

"Cut." Brenden walked toward me. "Courtney, I've decided since the challenge time is short, you won't be interviewing the contestants as they work."

Dumbfounded, I stared at Brenden. His instructions were the complete opposite of what Kinzy told me in the dressing room. I chose not to point that out. Instead, I said, "Okay. I'm going to head to the resort on an errand. I'll be back within the hour." With quick steps, and a glance over my shoulder to see if Kinzy and Quintin were focused on something elsewhere, and they were, I exited the building.

Immediately, I wished I'd brought along my purse with my phone and a light jacket. I hesitated and looked at the closed door. Deciding not to chance getting caught in a difference of opinion on my hosting duties for the day, I rubbed the chill off my upper arms with cupped hands and started down the main path to Coal Castle Resort.

It wouldn't take long to find Chef Hartsall and inquire about the wedding cake. A good chef kept their eye on the competition. If I described the one in Skylar's room, he'd know if it came from a bakery in the area.

Lost in thought, I didn't hear the UTV pull up beside me until Drake said, "Going my way?" His tone held a hint of suggestiveness.

I stopped. So did the vehicle. "If you are going to the resort, yes."

"I am going whatever way you need me to." Drake flashed me a hundred-watt smile that seemed to gleam in the sunlight and sent a delightful thrill coursing through me, creating a warmth that chased away the previous chill on my skin.

I climbed into the passenger seat and fastened the seat belt.

"You look lovely, and a little out of season." Drake chuckled at his joke while guiding the UTV down the path. His attire matched the fall weather, jeans and a long-sleeved royal-blue polo with "Nolan Security" embroidered over his well-developed left pec.

Smiling, I said, "The challenge theme is a tropical destination bridal shower."

"I see. Did you forget something at the resort? If so, all you have to do is call Pamela; she'll find it and get it to you."

"No, I need to talk to the bakery chef."

Drake flashed me a questioning glance. "Why?"

Oops! Should I tell him my concern about the wedding cake?

"Did you like something he served and want to replicate it?" Drake asked.

"Something like that." I turned and looked at his profile. My heart sighed. He was so my type with strong features and chiseled muscles.

Too soon, Drake pulled onto a cement pad by a side entrance I'd never used. He turned off the vehicle. Resting his left arm over the steering wheel, he angled in his seat to get a full view of me. He leaned forward. "I have to apologize. With this new murder, Security is on lockdown again. We can't do dinner off-site, which is too bad because there is a terrific French restaurant about twenty miles from here."

"I understand." I inflected my words with sincerity and noted that for as attracted as I was to Drake, my body registered relief instead of disappointment about dinner at a French restaurant. It was an odd emotional response that had more to do with Drake than French cuisine. Was it because I needed to talk to Eric?

"But." His features brightened. "We could have dinner at Fit for a King or . . ." He paused. His dark brown eyes, smoldering with attraction, locked on mine. "We could order room service."

Anticipation or panic, I wasn't sure which, shot through me at his suggestion. Although my previous thoughts about Drake had roved to adult activities, wouldn't we be skipping a few steps, like getting to know each other as more than acquaintances?

His eyes searched my face. I needed to respond. I pushed my lips into a smile. "I think Fit for a King sounds wonderful."

Disappointment flashed through his eyes before he straightened his posture, once again putting distance between us. "Sounds great."

The excitement in his tone didn't sound great. It sounded forced. Aggravation chased away the earlier thrill I'd felt. Was Drake a player? Did he only want to hook up?

"I'll look at my schedule when I get back into the office and text you a few dates to consider."

Unbuckling, I slipped from the seat. "Sounds great." I inflected the same tone he'd used in my response. I turned without saying goodbye and huffed toward the entrance door, wishing I had a car door to slam. I grasped the door handle and twisted. Nothing. I tried to jerk it open. It didn't budge. Then I realized I couldn't get into this entrance without the assistance of Drake and his security-level key card. Unbeknownst to me because I didn't look back when I exited the UTV, he'd followed me to the door. He swiped his security key and cranked the handle. As soon as I put a hand to the door, he was gone without a goodbye. I was peeved because he got to slam the proverbial door. My heart sank. We'd had our first rift, but not our first date.

I decided not to worry about either of those things now. Entering the building, I found myself surrounded by large, stainless steel appliances and a symphony of kitchen noise. I followed the music into a room lined with stainless steel counters and many sous chefs chopping. I inquired about Chef Hartsall and with the point of a knife tip, one of the chefs provided the direction.

Walking through the area, I left the savory scents of onion and garlic and was greeted with the comforting aroma of freshly baked pastries. Rounding the corner to another room, I approached a large, stout man wearing a red chef's coat rolling dough into a long log. "Chef Hartsall?"

He looked up and nodded. I walked closer. "I'm Courtney Archer." I extended my hand.

"Yes, the farmer's daughter. I know." His hands continued forming the dough log.

I understood. If he stopped and greeted me, it would require another handwashing.

"I'd like to ask you a question."

He stopped rolling and gave the wall his attention. I followed his head and saw why. A large magnetic knife rack hung on the wall. His disgusted huff filled the air. "Where is my favorite knife?"

He'd turned his eyes toward me. Did he want a response? I didn't know where the knife was. He frowned. "Ask your question." He bit out the words with a disgusted tone while he rubbed his palms together, showering the counter with flour.

Flabbergasted by his rudeness, I stammered, creating noises, but no words.

Anger settled on his face. "I am an actual chef who runs a busy kitchen. Ask your question or leave."

My eyes widened at his inference I wasn't a chef. I was! I just didn't run a busy kitchen. I found my voice and it held no friendliness. "I want to know about the cake you baked for *The American Baking Battle*."

"Which one?" His gaze dropped to the shelf under the

workstation. He rummaged through utensils and pans. "I made three."

Three? "Three?"

He pinned me with a droll look. "Yes, two large and a miniature."

"Two large?" Now I voiced words that I intended to stay thoughts.

"Yes, as instructed, I made two very beautiful and very different wedding cakes. The director chose the one to use; then I baked a miniature. Why? Did you not like it?" His features and body language turned confrontational, he waited for my response.

"I loved it. It was delicious." I hoped the compliment would warm him up to me and my questions. "What happened to the other large cake?"

He waved a hand in the air as he walked past me. "Taken to a local assisted living facility." He called his answer over his shoulder. He'd left the room, the conversation and me standing dumbfounded staring at the magnetic knife holder, wondering which of the three missing knives was his favorite.

Unsure if I should leave or stay, I took the time to look around the bakery area of the kitchen. The room wasn't large, but it was efficient. Chef Hartsall's work counter jutted from a wall into the center of the room, giving him sufficient workspace. Several baking racks stood behind it filled with all the small and large utensils, like whisks and mixers, required to prepare bakery delicacies. I turned to find ovens lined the far wall while the refrigerator, proofer, chiller and stovetop took up the wall facing the chef's workspace. The third wall housed racks and racks of prepared baked goods I surmised were for the events in the resort or maybe our commissary table. Somewhere there had to be another room for his assistants; perhaps that is where he went in search of his knife.

After a few minutes when Chef Hartsall didn't return to his work area, I exited the room through a small side door rather than the way I'd entered. I stepped into a narrow hallway, the secret passage. The door clicked closed before I remembered you needed a pass key to open doors from the hallway. Without my cell phone, I was stranded. Unless I could get to the office area. Someone would hear me knocking on the door and answer, right? Looking up and down the dimly lit hallway, I wondered which way led to the office.

I closed my eyes and pictured the direction I'd entered the castle, a side entrance toward the back of the building, which made sense for the kitchen area because delivery trucks would use the service road that ran behind the main property. Now, I was on the other side of the rear of the castle, so I turned and walked what I thought was the length of the building toward the front of the castle, where the lobby office was located.

Cleaning and security personnel both used this passage. I was confident I'd soon meet up with someone to help guide me or key me out to a public hallway. Minutes and steps passed with no one to be seen. I continued on and allowed my mind to wander to my conversation with Justin and Chef Hartsall about the cake. Their stories were in direct opposition. Justin stated it wasn't baked on-site, while the chef admitted to baking two large cakes, one used by our show, the other sent to the elderly to enjoy. One of them had to be lying, right?

I shook my head. No, why would they? Justin told me

the chef knew nothing about the cake found in Skylar's room. If it hadn't been baked on-site, it stood to reason that was the truth. A chef wouldn't approve a delivery of anything to a room. If a guest had ordered it, the delivery wouldn't have come through the kitchen. Did Chef Hartsall oversee the delivery to the assisted living facility? Or could the second cake he baked have been intercepted by a crazed fan? Had Lisa stolen or perhaps paid off a kitchen staff member for the cake? Or had she brought one with her? She was dressed in a bridal gown and had tried to force Skylar into marriage before. Had she thought this time it would work?

The cake at the scene of the crime bugged me. A bakery wouldn't keep an extra five-tiered wedding cake in stock. If Chef Hartsall knew nothing about it and the cake he baked was sent to an assisted living facility, Lisa had to have ordered it. Had Sheriff Perry or any of his investigators considered the cake? Or had they gathered enough evidence that pointed to Skylar and stopped investigating?

I needed to talk to Sheriff Perry. Bring this detail to his attention. He or one of his investigators could call or visit area bakeries to see if Lisa had ordered a cake to be picked up and delivered. He may want to check a larger radius. Bakeries Lisa had been familiar with, like Marco's family bakery. My eyes widened in a lightbulb moment. Marco might have easy access to a wedding cake, the ability to ship it and the know-how to assemble it. Could he have traveled with the cake and assembled it on-site? I pondered my suspicions. Would either of those scenarios be likely? Shipping would leave a paper trail. Air travel with a five-tier wedding cake seemed very unlikely. A better possibility was that he rented a kitchen after he arrived, baked then transported the cake to Coal Castle Resort. Still trying to sell myself on any of those theories, I knew one thing for sure. In my mind, it wasn't coincidental. I needed to bring the connection Lisa might have to Marco to the attention of Sheriff Perry. I'd text Eric to call him and set up an appointment as soon as I got back to the workshop and my phone.

Which reminded me, I'd been walking lost in thought for a long time. I stopped. When was the last time I passed a door? I peered behind me, then in front of me. Was I going the wrong way? Should I turn around or continue forward? I tried to recall the trivia I learned about Coal Castle Resort before and during my last visit. Drake had said Mr. Cole built a secret passage to his workshop. Is that where I was, because there were no longer entry doors in the hallway, not to mention no cleaning, maintenance or catering staff?

Panic stabbed at my insides. I needed to get back to the set. Should I backtrack and try to find my way to the lobby office or an entry door and pound on it? Should I continue forward and hope the secret passage led to a door in the area of the workshop the show was using?

Taking deliberate deep breaths, I decided to push forward. After all, this had to be the way catering transported food to the set, right?

A noise echoed in the hallway. Not a voice, a *click*. Maybe like a door opening? I hurried forward and was greeted with a hushed voice. From my vantage point, I saw the hallway curved. I needed to get to the door. The voice, still muffled, grew louder. I heard only one voice. When I reached the curve, I stopped. Closer, I recognized the voice. It was Marco. Was this the entrance area for the contestants?

The carpet muted my footsteps so he didn't know I was there. I didn't want to startle him. I opened my mouth to call out when he raised his voice.

"I said she was taken care of. Don't worry. Everything is handled. Everything went according to plan." He laughed.

My eyes grew wide. Flattening my body to the wall, I hoped he didn't pace while he talked on the phone. Which was now obvious to me because I heard only one voice, his. Was he talking about Lisa? Had I been right about his girlfriend, Lisa, being Skylar's stalker?

I swallowed hard. Why hadn't I told Sheriff Perry about that? I needed to talk to him. I needed to get out of this hallway. I needed to make sure Marco didn't see me while I inched along the wall to make certain it was him. I caught sight of his back. Still apron-clad, he held his phone in one hand and the door handle in the other to keep it from locking.

"No one knows. Yes, I'm sure. I've got to go." He pulled the phone from his ear and the door open the width of his body. Without looking back, he slipped out of the hallway.

I had a short window of time to catch the door before it locked. Thankful wardrobe dressed me in flats, I ran toward the door, watching the crack of light grow smaller and smaller with each running step. Just as the latch clicked against the strike plate, my fingers made contact with the door handle.

Breathing a sigh of relief, I stopped the motion of the

door. My heart raced from the conversation I'd overheard and adrenaline from trying to reach the door. I wanted to catch my breath before I entered. I also wanted to wait a few minutes to avoid running into Marco or having him see me since I thought my suspicions were true.

Marco murdered Lisa.

Chapter Seventeen

I stood alone in front of the contestants, glad it was the last shot of the day.

The day had been filled with tension. The door I'd followed Marco through led to the hallway in the workshop where the restrooms were located. I knew without checking that the label on the door would say "Janitor's Closet." I checked anyway. It did. When had Marco figured that out? Or had he just tried doors to find a private place for his phone call? It had a card scanner. Didn't it work, or had Marco found a way to disarm it?

Once I was back at the workshop, I'd managed to slip up to the makeup room, retrieve my phone and text Eric about needing to talk to Sheriff Perry. On my way down the stairs, Quintin had spotted me and stomped over to the bottom of the staircase. He reminded me in a loud voice, almost a shout, Kinzy had told me to stay on set and interview the contestants, and that even if I wasn't interviewing the contestants, I should be in a chair in the wings, not in the makeup room. Before I could tell him I wasn't in the makeup room or even on the premises of the set, Brenden cut in and told Quintin he'd decided not to interview the contestants during the breakfast challenge, which made him the subject of Quintin's berating.

From that point on, they argued about everything—when to break for lunch, the camera angles, even the thematic aprons the contestants wore. The tension created by the two of them set everyone's nerves on edge, especially the contestants, who were nervous enough.

Harrison and Shannon admitted to having their work cut out for them to choose a winner of the day and the person to send home. In their estimation not one person completed or succeeded at any of the recipe challenges. In addition, they'd received attitude from Marco, Lynne and Miller when they critiqued their offerings. After his critique, Miller had a meltdown, which turned up the heat and tension in the kitchen.

Standing still while I waited for lighting and camera adjustments, I eyed Marco. All of the contestants stood next to their creations and visited quietly, except him. He leaned against his counter, arms crossed over his chest. Impatience rested on his features, which struck me as odd since the baking competition was the reason he was here. Or was it? Had he only entered to kill Lisa and frame Skylar?

I had no idea whose names I'd announce, but deep down, I didn't want Marco to be baker of the day or the contestant going home. With my suspicions about him, I thought it best he remain on the resort premises, at least until I'd discussed my misgivings with Sheriff Perry tonight after we'd wrapped filming. If his girlfriend was Lisa Mackliner and he murdered her, we certainly didn't want to send him home or give him access to flee the country.

"Courtney?"

Hearing my name pulled me from my reverie. My eyes shot to Brenden, then his hand. He began a finger countdown. The monitor flashed to life. I smiled and slowly looked at the contestants from left to right. Marco had straightened up. His arms remained crossed. All the contestants stared forward.

"Most of you found today's challenges problematic." I paused and fought the urge to flash a narrow-eyed look at the culprit, Quintin. The challenges weren't the problem, it was the tension on set. "Which made the judges' decision difficult. The winner of today's challenge scores points from the judges for striving for tropical flavor and flare. Although your banana pancakes were tough, the starfish shape won praise. The tartness of your fruit salad puckered the judges' lips, yet serving it in hollowed-out coconut shells drew smiles."

Her glee started when I said the pancakes, and now covered every inch of her features.

"Baker of the day is Donna."

I waited for the congratulations to die down. "Now comes the hard part, sending someone home. The most skilled chef will not succeed in the kitchen if they can't control their frustration levels when, for whatever reason, the recipe isn't working out." My eyes glazed with moisture when I read ahead to the next line. "The tools of your trade demand respect. Not to mention, tossing some of them . . ." I stopped and swallowed hard. I'd seen the misuse of chef's tools, a cast-iron fry pan and a serrated knife, turn fatal. "Can cause injury or fatality. Miller, you are leaving the kitchen."

"Oh, baby." In an instant, Mary stood beside him and wrapped an arm around his shoulders. Miller hung his head. Most of the other contestants surrounded him with pats on the back and words of sympathy. Marco remained beside his counter, arms crossed. Lynne hung back from the crowd with an expression that showed her disapproval of something. If it was Miller's action, throwing a wooden spoon on the floor and then kicking it, or him being the cook sent home, I wasn't certain.

My cameraman cut filming. I stepped off my mark and over to where Shannon and Harrison stood in the wings. Normally, they were front and center during the announcement of their judges' verdict. Today, Harrison refused.

"That went better than I thought it might." Harrison tugged on the hem of his shirt, clearly uncomfortable in casual clothes.

"I suppose he'd calmed down some." Shannon started to walk toward the stairs. Harrison and I fell into step behind her. "He's lucky he didn't hurt anyone when he threw, then kicked the spoon during our critique."

Glancing at Harrison, I saw his lips draw into a thin line. "I thought we had a better group of contestants this time and they were bonding." We stepped up and entered our makeup room. "Now, I'm not so sure."

"Y'all, compared to last year, they're a much better group. I think Miller picked up on Quintin and Brenden's bad feelings, but in all honesty, I don't know how a few of the contestants made it on the show."

"Agreed." Harrison grasped the doorknob to his dressing room. "There are at least four people who are very inexperienced in the kitchen. Truth be told, Miller wasn't one of them. I actually thought Miller and Mary might have been given a spot as a screen test for a show of their own because they have terrific banter. His actions today were disappointing."

Before Shannon or I could respond, Harrison turned the knob and was gone.

"What are you doing tonight?" Shannon asked.

"Oh!" I hurried over to the door of our dressing room. "I'm meeting Sheriff Perry on my set. I'd better get a move on."

Both Shannon and I quickly changed into our own clothes. Shannon wore a denim skirt with a front vent, violet long-sleeved T-shirt and matching denim vest with low-shaft cowgirl boots. My black leggings and pink cotton sweater provided the right barrier layer to the cool fall air. My pink flats with cushioned insoles made the walk to the resort enjoyable. We parted ways in the lobby. She had a room service and Skype dinner date with her husband. I planned to do a run-through of tomorrow night's filming and convince Sheriff Perry my theories about Lisa Mackliner's murder were more than hypothetical.

Swiping my key card through the scanner, I waited for the flash of green and opened the door. Eric, Sheriff Perry and Pamela sat on the chairs used for the studio audience, drinking coffee and conversing. I hadn't planned on a trio. At least the duo knew I played with theories and what-ifs in my mind when it came to murder. One of us would have to bring Pamela up to speed. Unless she left.

"Hi, Courtney!" Pamela stood. "We were just talking about you."

I approached the chairs and looked down at Sheriff Perry. "I'm sure it all was good."

An ear-to-ear grin spread across his face, deepening the age lines around his mouth and eyes. "Oh, it was."

Eric rose. "Have a seat." He palmed a hand toward the chair he sat on and started to drag another one to the group.

I took the chair directly across from Sheriff Perry, which put Pamela on my left and Eric on my right. I opened my mouth.

Sheriff Perry held up a halting hand. "I didn't come here because you beckoned me with your theories on the murder investigation."

I closed my mouth. With lips drawn in a tight line, I crossed my arms over my chest and glared at him.

He chuckled. "Good. Your guard is up. I need to tell you both something." Sheriff Perry moved his eyes from me to Eric. "One of your audience members broke the gag order. They sold their story to a rag magazine, which hit the store shelves sometime yesterday. My county is abuzz with reporters. So, once again because of you, I have barricades blocking the entrances to Coal Castle Resort, not to mention extra manpower, which zaps my budget and makes my job more difficult because the press is bound to find out about the murder." When he was finished speaking, he rested his glare and perturbed expression on me, letting me know he considered me trouble.

I had to hand it to Sheriff Perry, he had a knack for keeping things that happened in his county from the press and when they did find out, he kept them on the fringe instead of in the fray.

Eric let out an audible sigh of disgust. "Do you know who?"

"Not yet. I need a list of the people in attendance and copies of the gag orders. Think your network will want to enforce it?" Sheriff Perry looked back at Eric.

"I don't know. I am surprised they haven't contacted me yet." Eric rose and walked to the counter, where his laptop rested.

While Eric perused it, Pamela addressed Sheriff Perry, "Do you think Courtney is in any danger?"

"In this situation, only of losing her livelihood." His lips twitched as he fought a grin.

"Nothing about this is funny." I stood and glared at him.

"Well, if you had told the truth." He stood and pinned me with a look that resembled more of a parent chastising a child than law enforcement staring down a trouble-maker. Of which I was neither. "Now"—he glanced at Pamela—"if she doesn't stay out of my murder investigation, she could be in danger."

Pamela's head ping-ponged between us while she wore an expression of utter confusion.

Sheriff Perry continued. "I don't want you interfering with my murder investigation. Understood?" When I made no motion of agreeing, he sighed and sat down. "What have you found out?"

I sat too. "It's not so much what I've found out. It's more of what I know."

Sheriff Perry rolled his eyes.

I cleared my throat and regained his attention. "Skylar has an aversion to weddings. We both know he can't stomach the sight and smell of blood. I don't believe he'd murder Lisa."

"Not even in the heat of passion or fear?"

"I suppose in those instances it'd be a possibility, but

here is what bugs me. Skylar doesn't like weddings, so why would there be a wedding cake and bridal gown?" Certain I saw a flicker of interest cross Sheriff Perry's eyes, I continued. "The cake really bugs me. Bakeries don't just have a five-tier wedding cake in stock. Wedding cakes are made to order and they're expensive. Would Lisa have the funds to purchase one? How did she get it here? Who set it up? I know food isn't your business like it's mine." A trickle of fear whisked through me, maybe not after my admission. I tamped it down and pressed on. "In addition, wedding cakes have to be assembled, and you need to know what you're doing."

I took a breath, which gave Sheriff Perry a chance to respond. He rubbed his chin in contemplation.

When he uttered no words, I continued. "I spoke with Chef Hartsall, the bakery chef at Coal Castle Resort; he baked two cakes for our show. The one that wasn't needed was sent to the local assisted living home, so where did the cake come from?"

Still no response from Sheriff Perry. His expression had turned thoughtful, though. "I haven't spoken to any front desk people to see if a local bakery delivered a cake to anyone staying on-site that day. . . ."

"And you won't." Sheriff Perry's voice boomed through the room. "Stop nosing around and asking questions. Do you remember what happened the last time you did that?"

Of course I do. I didn't dignify his question with an answer. How could I forget someone tried to kill me?

He stood and stepped closer to me, trying to intimidate me with his bulk, which didn't work. He looked down at me. "I am not telling you again. Stay out of my investigation. This time you might not be so lucky. And you"—

Sheriff Perry looked at Pamela—"keep her in your sights." With a hitch of his waistband, he turned, strode across the room and let the door bang behind him.

Pamela actually took ahold of the seat of her chair and scooched it closer to mine. "I am sorry if I let you down. I was sure Drake said to be present in your set area, not everywhere."

"I think Sheriff Perry got a little dramatic." I gave Pamela a back-off hand sign. "I don't need a bodyguard."

"I agree you don't need a bodyguard if you listen to Sheriff Perry," Eric admonished me while he walked back to the chairs, his laptop in hand.

"I did listen to him." I didn't add what I'd actually heard when I listened to him. He told me this time I might not be so lucky, which meant he didn't believe Skylar was the killer either. Because Sheriff Perry and I both knew Skylar would never hurt me.

The next morning I arrived on set in a cranky mood. I woke up that way and contributed it to Sheriff Perry's attitude about my help with his investigation and the fact that someone leaked my apology. When Pamela and Eric showed up at my suite to escort me to the set, it increased my negativity. Pamela walked so close to me we were almost joined like rising biscuits in a round baking pan.

Eric, dressed in black pants and mint-green pullover sweater, came armed with a hazelnut latte and a promise he'd call or text after he spoke with the network concerning the information leak. His words sparked my worry of losing my show, my cohosting gig and any prospects of sharing a show with Shannon. Not to mention the knife set I wanted to develop. Had the news of the leak made it to Quintin yet? Would I be banished to the sidelines with Skylar so I could easily be written out of this season if need be?

By the time Pamela stopped the UTV, tension knotted my muscles and stomach. My mood darkened to thunderstorm proportions. Eric and I never did develop an aftermath plan. What would we do for a living? He could still be a producer, but me, I'd have to start with an entry-level chef position somewhere. An intense throbbing pounded behind my eyes.

Pamela had the nerve to walk me to the entrance door of the workshop. I mumbled a greeting to Kinzy, who answered with a perturbed bend of her tightly closed lips, as I passed on my way to the stairs. Was Kinzy in a bad mood too or angry with me for not following her orders yesterday? I swung open the door to the makeup room to find Skylar sitting in a swivel chair and a sheriff's deputy standing at attention beside the wall.

"Skylar!" I stepped over to him and hugged his neck. My mood lifted a little knowing Skylar hadn't been arrested for the murder of Lisa Mackliner.

He patted my arm. "Good morning, Courtney." We made eye contact in the mirror.

"What's going on?" I shifted my eyes sideways in the direction of where the deputy stood.

"I'm not sure." Skylar looked at the deputy. "Sheriff Perry assigned him to me. I guess I must be a flight risk." He rolled his eyes.

I frowned. If the road leading into the resort had a barricade, how could Skylar leave? Scale the Poconos? I wondered why Sheriff Perry would have Skylar watched.

Did he think there was an accomplice? Or did he think Skylar was in danger? After all, he had somehow been drugged.

My eyes returned to the mirror and I studied his face. Deep lines creased his forehead, and dark circles half-mooned his eyes. He hadn't shaved in days; his stubble had turned into a short beard.

When our eyes met again, sadness veiled his blue irises. "I'm a doomed man." His tone, which held a level of acceptance, unnerved me.

"Not if you're innocent." I moved from behind him and took a seat. We swiveled to face each other.

"The evidence is stacking against me." He dropped his gaze to his lap.

At that moment, I realized my situation wasn't dire. People switched careers all the time. I was a trained chef with cooking experience and connections. I had options, even if I had to start from the bottom up in a restaurant kitchen. My apology and the leak could alter my career path, not my life.

Pushing my blues to the side, I inflected support in my tone when I said, "Skylar. I know how you feel. I do. You are innocent. Don't let them brainwash you into thinking you aren't." I cast an accusatory glance over my shoulder at the deputy. I knew he was listening because he shrugged.

"I am innocent. I didn't kill Lisa Mackliner. I wanted her to leave me alone. I wanted her to get help for her obsessive behavior. I wanted her to find someone else to love." He heaved a loud sigh. "But all the evidence points at me." Skylar stood and walked out the door. The deputy followed him.

Questions concerning the murder of Lisa Mackliner

nagged my mind while I changed into my wardrobe for the day, black leggings with long shafted black boots and a fuchsia T-shirt with "Bridal Party" emblazoned in glitter across the front. I hadn't had enough time to research Lisa's background. My intuition told me she didn't come from a wealthy family. If Lisa had been released from prison, would she have the funds to purchase a cake and dress? I should have asked Skylar if she had to pay restitution or anything along with the prison time. She could purchase a bridal gown cheap at a thrift store. But not that cake. Also, if money was an issue, how did she reserve a room at Coal Castle Resort? My mind stopped whirring. That was something I could check with the front desk even if Sheriff Perry warned me not to. If she hadn't reserved a room, then where was she staying? Had she sneaked onto the premises and slept in the wooded area or one of the benches around the pond? How had she gotten from prison to the resort? Skylar lived clear across the country. She had to have an accomplice. Someone to help her get a room, a best friend or sister? Or boyfriend? Like Marco.

I caught the gasp in my throat. In light of the lecture I'd received from Sheriff Perry, I'd forgotten to tell him about Marco having a girlfriend named Lisa, his odd behavior and incriminating phone call. My heart sank. I wasn't helping Skylar by withholding that information. Sometime today, I had to make contact with Sheriff Perry again. I'd probably endure another lecture, but Skylar's freedom was worth it.

My stylist added my accessories, bangle bracelets and gold hoop earrings and sent me out to makeup. Shannon and I hit the chair at the same time; instead of leggings, she wore skinny black jeans with ankle boots. Our stylists had perfected our makeup when Kinzy swung the door open.

"You need to be on set in five minutes."

The stylists argued they couldn't do much with our hair in that amount of time, lost the battle and decided on a sloppy bun for me and side braid for Shannon.

Kinzy stayed in the area and paced the entire time. Her sour expression matched the one Quintin wore most days. His presence on the set obviously influenced Kinzy to do the same. Did she really find him a role model?

We made it down to the set with thirty seconds to spare. Kinzy joined Quintin. Harrison and Skylar waited in their chairs with the deputy standing behind Skylar. I'd wondered how Harrison fit into the bachelorette party theme. Dressed all in black, his T-shirt stated "Designated Driver" in bold white non-glittered letters. A chauffeur hat rested in his lap while disgust rested on his face. Harrison didn't get into dressing in theme.

"There you are." Pamela stepped up beside me. She held a catering cup of coffee.

"What are you doing here?" I didn't add, *And standing so close.* Instead, I took one side step away from her.

She crunched her features into an are-you-crazy expression, then said, "My job. Sheriff Perry told me to guard you."

"I don't think he meant literally."

"I think he did since he phoned Drake with specific orders." Pamela smiled. "Don't worry. You're safe with me."

I was ready to say that I wasn't worried about being safe when Quintin stormed across the room. The heels of his dress shoes beat down on the wooden floor. "Who are you?" He looked at Pamela, then at the deputy.

"Security for Miss Archer." Pamela used a very professional and authoritative tone. I was impressed. The deputy followed suit.

"I want you both gone." Quintin rose to his full height and rested his hands on his hips. He cast a formidable shadow over Pamela and me.

She didn't back down. "I am following my orders, as I'm sure the deputy is doing." The deputy nodded. "You will have to talk to our supervisors."

Quintin stuffed his hands into his pockets and began to pace. "I don't want security or law enforcement personnel on the set. Outside is fine. Inside, I run the show. So get out!" He stopped pacing and pointed toward the door.

"No." Pamela pulled her phone from the case on her belt and started to dial.

Glowering, Quintin spoke through clenched teeth. "Put that away. I don't need more cops descending on the set. Stay, but don't get in my way." He stalked back to his chair.

My respect for Pamela shot through the ceiling. For a small woman, she'd held her ground. Sliding her phone back into the holder, her eyes met mine. She quirked a brow and gave me a lopsided grin.

I smiled back at her, yet I couldn't help but wonder about Quintin's reaction. Why wouldn't he want security on the set? Did he really not care about his talent and their safety? Or was he guilty of something?

Chapter Eighteen

It took three takes to kick off the challenge because I flubbed my lines. My mind was on other things, namely, the actions of Lisa, Skylar, Marco and Quintin. While doing the interviews, I noticed Skylar at the catering table. He spoke with Justin. Justin wore an expression of sympathy as he listened to Skylar, yet he kept looking over his shoulder during the conversation, like he was torn if he should stay or walk away. I was sure he wanted to talk to Skylar and keep his job. With the new protocol laid down by his manager, he couldn't do both. Sadly, everyone felt the strain of this murder and the aftermath.

Brenden gave me leeway on the interviews this round. They could be brief or long, which I was fine with because most of the contestants preferred to work rather than talk. I interviewed the contestants in a haphazard order. I kept the interviews brief. With a lower number of contestants, they went fast, which was good because my mind really wasn't on my work. I had two contestants left, Mike and Marco. I'd saved Marco for last, hoping to glean some information from him.

Their challenge had been a sweet and savory snack that was transportable for the bachelorette party to munch on in the limo.

Mike stood in front of his stovetop. "What are you making?" I sidled up to his kitchen counter so the cameraman could capture us both in his shot.

He glanced up and continued stirring the contents of the saucepan. He smiled. "A chili coating for snack mix." He nodded toward a large bowl filled with pretzels, bagel chips, nuts and chunks of cooked bacon waiting for the spicy seasoning. He wiped his hands down the fuchsia apron, which matched my T-shirt to the letter. "Once it's coated, it needs to bake."

"Sounds good, and very savory. Any ideas on your sweet snack?"

He nodded. "Something with oatmeal to help soak up the alcohol." His attention returned to the pot. "One thing at a time. One thing at a time," he answered, watching the bubbling liquid instead of looking at me or the camera. Since he hadn't started on his sweet, I gave the cameraman the signal to move on to Marco.

As soon as the cameraman moved, Mike became chatty. Looking directly at me and paying no attention to his recipe, he said, "Maybe you can tell me something." Mike stirred while he spoke. His spoon knocking into the side of the stainless steel pot. "Why hasn't Skylar been arrested? All the evidence points to him."

What? Why would he think he could ask me that question? "Obviously, all the evidence doesn't point to him or he would be arrested. You know he is innocent until proven guilty."

Mike shrugged like he didn't notice the sass in my tone. "Well, he shouldn't be on set. It creates tension. A cooking competition is tense enough. We don't need two layers of tension. Could you talk to the higher-ups about it?" Mike turned his focus back to the now-boiling sauce and muttered, "Like they care. All they're worried about is who has the upper hand in their struggle for power."

My eyes widened in disbelief at his choice of conversation about Skylar being on set and Brenden and Quintin's continual differences of opinion. Did he think I could do something about either? I could do one thing, set him straight on Skylar's character. I opened my mouth to do just that but didn't get the chance. My cameraman beckoned me over to Marco's kitchenette. I complied while seething over the previous conversation. Halfway there it hit me. Something I said rang true. All the evidence couldn't point to Skylar, or Sheriff Perry would have arrested him by now. Right? Or was he going through proper procedure to make sure the charges stuck?

Still pondering, I walked over to Marco. Glancing up from his cutting board, he grimaced. An odd reaction unless he'd seen me in the hallway and knew I overheard his call. A very incriminating conversation, in my opinion.

"Not a good time for an interview?" I asked.

"Not really. You should have started with me." Marco continued to cut figs.

"We need to get footage of everyone."

Marco rolled his eyes.

I pushed on. "Tell us what you are making?"

"Candied bacon-wrapped figs." Marco stabbed a fig with the tip of the knife, then sliced down so hard the knife blade hit the wooden cutting board with a loud *crack*.

The action sent shivers of fear dancing up and down my spine. Had he used the same technique on Lisa? If Lisa Mackliner was in fact his girlfriend. His knife punctured another fig and guillotined it in half. My suspicion grew stronger than my fear. Now was my chance to ask him a few questions, so I took it.

I swallowed hard. "Is your girlfriend excited you've made it this far?'

"Yeah." He stopped cutting and started wrapping bacon around the halved figs.

"Did you give her Skyler's autograph?"

He snorted. "No."

Even though I wanted to, I couldn't outright ask his girlfriend's last name. I decided to try a different line of questioning. "Does your family bakery make and ship wedding cakes?"

Throwing me a confused look, the cameraman turned off the camera and held it lens down. He knew the last two questions weren't for the viewers.

Marco stopped working and pinned me with a look that could kill.

I took a step away from the counter.

"Why?"

Before I had a chance to respond, Brenden hollered my name. When I looked at him, he said, "Looks like you're done. Take a break."

Had he caught Marco's facial expression? My conversation with Marco was over. If you could call his one-word answers conversation. His vagueness led me to believe he was hiding something. Judging by the phone conversation I overheard, I thought it had to do with Lisa's murder. He knew if he talked too much, he might incriminate himself. I really needed to talk to Sheriff Perry and tell him about this situation.

Following Brenden's orders, I walked over to my canvas chair and pulled it close to Skylar. He sat in a slouched position, staring into space. Harrison and Shannon were nowhere around, so they were probably at the bistro table shooting their judges' conversation. The deputy assigned to Skylar and Pamela were missing too. I surveyed the area and found the deputy at the catering table filling a plate. Pamela had either stepped outside or into the ladies' room. I had a short window of opportunity to talk to Skylar. I took it.

"Skylar."

Hearing his name, he looked my way and seemed surprised I sat beside him. I so understood his foggy daze.

"Do you know anything about Lisa Mackliner's background?" I spoke in a hushed tone not quite a whisper.

He nodded. "She came from a middle-class family. Her parents were both teachers, father high school, mother elementary. She'd went to college and graduated with a business degree." He blew out a breath. "I guess college is when she became obsessed with me. She wasn't very active or social there so she started living in a fantasy world."

"Did she have a drug problem or maybe a medical condition which required a prescription she'd stopped taking when she became obsessed with you?"

He turned in his chair. "Not before she was arrested for stalking me. After that she was tested and diagnosed with a mild mental health disorder. Her attorney used the diagnosis to get her a lenient sentence when I and the network filed charges."

"Interesting. Did she have to pay a monetary restitution to you and the network?"

"Yes, she had to pay the network for the damage and me for pain and suffering. Her bank accounts were exhausted, and it wasn't enough to cover both settlements. There is a court-ordered garnishment of her wages until her restitution to the network is paid in full. Including what little she earned at her job in the prison library. The court granted me my full settlement, which I donated to a facility that treats mental disorders like hers. I was happy she'd found help and hoped others could too. Again, I just wanted her to leave me alone. I never wished her harm." A gag punctuated his sentence. I knew the murder scene popped back into his mind. "I mean, she was murdered in such a tragic and bloody—" Another gag interrupted him. He arose and ran toward the restroom area. The deputy, who still stood beside the catering table nibbling, saw Skylar move and followed him at a leisurely pace. It was obvious to me the deputy wasn't guarding Skylar because he was a flight risk.

I sighed. My chance for more information was gone. At least I did know a little more about Lisa from the background sketch Skylar provided. Her previous employment and legal restitution indicated to me someone, somewhere helped her get here. Maybe a boyfriend? Which circled my thoughts back to Marco and his phone conversation.

"Hey, girlfriend." Shannon squeezed my shoulder before she sat in the chair Skylar vacated. "You are lost in thought. What's up?"

So I told her and ended with: "We need to somehow find out the last name of his girlfriend."

"Well, you didn't have any luck trying to get other answers out of him. How could I work that into a conversation with him? Would he be more forthcoming with me?"

"I don't know. We don't want him to catch on that we're after information." Although I felt certain he already had by his one-word answers to my questions. "I think we should try doing an Internet search. Maybe we'd find a picture that would lead to a name. Or face. Let's plan to do that during our lunch break."

"I'm in." Shannon flashed me a conspirator smile.

Unfortunately, lunch break came and went for us because filming demanded our time. We were able to grab quick bites of food off the catering table while waiting for a repairman to fix a broken refrigerator. Quintin demanded everyone stay on the set, even the contestants. After a slight delay, their catered lunch was brought to the set and eaten in the area where we usually shoot the opening sequences, something that had been done only once since the murder of Lisa Mackliner.

In the chaos of the broken appliance and Quintin barking orders, neither Shannon nor I made any progress on researching Lisa Mackliner. Now, I stood with toes to tape knowing I couldn't blow my lines because I was due on my *Cooking with the Farmer's Daughter* set in forty minutes.

I hit my cue when Brenden closed his fist, and read the lines perfectly, announcing that once again Mike made baker of the day. When the congratulations died down, I read the monitor in an even tone, although a hint of disappointment touched my heart. Nadine, who struggled with every challenge today, had to leave the kitchen.

As soon as I was cleared to leave, I hurried toward the stairs. Pamela entered the workshop, holding the heavy wooden door open. "Are you ready?"

I looked down at my clothes and fought the urge to ask if I looked ready. "I'll be five minutes tops." I flew up the stairs and into my dressing room, thankful our wardrobe hadn't been formal today. True to my word, Pamela and I headed out of the door in exactly five minutes. With the pedal to the floor, she maneuvered the path like an experienced race car driver so I would have plenty of time to get into wardrobe for my show and to wonder if my audience would mention the article in the magazine. Maybe my viewers didn't read those types of magazines. A girl could hope. Another thought struck me. Someone affiliated with entertainment news programs probably read those rags from cover to cover. Had they picked up the story yet? Was Eric prepared for something like that? Was our network? I had no idea. Eric had spent so much time with Pamela, we'd not had the time to discuss what we should do. Guilt snaked through me. I needed to focus on my career. There were many jobs riding on the line for *Cooking with the Farmer's Daughter*, not just Eric's and mine.

Eric and I might have time to meet and discuss my concerns before filming began, a private conversation in my dressing room. Pamela could wait on the set. Our studio audience wouldn't be led into the suite until minutes before filming started, which would give us about ten minutes.

I hit the suite on a run, Pamela close behind, hoping my stylist could work fast. "Hi, Eric! I'll try to hurry. We need to talk." I slipped through the door in the portable wall so my stylist could work her magic.

In no time, I'd tucked a blue bandanna print blouse into a denim skirt and slipped into low-shafted cowgirl boots. The curlicues on the soft brown leather matched the print in my shirt. My stylist parted my hair into two pigtails, attaching the holder just under my earlobe. She covered the elastic band with blue ribbons that matched my shirt.

"Eric." I opened the adjoining door as I called his name. When he didn't answer, I looked around my crew members readying my set. Harrison, Shannon and Pamela huddled around Eric in a far corner.

"There you are." Harrison came toward me. "Shannon and I are here for moral support. Since a fan leaked your secret you may get questions concerning your apology. Once your confession and apology air, your life is going to change. Tonight could be the start of it." He took my hand and we stepped over to the gathering of friends.

"I know. I could lose my show and put many people on unemployment." I sighed and looked at Eric. I didn't want to have this conversation in front of everyone other than Pamela, but they were my friends and colleagues.

"Not what I meant." Harrison released my hand. "I mean you need to prepare for the worst—paparazzi, hate mail or an outraged fan approaching you in public. Once the press gets word about your lying to the public, they will look for everything and anything bad you've ever done."

"Thanks for giving me more to worry about." Fear edged my words.

"Courtney." Eric wrapped me in a side hug. "Everything Harrison said will probably happen. He told you those things so you are prepared and not taken by surprise." I looked at Eric, more than a measure of concern filled his eyes and mixed with another emotion. Was it love?

"Y'all, I don't think Courtney has to worry about past mistakes showing up in the press. She is squeaky clean." Shannon side-hugged me on my free side.

"I'll say." Pamela laughed. "Her background check is boring reading."

My eyes snapped to Pamela; then I grinned. Not because she'd just pointed out I was a boring person, but I might have another avenue to find out Marco's girlfriend's last name.

"So, to recap our show today." I threw a lemon in the air and caught it. "Oh my gravy, there are many uses for lemons in the kitchen from cleaning the odor of fish off your hands to reviving wilted lettuce to making a splendid lemon curd for pie or other desserts." I held the lemon chin height and smiled into the camera.

Our director yelled, "Cut," and the filming ended.

Eric stepped front and center. I walked around the kitchen counter and joined him, wishing I could have done a carving in the lemon peel. I knew a neat technique where I carved a duck shape, bent the peel a little and it looked like it was standing on the lemon. Really basic stuff, but cute.

"Now we have time for questions and answers."

Drake had joined us. He and Pamela stood flanking the chairs. Harrison and Shannon had separated so I'd have a friendly face to seek out on each side of the audience if need be. I smiled. I had great friends.

A young man stood. "I have a question for Miss Archer."

Eric moved with the microphone and the audience member waved him off.

"I know how to project my voice. I want to know what happened on the premises of Coal Castle Resort. I heard there was another murder. Are you involved again? Was it aimed at you? Do you have enemies?"

Stunned, I moved my wordless lips. I'd braced for questions about my career, not the murder. "I . . . um . . . can't . . ."

I never saw Pamela move from her post, yet in what seemed like an instant she stood in front of me. "Sir, Miss Archer is taking cooking questions."

"But our local news station wants to know what's going on. We have word the coroner came here and Miss Archer seems to . . ."

Drake approached the young man and took ahold of his arm, stopping his argument with Pamela. I really wanted to know what he was going to say next.

"That's enough. Let's go." Drake pulled until the reporter took a step.

"You can't arrest me and I have a ticket to be here," the reporter argued while Drake practically dragged him from the room.

The remaining audience members began to murmur.

"All right." For a small woman, Pamela had a commanding tone. "We'll take any of your cooking questions."

For the next twenty minutes, I answered questions about gardening with Eric's help, gave tips on less stressful holiday cooking and listened to a few ideas on what they'd like to see on the show. Shannon and I made eye contact on a couple of the suggestions because they would be perfect for the joint show that we hoped the network would pick up if my apology didn't crush that dream. The audience must have taken the reporter incident and Pamela's warning to heart, because no one asked about my background or the story in the gossip magazine.

During the autograph and picture session, Eric and Pamela maintained a deep conversation that wasn't about the show because she inserted flirty giggles and Eric's normally fair skin deepened to dark red several times. Yet, Pamela kept a close eye on the crowd and me during this time too.

The last autograph I signed was for a middle-aged woman who inquired if I planned to release a cookbook of the recipes on my show. I explained there was none in the works. As she walked away, I wondered why Eric and I hadn't considered that along with my knife set. I stored the request in the back of my mind.

Just as I stood up and stretched, Sheriff Perry barged through the door. His gaze swept the room, then landed on me. "Where's Drake and that reporter?"

"I believe he took him to the suite we use . . ."

Sheriff Perry waved a hand at Pamela, which stopped her explanation, and addressed me. "So you're associated with a murder again." The corners of his lips quivered, but to his credit, he didn't give in to a smirk.

"You seem delighted by that."

He shrugged and for blasting through the door, didn't turn to go find Drake. Then it hit me. He would know where Drake and the reporter were. Putting my hands on my hips, I said, "Do you have another reason to be here other than to harangue me?"

A smirk deepened the parentheses around his mouth. "I need to interview the five of you." He indicated Eric, Pamela, Harrison, Shannon and me with head nods. "I want to collaborate Drake's account of what happened. You'll be last." He pointed at me.

I watched Sheriff Perry pull each person aside until it was my turn. I told him what happened.

He pinned me with a stern look. "From what I can attain, the reporter only knows the coroner came out here. He really had no idea why. Someone could have had a massive heart attack or died from natural causes, yet he jumped to the conclusion *you* were involved with another murder. Which substantiates my opinion, you attract trouble."

"I wholeheartedly disagree with your opinion." My words didn't faze him. I decided to turn the tables on the conversation. "Have you found anything out about a nearby bakery making a wedding cake?"

He scowled. "I told you to stay out of the investigation."

"And I told you I think the cake is key to the murder. According to what I found out here, the cake wasn't baked on-site. It was too large for one person, say Lisa, to sneak in. It would take two people to lift the bottom tier and a cart to transport it. Unless it was shipped here, it had to be baked and delivered locally."

Sheriff Perry sighed. "The only bakery in the vicinity is inside a grocery store."

"Great. You can check it out."

"We have." Sheriff Perry pinched the bridge of his nose and closed his eyes like he was trying to relieve the pain of a headache. I was ready to ask him if he needed aspirin when I realized I was probably the cause of the headache. That brought a smile to my lips.

He continued, eyes closed, bridged pinched. "They haven't made a wedding cake for two months."

"That means it was baked . . ."

He opened and bore his eyes into mine. "Stay out of the investigation." He flipped his gaze to Pamela. "Watch her." He stood and headed for the door.

"Sheriff Perry. Sheriff Perry! I have—" The click of the suite door closing cut me off. Once again, I didn't get the chance to tell him about Marco having a girlfriend named Lisa. I started to run after him. Harrison grabbed my arm and stopped me.

"It's been a long day and I have a treat for everyone." Harrison went to the refrigerator and retrieved a small box. "Petits fours." He opened, then tipped down the box to display a colorful assortment of the dessert. Eric retrieved paper plates and plastic ware from the adjoining suite. After Eric passed around the paper and plastic ware, Harrison served each of us by offering the box. He started with me. I took a mint-green frosted treat, hoping the flavor matched the color. White icing had been piped around the edges with a yellow flower centered on top. I noticed a familiar heart design in the corner and marveled at the intricate miniature. "Chef Hartsall made these."

"Yes, we are old friends. He has used the same insignia for years to indicate his work."

I cut through my dessert with my fork, breaking the

pristine piping that was the chef's signature. The squiggles that once formed the heart now looked odd on the cake. Like half-coiled snakes. I lifted my plate to eye level.

I studied the odd-shaped squiggles.

I'd seen them before and I knew where.

On the cake that became Lisa Mackliner's deathbed.

Chapter Nineteen

The crime scene cake had to have been the backup cake Chef Hartsall mentioned. The thought had been my mantra since I sliced through the petit four last night. I'd snapped a picture of the broken heart before I ate the treat.

It kicked me into research mode. I tried every possible search engine and combination of Marco's and Lisa's names. I found nothing because his social media sites were set to private and she didn't have any. At two in the morning, I decided to give up the search. I had to find a way to see the thorough background check the show completed on Marco. After last year, the background checks contained more information than financial or employment.

The cake niggled my mind, making it difficult to drop off to sleep. I had no idea how much sleep I'd gotten. All

I knew is it wasn't enough. To make matters worse, Shannon, Harrison and my stylist all stared at me with the same expression in the makeup room and inquired if I felt ill. Thank goodness my stylist is talented. When I left the makeup chair, my skin looked dewy and fresh.

Today the challenge revolved around the groom. All of the talent wore a tuxedo. Shannon and mine matched. A charcoal velvet stripe ran down the black skinny legged pants and outlined the lapel of the fitted jackets. Ruffled yokes and a pointed collar adorned our white blouses. A black bow tie replaced our normal accessories. Charcoal satin sling-back pumps with a three-inch heel finished our ensemble. They dressed Harrison in a traditional tux in every sense of the word.

The contestants' aprons mirrored Harrison's tux in color, black with a mint-green bow tie screen printed on the fabric. They faced two challenges today. A hearty dinner worthy of the best bachelor party and a groom's cake.

As tired as I was, I had a plan. I kicked off the challenge, then hurried to the corner of the set. I gave the room a once-over since I'd yet to see Pamela today and was glad she had shirked her bodyguard duty. I had a phone call to make and I didn't want her to overhear. When I didn't see her, I pulled my phone from my jacket pocket along with a slip of paper with the names of the two closest assisted living complexes.

I couldn't decide if Chef Hartsall had lied to me or someone highjacked that cake. Had Lisa bribed the delivery person? Had she stolen it? Or had Marco? I pressed in one of the numbers, stated my business when they answered and was transferred to the kitchen.

The transfer call rang and rang; just as I thought it'd cycle back to the receptionist, someone picked up. I asked for the manager, waited a few minutes for a female voice to say hello, then launched into the spiel. "This is Courtney from Coal Castle Resort. We wondered if you had any feedback on the cake we sent for your residents to enjoy."

My bubbly tone was met with a gruff, "What? We didn't receive a cake from you this week."

Hmmm. "My records show we sent one over on Monday."

"Your records are wrong. The last thing we received from your chef was cream puffs about a month ago." The manager hung up before I could say thank you or have a nice day.

To cover all my bases, I dialed the other facility, which resulted in me hanging up because their kitchen manager cussed me out because their facility should be on the receiving end of the resort and was not. I slipped my phone in my pocket, knowing I might have stirred up a bad batch of not being a good corporate neighbor for Coal Castle Resort.

The next call I made was to Sheriff Perry on his cell phone, which went straight to voice mail. I left a message to check the crime scene photos of the cake. I knew the investigators took pictures from all angles. I added that I'd send a picture I'd taken of the broken heart on the petit four so he could compare them. If the design matched the one on the crime scene cake, it was baked on-site and high-jacked from its intended destination to Skylar's room. Before I said goodbye, I assured him I was checking things out on this end; then I sent the picture.

I thought a minute. Would Drake have access to the crime scene photos? Would he remember the squiggle? It wouldn't hurt to ask him and alert him to my suspicions about the cake and Marco. I sent him a text, to which I received an automated message about him driving and would answer later.

In the meantime, I decided the person I needed to talk to about the cake was the kitchen manager. I could check worker shifts and inquire on whose job it was to deliver the cake. I was sure that information didn't fall into Chef Hartsall's job description, and to be honest, he bordered on rude and I wasn't sure I could trust him anyway.

I was certain the cake was baked on the premises and its destination had been diverted to Skylar's room. What I needed to find out was how and by whom.

Stuffing my phone into my pocket, I hurried out to the main set and catering table to find Justin. The staff usually stuck around at least an hour to ensure the food stayed hot and plentiful. My gaze locked on to him as I walked toward the table. I hadn't eaten yet, so I grabbed a plate and began to fill it with a scoop of corned beef hash with a poached egg in the center. "Good morning, Justin."

He stopped swiping at the crumbs and food bits left on the table by others. "Good morning." He briefly met my eyes, then returned to his work. I remembered what he told me and would keep the conversation brief while I continued to heap my plate with fresh fruit.

"Could you tell me the kitchen manager's name?" I snagged a small Danish and took a bite.

"Why?" Another glance at me, then over his shoulder. "Is something wrong with the food and service?"

"Oh, no! Nothing like that. I'd like to compliment him."

A loud crack of stainless steel hitting tile-covered cement and a very loud cuss word pulled my attention from

Justin. Lynne stared down at her feet, her skin red and her face scrunched with anger.

"You okay?" Afton ran to her side.

"Yes." She spat out the word. "Not my salmon tartare, though."

Afton gave her a hug. Jeremiah ran over, wiping his hands on a towel. "How can we help you?"

Lynne looked up in disbelief.

"Hey, I have seven minutes of cooking time before I can do anything to my food. Tell me what you need and I'll help." Jeremiah threw the towel on her counter.

"Me too," Afton offered, then smiled at Jeremiah.

Mike came over loaded with a roll of paper towels. "Let them help you restart. I'll clean up this mess." He disappeared behind the counter.

"Thank you, thank you." Tears streamed down Lynne's face. She started listing things she needed, sending Afton and Jeremiah scurrying off to the pantry and the refrigerator.

My eyes sought out Brenden, who wore a huge smile to match mine. This was exactly the show he'd hoped for last time. A friendly competition with people willing to help their fellow contestants. For some reason, I looked at Quintin. His normally sour expression had softened into appreciation. Cameramen followed all four contestants, capturing the scene. I knew some of, if not all of, this footage would appear on the show.

When the hubbub on set died down, I turned back to finish my conversation with Justin. He was gone. I searched the area to find all the catering staff had taken their carts and left. I shrugged. I'd have to catch him at lunchtime. A quick glance at the clock told me I needed to eat my breakfast because I'd be needed on set in a few minutes to give a ten-minute warning. I stood and watched all the contestants start to plate or put the last-minute finishing touches to their meals.

"Courtney, did you see that?" Brenden asked with the wide smile still plastered to his face.

"I did." I pitched my plate in the trash can. I put my fingers to my lips.

"Don't worry. The lipstick we use is supposed to stay on all day. It still looks great. Are you ready to call time?"

"I am." I hurried over to my mark. The cameras set up for the shot and I said, "Bakers, you have ten minutes."

Lynne hollered, "Thanks to everyone, I'm going to be able to plate my food." She didn't look up or quit working. Neither did the contestants who hollered, "You're welcome," or "No problem."

Time ticked by slow for me under the arch covered with carnations in fall hues of yellow, peach, deep orange and red. Pheasant feathers and pussy willows rounded out the arrangement, giving it a masculine feel except for one thing. It smelled feminine. "Two minutes." The contestants started to hustle. "One minute." Hands moved faster, features pulled into stressful expressions. "Time's up."

Everyone stepped back from their work. Cameras stopped filming. Kinzy waved the contestants out of the kitchenettes while a crew came in and cleaned up the area. The contestants nibbled at what was left on the catering table and hydrated themselves with juice or water.

Brenden and Quintin had what appeared to be a cool conversation, then Brenden approached the talent. "Courtney, you will accompany Harrison and Shannon during the judging."

Once the set was spiffy with the bachelor party meal

waiting on the edge of the counter, Kinzy waved the contestants back to the area to stand behind their offerings. Marco lagged behind the group. Again, he took the stance leaning against the counter until Brenden hollered, "Action."

"You had an issue this morning." Harrison flashed a sympathetic look at Lynne before turning his attention to her plate.

"I did." Her face flushed. "Thank goodness others helped me, or all I'd have plated was the vegetable. They're a good group of people."

"I find steak and salmon tartare an interesting choice." Shannon peered down at the salmon, her expression stoic.

I knew when she sampled it, her face would be green with sickness versus red from embarrassment, like Lynne's. Shannon didn't like raw fish.

Harrison loaded a grilled crostini with the salmon and steak. He waited for Shannon to do hers. She spread a thin layer of each on the ends of the bread, leaving most of the crostini to cover the taste.

"Delicious." Harrison nodded after his sample. "I'd make sure everyone in the party liked tartare meat before serving, though."

Shannon covered her choke, both on the steak and the salmon, with a cough. "Again, interesting choice." She took a large bite of the stuffed baked potato and gave Lynne a thumbs-up. Harrison liked it too.

I knew Shannon needed to cover up the taste of the salmon. I saw her peruse the rest of the offerings and breathe a sigh of relief. No one else prepared seafood. Mike and Jeremiah went with barbeque ribs with the help of an instant pot, which was so much safer than the earlier prototypes, yet an old-fashioned pressure cooker saved my life, so who was I to play favorites? Afton, Donna, Mary and Alex played it safe with different cuts of steak. Donna overcooked hers, while Shannon insisted Mary also prepared steak tartare hers was so undercooked. Shannon didn't like the blood running into the mash potatoes. I agreed.

Marco kept to his roots serving veal parmigiana with a side of spaghetti and earned praise from Shannon and Harrison. I snuck a bite. The veal melted in your mouth, and the mild sauce complemented the meat. It was wonderful. Marco beamed.

A phone ringing stopped our judging session. All heads turned toward Quintin when he bellowed, "Now what?" into his cell phone. His deep frown softened while he shook his head in understanding during his one-sided conversation. He headed toward the workshop door while pocketing his cell phone.

I knew the door opened and closed by the change of light inside the workshop. Quintin, accompanied by Drake, entered the set area. "Cut the action." Quintin barked the order even though the cameras weren't rolling, no action had happened since he took his call. "Mr. Nolan has an announcement to make."

By the somber expressions on their faces, this wasn't going to be good.

Drake cleared his throat. "Sheriff Perry has notified me that Skylar Daily is no longer suspected of murdering Lisa Mackliner."

A round of cheers and some applause sounded through the set. Most of the cheers were from the cast and crew, while the clapping came from everyone in the kitchen except Marco. He glowered.

"Will he be returning to the set?" Mike asked, and sounded happy about it for being a person who thought Skylar was guilty.

"That is up to Mr. Shepherd." Drake deferred the question with a jerk of his head toward Quintin.

"I don't see why not." The wide smile stretching across Quintin's face made him look like a new man.

More cheers and applause and glowering.

"Courtney." Shannon touched my arm. "You don't seem pleased."

I pulled my eyes from Marco and smiled at Shannon, whose face beamed with happiness for Skylar. "I am, it's just . . ." I turned toward Drake. "Did you find new evidence?"

Pushing his palms down in the air to quiet the group, Drake said, "I'm not at liberty to say." He hesitated. "I'll tell everyone that Sheriff Perry and his department confirmed Mr. Daily had no prescription for a sleep aid, the blood on his clothes wasn't fresh and the knife that delivered the fatal wound was an eight-inch butcher's knife, not the serrated knife which bore his fingerprints."

An eight-inch butcher's knife? I caught my gasp in the back of my throat. Could it be the one missing from Chef Hartsall's magnetic holder? The one he was looking for? Was it used to kill Lisa? I grimaced recalling the scene. So much blood! Was it because someone removed the butcher knife and inserted the serrated one? Or was the blood loss normal for a stabbing victim? My head swam with questions, but two things were clear. If the knife was switched, this murder was premediated and I needed to talk to Chef Hartsall or the kitchen manager now more than ever.

"This is wonderful news." Brenden smiled, draining all the tension from his features.

I forced myself to smile with the crowd. It's not that I wasn't happy Skylar had been removed as a person of interest in the murder. I was. I'd never thought he had it in him, but what people weren't considering is, who did murder Lisa Mackliner? Was the murderer among us? Or long gone? Should I ask Drake? I decided not to be the buzzkill in our small celebration. Instinctively, my eyes rested on Marco. Had anyone else noticed how unhappy he seemed with Drake's revelation? His mouth had drawn into a tight-lipped frown. He flexed his hands into fists, then released them while pacing back and forth behind his counter. I needed to keep my eye on him. I also needed to tell Sheriff Perry my suspicions about him.

"Instead of announcing the winner of this round now, we are going to break for a long lunch. Kinzy, please call the resort and tell them to deliver the contestants food and the cast and crew catering early, if they can. We'll reconvene at one."

Wow! A two-hour lunch and it was Quintin's suggestion.

"Super news, super news." Harrison looked at us. "Our gang is back together." He smiled as he walked toward the stairs.

"I have some phone calls to make." Quintin gave a slight bow in Shannon and my direction. "If you'll excuse me."

"Of course." My tone showed my shock in the turnabout of his demeanor. But his admission about the call turned my thoughts to a call of my own. I needed to phone, not text, Eric to fill him in on what was happening here.

"What a switch!" Shannon exclaimed. "Do you think his worry came out as anger?"

I watched Quintin disappear around a corner. I knew he was heading to the set in back to make his calls. "I don't know." I shook my head. "Something seems off with him."

"Want to get some lunch?"

"You go ahead. I'm going to call Eric; then I'll grab a plate and meet you upstairs." I pulled my phone from my jacket pocket, found Eric's number and tapped it.

"Sure. Maybe we have time for a walk afterward."

I nodded as I held the phone to my ear and listened to the ringtone.

"Courtney, is everything all right?" Concern filled his voice.

"Yes, I'm fine." I paused, realizing the past few phone calls I'd had with Eric revolved around bad news. "It's actually good news this time."

Tinkles of laughter, feminine laughter, floated over the connection. Pamela. My insides twisted when Eric chuckled too. What was going on there? Before I could stop it, jealousy huffed from me.

Eric caught the audible huff and said, "I thought you had good news."

"I do." The words spat from my lips; then I caught sight of Drake talking to Brenden and all my nerve endings danced with attraction. Shame replaced the jealousy. I couldn't have it both ways. I couldn't expect Eric to wait for me while I dated other men. Of course, who knew if a date with Drake would ever materialize? We hadn't had a personal conversation since we'd disagreed on a dinner location. Softening my tone, I said, "Skylar is no longer a suspect or person of interest in the murder of Lisa Mackliner."

"Fantastic." Eric relayed the info to Pamela before he continued. "Now you can focus on cohosting duties and forget the murder."

Sure, I *could* do that, but the knife and cake, along with a murderer being on the loose, gnawed at my brain. I decided to stop the conversation before Eric made me promise. "Well, I'm going to get lunch now. I'll talk with you later."

We said goodbye and I ended the call. I stood wondering if I could get Eric alone tonight. We'd have a serious talk about our personal and professional relationship. Drake definitely had a lustful effect on me that left me wanting to get to know him. I wasn't sure I elicited the same feelings in him. Lustful, yes, but a serious relationship, I wasn't sure. Although it would be fun to find out if we were compatible, I didn't want to do it at Eric's expense. After all, it had been his arms that caught me as I collapsed when an attempt was made on my life. He'd always been there for me and stuck with me through thick and thin. After Shannon had mentioned he was interested in me, I'd thought I'd seen it in his eyes several times. Most recently on the path to the workshop when Pamela interrupted us. Before I could talk myself out of it, I shot a quick text off to him to see if we could have a private conversation over dinner tonight.

Turning, I saw the line had dwindled at the catering table. Skylar stood behind the table chatting with Justin while he worked. I pocketed my phone and joined them. I filled my plate with chicken salad dressed with Greek yogurt instead of mayo. I passed on the bread and added a large scoop of sautéed veggies.

"Hi, guys." I stood beside Skylar. "I am happy for you and never thought for one minute . . ."

"Thanks, Courtney. I know you stood behind me all the way. So did Justin." Skylar smiled at his friend. Justin's cheeks colored. "He told me early on he didn't believe I killed Lisa and just now, he congratulated me."

I smiled. It made me happy to know Justin took my advice and talked to Skylar himself. "Justin is a good guy. What would we do without him?"

"Starve!" Skylar chuckled.

Justin laughed too while looking over his shoulder. Which reminded me that they probably hadn't been given clearance to talk to the rest of us.

"Are you going to head upstairs to eat your lunch?" Skylar asked while he turned away from the table.

"I am. I need to grab a drink and a dessert. Meet you there?" I wanted to ask Justin a question or two since he disappeared on me this morning.

Once Skylar was out of range to hear me, I approached Justin. "Do you know who delivers the cakes to the assisted living facility?"

"Sure do. Roger. It's the last thing he did before he left for his honeymoon on Monday. Why?" Justin made no eye contact with me. He focused on straightening spoons in the entrées.

I fought to keep my face expressionless in case Justin glanced up. I knew the cake had never been delivered. I didn't want to let on I knew Justin gave me the wrong information. Whomever he asked, I was certain it wasn't

Chef Hartsall, was misinformed. I found Chef Hartsall rude and intimidating, so I could only imagine how unapproachable he was to the kitchen underlings like Justin.

"I just wondered. I think it's a very nice gesture on Coal Castle Resort's part. They're a good corporate neighbor."

Justin looked at me. He didn't fight his eyebrow pull. He obviously didn't know about good corporate neighbors. "Oh." He fussed with the napkins.

I knew I had to wrap this up because I didn't want him to get into trouble. "What kind of working hours does Chef Hartsall keep?

Justin looked directly into my eyes and smiled. "He gets here really early and is the last person out of the kitchen at, like, seven o'clock in the evening. Why?"

"I need to talk to him about a recipe." I returned his wide smile. He didn't need to know the real reason. "I'll head over there when we're finished filming today."

"I see." Justin cast a glance over his shoulder at his coworkers. "I'd better go. It's been a good news day. Right?"

"Right!" I watched Justin lift empty trays and carry them over to their catering cart and work with the kitchen staff.

I hoped the day remained that way. I started up the stairs to the makeup room to celebrate Skylar's return to the set and name removal from the suspect list. Halfway up, I paused. A very gruesome thought popped into my mind. I really needed to talk to Chef Hartsall about his missing butcher knife. Was it still missing? Or had the murderer cleaned and returned it? After all, a good commercial kitchen thoroughly sterilized all the cooking utensils, which would remove any fingerprints or blood residue, making it hard to tie to the murder. The thought of a knife used to take a life then returned to its normal purpose, coupled with the knowledge Sheriff Perry couldn't solve the case without a murder weapon, turned my stomach and made me wish I hadn't eaten lunch.

Chapter Twenty

I pushed my thoughts about the knife and Chef Hartsall to the back of my mind once I joined my coworkers to celebrate Skylar being cleared of any murder suspicion. We toasted to his freedom with sparkling water in disposable cups.

"Let's all have dinner together tonight so we can make an official toast with champagne in crystal flutes." Harrison looked at each of us for confirmation. My heart twisted. I'd already texted Eric and made a dinner date. I'd been adamant about having dinner alone, so I didn't want to cancel. Besides, I did need to speak with him. I needed to either confirm or put to rest Shannon's opinion about his feelings for me. Until I knew how he felt, I couldn't deal with my own budding feelings for him or my interest in Drake.

I winced. "Sorry, I have dinner plans with Eric. Could

we meet for drinks to make the toast official instead of dinner?"

Shannon flashed Skylar an apologetic look. "Sorry to say, Skylar, but that works better for me too. My husband set up a Skype session. We need to discuss my cookware and the release date. I guess I need to do some promos for marketing."

"Drinks it is!" Skylar raised a fist in the air. "Harrison, I'm willing to have dinner afterward."

"It's a plan." Harrison lifted his glass. "To Skylar and *The American Baking Battle* for bringing new colleagues and friends into my life."

"Here, here." Skylar, Shannon and I spoke in unison.

"Shall we meet in The Queen's Sacrifice thirty minutes after filming? That should be plenty of time to change and freshen up," Harrison said.

"Where in the resort is The Queen's Sacrifice?" I knew by the name it was somewhere on the premises.

"In the basement close to the bowling alley." Skylar looked at me. "You haven't checked the lounge out yet?"

I shook my head. "But I will tonight!" I didn't get a chance to investigate the amenities either time I stayed at Coal Castle Resort. I'd been too busy investigating murders.

We spent our remaining lunch break chattering about the contestants, the baking competition and our respective shows. Shannon and I kept mum about the show we planned to pitch to the network because Harrison, once again, reminded me how my professional life might change with my announcement, which dampened my spirits a little bit and reminded me of another topic Eric and I needed to discuss. He'd never texted or called with any news from the network concerning the leak of information regarding my to-be-aired apology. I made a mental note to discuss that first and romantic feelings second over dinner tonight.

The long lunch went fast and too soon Kinzy knocked on the door and entered. Quintin had sent word via Kinzy to get Skylar into wardrobe so he could start his cohosting duties immediately, to which he happily complied. She told the rest of us to return to set.

I'd tried hard not to let Harrison's warning dampen the festive mood. I must have failed. On our way back downstairs, Shannon reached for my hand and gave it a squeeze. "You know," she whispered, "your admission might bring new fans and opportunities your way. Industry professionals will see your true training and talents. You will gain the respect you deserve as a trained chef versus a home cook from your colleagues."

"Thanks." I returned the squeeze. Other than Eric, Shannon was my most supportive friend. She always saw the bright side of the situation, yet I saw an emotion cross her features. I pinpointed it to longing. Shannon wasn't a trained chef. Since Shannon was always upbeat, I never considered she had faced prejudices in the industry. Judging by her reaction, she had. "And you need to know this trained chef has respect for home cooks. So do many others."

A soft smile settled on her face. "Thank you."

We didn't wait long for Skylar. I suspected he was anxious to get back to work. As Brenden directed, our foursome stood centered in front of the contestants. Even though Skylar and I knew who Harrison and Shannon awarded as the winner of this round, we read our lines from the monitor, our tone inflected with mystery and suspense.

Skylar had the honor of telling Marco his entrée stood out among the others not only in taste but also originality. Harrison ad-libbed and pointed out to the contestants who'd prepared steak that it wasn't always synonymous with a male's taste. Many women enjoyed steak, while many men preferred seafood, ribs or veal.

A smug smile settled on Marco's face. He looked around to the other contestants who expressed their congratulations. The cameras cut. Harrison and Shannon stepped into the wings. Crew members removed the entrées from the ends of the counter while the contestants took their places more to the center of the kitchenette, ready to begin the second challenge.

Satisfied with the shot, Brenden gave the countdown and yelled, "Action."

"Bakers, this may come as a shock to your system." Skylar smiled at the group. "For this challenge you will actually bake!"

The contestants chuckled.

I took over. "You have three hours to bake and decorate a groom's cake. Keep in mind you will be judged on creativity of design as well as taste."

"The one caveat to this challenge is the cake must have some type of filling." Skylar gave the instruction in a tone to rival any teacher.

Afton and Donna grimaced. I guessed that announcement changed their minds about what kind of cake to bake. I kept my eyes on them waiting for their next reaction.

"In addition to the cake being filled, you also have a mandatory ingredient to use." My tone expressed excitement. Most of their expressions did not. As I predicted, worry pulled at Afton's and Donna's features.

"Lift the covers from your mixers to reveal the ingredient to incorporate in your cake."

The contestants followed Skylar's instructions. They found squishie toys in the shapes of butter, a strawberry, a coconut, a donut, ice cream, a cookie, a chili pepper and a lemon. Their expressions were mixed as they stared at their secret ingredient. Jeremiah received the lemon and smiled with delight. I knew he had a very popular lemon cupcake at his shop.

Skylar and I didn't give them much time to ponder or grumble. Together we said, "The baking begins now."

Most of the contestants scrambled. Mike stood gazing down at his squishie, the cookie. I wondered if he even knew kids were nuts for these toys, maybe if he had grandchildren. In typical fashion, he shrugged and walked over to the pantry.

"Cut. Great. It's wonderful to hear your duet." Brenden came over to us. "You will need to interview the contestants. Let's give them some lead time. We'll shoot the opening for today's episode." Brenden waved a cameraman over. "We are behind on those." He smiled and led the way to the back-corner set.

"Don't we need costumes?" Skylar asked.

"Not today," Brenden said as we entered the area.

A long table held a prop for every kind of interest a man might have. We ran through our lines. Due to the puns the writers put in the script, our parts weren't interchangeable. When Brenden thought we had it down with the exact expressions to emphasize those puns, we started.

"Weddings are usually all about the bride." Skylar smiled into the camera. "But not today!"

I picked up where he left off. "Today, we are focusing on the groom."

"The bachelor party meal." Skylar waggled his eyebrows suggestively. "And the groom's cake, which should reflect something in the groom's personality. Like maybe this football." He lifted it and gave a little toss before assuming the Heisman Trophy stance.

"Or this farming tractor." I held up the red toy and winked into the camera.

Skylar laughed and resumed his normal posture. "Of course *you'd* suggest that." He sobered. "Seriously, Courtney, what item here would represent my personality?"

I reached for a fishing pole, which reflected his personality, in a fake-out move. "No." I shook my head, bent down and pulled something from under the table. A bright yellow child-size grocery cart filled with colorful cardboard boxes. I smiled brightly.

Skylar panned an annoyed looked into the camera. "I'm not sure about your grocery store ruse."

The camera focused on me. "Don't you mean gambit?"

"Cut. Perfect timing. This will be great." Brenden clapped his hands together. "Now get back on set and interview those contestants."

Skylar and I picked up his enthusiasm and hurried off to the set.

"That opening was so much better than smearing cake on our faces." Skylar adjusted his jacket sleeves. He wore a white tux with a royal-blue cummerbund and bow tie. Both colors popped his complexion.

I noticed the venom he'd had for weddings no longer dripped in his tone when he spoke. Had it been because of Lisa and her stalking, or had he heeded my warning it wasn't helping his case? Being suspected for a murder you didn't commit does make you rethink your actions. I could vouch for that.

"I agree. I'm anxious to see what the contestants come up with for the groom's cake. Especially filled. If the filling isn't stiff enough, the cake won't hold its shape," I said.

Skylar and I reached the set before Brenden. I took the opportunity to text Eric my plan to talk to Chef Hartsall and meet Shannon, Harrison and Skylar for a drink before dinner. Then I asked if he wanted to have room service deliver something to either of our suites or the *Cooking with the Farmer's Daughter* studio suites.

When Brenden still hadn't showed, I dialed up Sheriff Perry again. When his voice mail answered, I left the message concerning my suspicions about Marco, his girlfriend, the autograph and the overheard phone call. The message system cut me off, so I called back to tell him my plan to speak with Chef Hartsall to see if his knives were still missing since one of those missing knives was the same type that fatally wounded Lisa Mackliner. I managed to get in the name of the honeymooning kitchen worker who had access to the cake, the knife and everything wedding in before the annoying beep sounded and cut me off. Which it did before I could say, "Please return this call." I ended the call on my end and decided I'd given him enough information to peak his curiosity enough he'd return my call where I'd go into more detail.

I wondered if Sheriff Perry was aware of Roger. I wished I'd known about him sooner. There was a probability of him murdering his intended and leaving the country on what everyone thought was his honeymoon. It also explained the wedding gown and the cake. I chided myself for not asking Justin if he knew the honeymoon location. If it was out of the country, it was the perfect getaway. In addition to checking with Chef Hartsall about his knives, I'd inquire about Roger.

When Brenden called my name, I pocketed my phone and hurried over to the set.

"We're ready for your interviews." Brenden looked at the bakers. "I hope they are."

"Should Skylar take the lead? I mean, he hasn't had much camera time and we can't reshoot the last few days." I smiled at Skylar.

"Great idea, Courtney." Brenden motioned to us and our cameraman. "Do your thing."

We stepped over to Marco first. He glanced up and smiled at Skylar before making eye contact with me in a stony stare. His greeting confirmed my suspicion that he'd seen me in the passageway and knew I overheard his phone call. Or was I misreading the situation? Skylar didn't seem to notice Marco's reaction.

"What was your secret ingredient?" Skylar asked the question even though we could see his squishie laying on the counter.

A cocky smile appeared on Marco's face. "Coconut. Which is perfect for me." He looked directly into the camera. "Can anyone say Italian wedding cake?" He laughed. "It's a specialty at our bakery. I can make it in my sleep."

"Wow! Sounds like you have an advantage." Skylar smiled.

Marco shrugged while feigning humility.

"You do know grooms' cakes have to reflect the interest of the groom, right?" I knew most Italian wedding cakes were beautiful layered cakes.

"Of course." Marco rolled his eyes.

"What?" Alex bellowed across the aisle.

We all looked at him. He stood rigid with bugged eyes. Judging by his outburst, he had no idea a groom's cake was shaped like, or reflected in some way, the interest of the groom. "We'll come to your area next," I said, holding my palms up in a hold-on fashion.

Skylar wrinkled his brow. Since he wasn't a cook or baker, I don't think he'd figured out Alex was in crisis. In good cohosting form, he ended the interview with Marco by wishing him luck.

By the time we reached Alex, he'd looked around the kitchenettes and stood with his head hung.

I looked at the cameraman. "Don't film this." He nodded; then I addressed Alex. "You had no idea that a groom's cake is decorated or shaped to reflect their personality, did you?"

He shook his head. "I got butter and planned a three-layered maple cake with buttercream frosting." He sighed. "Now what do I do?"

"Well, you can still make that cake, just form the layers into something that would interest a groom." I hoped my words were encouraging. "Or decorate the cake to reflect that interest."

Alex stared blankly at me.

Skylar, now up to speed on what the problem was, added, "What would a cake for you look like?"

Alex lifted his brows, then smiled. "I can do this! Can you come back to do my interview?" Alex asked on a run to the baker's rack that held pans in all shapes and sizes.

We nodded and moved on to Mary. She'd received the strawberry and planned to use a play on strawberry shortcake using angel food cake. Her cake design would be a tribute to Miller and one of his interests, stamp collecting.

I was intrigued since most groom's cake that I'd seen

revolved around sports. We moved through the remaining contestants, learning Afton was making a Boston cream cake in honor of getting the donut squishie but had not yet decided on if she would make something that interested her father or her brothers. The rest of the contestants kept their cake idea hushed. Mike did say that cookies were perfect for a groom's cake that reflected his interest.

I found this challenge exciting, exhilarating and couldn't wait to see the end results, but for reasons involving another cake, I wished the challenge was over.

"Wow!" I read my instruction from the monitor and scanned the contestants standing beside their creations at the end of their counters. Alex made a layer cake cut into the shape of what else, a maple leaf. He air-sprayed the icing with fall colors. Afton's Boston cream became a sprint car track. "When we give bakers the chance to actually bake, they provide us with some spectacular cakes and sadly a couple of missed hits." I stopped, sobered my expression and looked at the contestants.

Since Skylar missed out on a few days of filming, he got to be the heavy today. He was sending a baker home, so I continued. "Contestants, you made it difficult for the judges with the groom's cake round but factoring in the bachelor party menu brought three contestants very close. Before the baker of the day is announced, you need to know Harrison and Shannon struggled with the winner. Mike, your entrée, barbeque ribs, lacked originality, but tasted great. However, the use of your secret ingredient put you over the top on the groom's cake. Crumbled cookies, not only as a crunchy layer giving your cream filling texture but as the jagged rocks on a rock-climbing wall pushed the limits of imagination. The judges wanted you to know you were in the top three and fell—pun intended—just short of winning the baker of the day."

I paused as the contestants chuckled at my pun and Mike nodded, his lips stretched into a wide smile. "That leaves two. Jeremiah, we all knew the Cupcake King of Chicago would deliver a visual and tasty groom's cake. Your signature lemon cupcakes, filled with lemon custard, arranged and sculpted to look like a muscle car with continuous smooth yellow icing gave the car a flawless paint job. Not to mention the modeling chocolate race strip and sugar glass for headlights, taillights and windows sped you to the head of the pack. Your bachelor menu, barbeque ribs, tasted okay, but your twice-stuffed baked potato and bacon-wrapped asparagus won the hearts of the judges."

Anxious, Jeremiah kept shifting his weight from foot to foot while I spoke. It kept his torso in perpetual motion and reminded me of women rocking their babies. I suspected he wanted his own cooking show or maybe to expand his business, and winning this competition would give him a step up.

Taking a deep breath, I continued. "Marco." A wide smile appeared on his face. "Your bachelor party menu reflected your heritage and was a unique offering prepared perfectly. The only thing the judges had to say about it was yum. Who knew an Italian wedding cake with the traditional frosting could be tinted with food coloring to look like a sandy beach covered with seashells? The marzipan beach chairs, towels and flip-flops accentuated your theme. And your use of coconut milk in the frosting between the layers." I kissed my gathered fingers and threw them into the air. "Magnifico. The judging was so close on these competitions it came down to technique." I kept my eyes locked on Marco, then said, "The baker of the day is Jeremiah."

To my surprise, and Marco's credit, the smile remained on his face and he sought out Jeremiah, wrapping him in a big hug. Mike, Marco and Jeremiah accepted the congratulations of the other contestants.

Skylar cleared his throat and the bakers gave him their attention. "Mary, your idea to create a postage stamp was unique. Your decorating skills to re-create Miller's favorite pastime and stamp were stellar. Unfortunately, his favorite type of cake, angel food, proved too light and airy for a heavy filling, and layers of frosting needed to create the design. Even baked in a loaf pan, cut and stacked, it lost its form, sinking in the middle. Mary, you are the baker leaving the kitchen today."

Mary swiped her eyes with the backs of her hand, accepted her consolations and abruptly exited the kitchen.

Brenden hollered, "Cut." Kinzy escorted the contestants off the set while the talent headed upstairs to slip into our street clothes.

Filming ended a little earlier than I thought it would, so I bid everyone farewell with a promise to see them later and stepped down to the first floor. Before going outside, I dialed up Sheriff Perry again. It went directly to voice mail, which left me perturbed. Would he have turned off his phone? Was he on the phone? Why hadn't he returned my call from earlier? When the buzzer sounded, I left the same basic message as before, then told him I was on my way to the kitchen to talk to Chef Hartsall and would call him with the information I'd found out. I wanted to add, but didn't, that I wished he'd call me with any information he found out or to at least acknowledge my calls. I hung up hoping he hadn't shrugged off the information or my opinions.

Eric had returned my text. He told me room service would deliver our dinner to my set at six thirty. I answered his text with a thumbs-up emoji. That gave me plenty of time to speak with Chef Hartsall, call Sheriff Perry and probably leave another message before sharing drinks with my coworkers.

I hurried on the main path back to Coal Castle Resort, taking the time to notice the new pops of color creating variegated swatches of reds, golds and orange leaves. The Pocono Mountains range made the perfect backdrop for the fall foliage. As I neared the castle, I noted the vibrant zinnias and mums bloomed in the same colors as the leaves on the horizon. The lush lawn remained green, I suspected, through the power of automatic sprinklers.

Finding the side door I'd entered before, I went into the castle. Instead of being met with a symphony of kitchen noises made by busy cooks, silence ensued. I walked through the empty kitchen where the sous chefs chopped last time and rounded the corner to the smaller room where I'd found Chef Hartsall. Like the other room, the stainless steel counters gleamed in the late-day sun filtering through the high windows.

"Chef Hartsall?" I called while I entered the room farther, being careful not to touch any of the cleaned surfaces. I was well aware of food contamination and illness. Since I was eating food prepared here, I preferred not to get sick. Standing in the middle of the room, I looked around. It appeared that all work had been done for the day. It was just a little past five. I was certain Justin said the chef worked until seven, which made perfect sense because some pastry dough needed to be prepared the day before. Was Justin wrong about the chef's end-of-shift time like he'd been about the second cake? I sighed. Sadly, he probably wanted to help but didn't actually talk to Chef Hartsall in either case. I'd interned in kitchens where the chefs barked out orders, then made themselves unapproachable to their underlings.

For good measure, I called his name again while my eyes searched the magnetic holder beside his work counter. Seven knives adhered to the holder in a perfect line. The eighth knife in the set was missing and was the exact type of knife that made the fatal wound in Lisa Mackliner.

The click of a door opening, the side door I'd exited on my first visit to the kitchen, startled me. My body jerked in an involuntary reaction that probably had more to do with where my thoughts had wandered than the actual noise.

I turned to see Justin enter the room. Putting a hand to my still-racing heart, I sighed. "Hi, Justin. The door startled me."

"Oh, sorry." Justin gave me a lopsided grin.

"I guess Chef Hartsall left early today?" My heart rate returned to normal.

Justin answered with a shrug of his shoulders.

"Well." My eyes surveyed the magnetic holder and the knives one more time. I had my answer. I turned and took a step, intending to exit through the door where Justin entered since I knew which way to head to get to the main lobby now. I noted Justin's gaze had focused on something over my shoulder, then returned to meet mine.

The only thing on the wall over my shoulder was the knife rack. He had obviously noticed the missing knife too, or maybe Chef Hartsall alerted the kitchen help it was missing and warned them to be on the lookout for it. Justin proved to be an unreliable source, but he'd noticed the knives and might be able to answer one more question; then I'd have two things to report to Sheriff Perry.

I glanced over my shoulder, then back at Justin. "Do you know how long Chef Hartsall's knife has been missing?"

Chapter Twenty-one

Justin fidgeted with the hem of his catering smock. "You'll have to ask Chef Hartsall tomorrow." He walked over to the door that led to the sous chef workspace. He pulled it closed and entered numbers in a keypad. "I'm on lockup duty tonight."

"Okay. I'll get out of your way." I went to take another step when a thought occurred to me. "Wait a minute. If you were scheduled to close up shop, you knew Chef Hartsall wouldn't be here." My question was rhetorical, an exercise in futility for me.

Justin planted himself back in the spot where he'd once stood between me and the side exit. His eyes darted to the knife holder and back at me. His nervous gesture flashed pictures of the emotional responses he'd shown over the past few days through my mind. Actions I'd reasoned away instead of trusting my first instinct.

"You do know when the knife went missing, don't you?" I gave my surroundings a quick once-over. Justin had locked the exit closest to me and blocked the only way out of the kitchen. I was trapped like herbs in a bouquet garni. My racing heart kick-started my flight-or-fight impulse. I needed to get out of here, preferably alive.

"Why are you so nosy? Always asking questions. Wanting to speak with people in charge." His eyes narrowed while his mouth pulled into a sinister smile. His eyes flicked to the knives. I followed his gaze. Any type of knife used correctly could make a fatal wound, but the cleaver hanging on the wall could do the most, and fastest, damage since chefs keep their knives at peak sharpness. Judging by his menacing expression, he was trying to figure out which knife to use on me. Luckily, he stood farther away from the magnetic holder than I did.

The rapid beat of my heart caused my pulse to create a bass drum rhythm in my ears. I found the missing ingredient in my sleuthing, Justin. Justin killed Lisa Mackliner and tried to frame Skylar. The scene at the wedding reception mixer the first day of filming flashed into my mind. Justin handed Skylar the serrated knife. The same knife found in Lisa Mackliner's body. But not the blade that made the fatal wound. That came from Chef Hartsall's favorite, and missing, knife.

Nosy or not, I had a few more questions for Justin. In addition to sating my curiosity, they'd help me buy time to figure out how to escape. Inhaling, I forced my tone to sound calm and collected. Justin might not realize I figured out he was the murderer. "Where is the eight-inch butcher's knife?" I knew it was hard to charge anyone without the murder weapon.

Justin laughed. "I don't know. Chef Hartsall must have misplaced it. Maybe it went out in the trash."

I fought to keep a grimace from my face. I hoped that wasn't the case. Maybe he was trying to throw me off like when he lied about the honeymooning employee who should have delivered the cake. I wasn't quite ready to let him know I'd figured out his secret. "Who did you tell me delivered the extra cake to the assistant living facility? I want to make sure I get the correct name when I speak with Chef Hartsall tomorrow." I took a few steps closer to him as if I was leaving the room.

He pulled his body into an intimidating stance, legs spread, fists on his hips with his elbows jutted out. He had no intention of letting me leave this room. The drum solo in my ears grew louder. I had to figure out how to get away. I had my cell phone with me, but there was no way I could sneak a text for help.

"Still asking questions?" He huffed. "His name is Rodney." He spat out the words.

Again, his gaze flicked to the knife rack. If he made a move toward it, I could run for the door. His eyes darted back to me. I was certain his thoughts mirrored mine. I retreated back to the spot where I'd stood when he'd entered the room. "I thought you told me his name was Roger."

Justin's eyes widened and blazed with anger. He took a side step toward the wall. So did I. Twisting a little to my right, I double-checked what was behind me. My memory recalled baker's racks filled with small and large kitchen utensils and appliances. I was right; however, the quick glance I'd allowed myself didn't reveal anything I could use to deter Justin while I ran to safety.

A disgusted snort echoed through the high ceilings of the room. “No, I didn’t.” Justin dug into his pants pocket and pulled out latex gloves. Pushing one hand and then the other into the gloves, he snapped the open ends against his wrist.

Although the sound unnerved me, it didn’t build my fear as I thought he intended to do. It had the opposite effect. My fear shattered. I’d had enough. A quick glance over my left shoulder gave me some comfort. Perhaps if I threw a larger appliance at him, it’d knock him off balance and I could escape. In the seconds it took me to look at the baker’s rack, Justin had stepped closer to the knife holder. Would calling his bluff help?

Squaring my shoulders, I tried a different tactic. “I think the name of the kitchen employee who delivered the cake is Justin Henry.”

Dawning settled into his features. He’d figured out I knew he killed Lisa Mackliner.

“You kept the cake because you and Lisa were going to be married, right?” I held his gaze and took a side step closer to the appliance-laden metal baker’s rack.

“No!” He shouted the word. Rage morphed onto his face. He lunged toward the magnetic knife rack, grabbed the cleaver and rolled over the stainless steel work counter.

The soles of my shoes tapped on the tile floor in a quick succession of small steps trying to put space between us. I knew after seeing his agility, I’d never make it to the door in time if I ran and I didn’t want to turn my back to him. I’d managed to get to the other side of the appliance rack. I grabbed ahold of the metal shelving to steady my shaking legs. Why didn’t I listen to Sheriff Perry and Eric? If only Sheriff Perry had answered my call.

Justin swished the knife, cutting through the air, perhaps showing me moves he intended to use on me.

I released a shaky breath.

He laughed. "Being nosy gets you into trouble." The blade whooshed through the air.

I glanced up. Three heavy kitchen mixers sat in a row on the top shelf. I couldn't reach them, but I knew what I could do. I just needed to figure out when. Justin wasn't quite close enough yet.

"I guess." I shrugged like it was no big deal.

"Don't you want to know why I killed her?" He took a step closer.

I did want to know, but not as much as he wanted to tell me. His expression turned from anger to that of a man needing to confess his sins. "Because she wouldn't marry you?" I used a goading tone, hoping it would spur him forward both in confession and movement. Marriage had to be a part of the murder or there was no reason for him to steal a cake or her to be dressed in a wedding gown.

"No." He momentarily closed his eyes and gave his head a shake. "I mean, yes. I kept the cake because we planned to be married." His features softened. "For months we planned our wedding and our future together."

"Really?" I kept my tone sympathetic. Lisa had been in prison. Had Justin known her before her incarceration?

"Yeah." He sighed. "I met her online. I like hardcore chicks, so I troll some social media sites that help you get in touch with inmates. She said she was interested in me because of my kitchen staff background at Coal Castle Resort. She liked men who cooked." His mouth set in a grim line, and hatred veiled his eyes. He snorted. "I was stupid and believed the psycho."

"So, she didn't like people in the food industry?" I

stepped back a little bit, keeping my hand on the baker's rack. I hoped he'd notice and step toward me.

He didn't. He stared at me, but I was unsure I was who he saw. Next time I'd make the move less subtle.

"Oh, she liked guys or a guy in the food industry." The corner of his lip curled into a snarl and focus came back to his eyes. "Just not me. I wasted all of my time and money flying back and forth between coasts to visit her in prison. When her release date grew closer, I went out and proposed. She accepted and I bought her a plane ticket to come out here. She didn't care if it did break her parole."

"She used you to get access to Skylar, didn't she?" My tone still held sympathy. I was sure my plan to escape would work and I wanted to hear his full confession even though I had a good idea how the rest of the story played out.

"Yes." The word hissed from his lips. He cut air with the cleaver. "Not the first couple of weeks. It was all about us. We shopped for rings and a wedding gown. She applied for jobs, and we drove around neighborhoods dreaming of the type of house we'd own someday. Then, as the day of filming for the second season of your show approached, all she talked about was Skylar. She'd record his weekly show and watch it over and over. When I said something, she convinced me she watched the show because she was proud her soon-to-be-husband knew a celebrity."

"She didn't care that you knew the rest of us?" I inflected hurt into my tone this time, even though I was not hurt and knew the answer. I knew it'd keep him talking.

"Sorry, no." To his credit, he looked very apologetic when he answered me.

"When did you find out she was really here to see Skylar?" I took a bigger step backward and let go of the baker's rack.

Justin noticed and took two steps forward. I glanced at the baker's rack and judging by the distance between us, he was in the right position.

"Stop! I don't want to kill you. You've always been nice to me, but you asked too many questions. I don't want to go to prison so I can't let you live." Justin swung the cleaver back.

I swallowed hard and hoped he didn't make his move yet. I needed to get more information out of him like how he actually killed Lisa. Holding my hands up in a surrender fashion, I said, "I won't move again." I didn't need to. I repeated my question.

Justin continued to hold the cleaver high over his shoulder. "The day before filming began, Lisa insisted we get a room at the resort, so I used my employee discount and reserved a room. We got here and she begged me to swipe some kitchen clothing so she could sneak onto the set. I refused because I like my job and didn't want to lose it. I told her I needed to have a job to buy the little bungalow we'd found. She tore into me, then laughed and asked me why I thought she'd marry me when a god like Skylar was available." Justin paused and swiped at his eyes with the fingers on his free hand.

He had really cared for Lisa. "Is that when you killed her?"

"No, I was heartbroken, but I went to work. The longer I thought about the situation, the hurt turned to anger. Then she showed up in the kitchen being all sweet and lovey like nothing had ever happened. When she asked for a catering smock, I snapped. I told her to go back to our room and I'd bring one. I continued with my kitchen duties, which included delivering the wedding cake. I found a pass key the waitstaff use for room service and slipped it into my pocket along with a can of cooking spray. When Chef Hartsall left his workstation, I grabbed the knife and the cake cart. I knew the talent had early calls for hair and makeup, so it'd be easy to get the cake into Skylar's room. I used the service elevator to get to his suite."

"Aren't there security cameras in the elevators and hallways?" I asked the question out loud but really hadn't meant to.

"That is what the cooking spray was for. I knew which angles to take to avoid the security cameras. I used that advantage to spray the lens to distort the picture. Then I took the cake to Skylar's room and put it on the glass-topped coffee table. After that, I used the backstairs and went to Lisa and my room." Justin started to chuckle. "She thought she was so smart. I convinced her that I'd spoken with Skylar and he wanted to see her in his room with her wedding dress on. She took the bait and changed. Man, she looked pretty in that dress."

Justin had a faraway look, so I used it to my advantage and stepped backward to put more space between me and the baker's rack. I knew I'd need to take a run at the rack in order to push it with enough force.

Not noticing, Justin continued. "I made one last plea for her to marry me. She laughed and told me I was a swell guy, but not her type. I begged her to have one last drink with me. She finally conceded. I got beer out of our mini-fridge and used the plastic glasses from the bathroom. While I was in there, I dumped five Ambien into her cup and poured the beer over it." He paused and shook his head. "Who knew having insomnia would come in handy?"

The picture of Lisa sprawled on the wedding cake with closed eyes flashed through my mind. Now I knew why. "After she finished drinking it, she fell asleep?"

"Not right away. I got her to Skylar's room. Once she got drowsy, she couldn't stand and her words were slurred. I lined her up in front of the cake and stabbed her. I'd paid for her travel, the wedding gown, the ring and I stole a cake, all because I loved her. She'd played me for a fool and I couldn't let her get away with it, you know?"

I didn't, but I had the good manners to nod my head in agreement.

"I am really sorry I have to kill you. You had nothing to do with my failed relationship. You just asked too many questions. Now that you know the truth, though, you have to die."

I glanced at the baker's rack, top heavy with industrial mixers. I had only one shot for momentum and a hard push. I changed my stance so I could make a run at it just as Justin made a rush toward me. Even if the mixers didn't wallop him in the head, the rack should knock him down, or at the very least tangle him in cooking appliances, giving me enough time to get out of the door and run for safety.

Justin didn't rush me. Instead, he continued with his confession. "Because Lisa was drowsy, there was no struggle, which resulted in no blood splatters from the stab wound. Not even when I loosened the knife enough for her to bleed out."

I remembered Justin handing Skylar a bottle of water and then a cinnamon roll and coffee. Both times, Skylar became ill. "You laced the food and drink you gave to Skylar with Ambien, didn't you?"

Justin nodded. "I didn't plan to at first. I went to our room to change my clothes and thought why not? He had ruined the best relationship I'd ever been in."

"But did he? Skylar never wanted Lisa."

"Not intentionally, I guess. But I wasn't going to jail over Lisa, a woman who didn't love me and tried to ruin my life. I knew Skylar didn't like to be waited on, so I made sure I had on gloves and he touched the serrated knife and tucked it away before anyone else could touch it. I hadn't counted on his hatred of weddings or the lucky break when your producer sent us away."

"You switched the knives."

"Bingo. Now you know everything, it's time for you to forget." Justin took a step.

I stepped back. "You forgot one thing. Where is Chef Hartsall's favorite knife, the one you used to kill Lisa Mackliner?" I planted my feet and positioned my arms. I could tell Justin grew impatient. He started shifting his weight from one foot to the other.

A beep sounded like a card opening the door. Involuntarily, I twisted my head in the direction of the door Justin had entered through. Hope sprang through me, then evaporated. No one came through the door.

Justin had heard it too. When my eyes returned to him, he craned his neck to see around the corner. "Time to end this."

The pounding of my heart made my breathing heavy. I'd only have one chance. I had to keep my eyes on him so I could spring into action at just the right moment. "But you didn't tell me where you hid the murder weapon." I really needed to know this information because I planned to survive.

"In the toilet tank in the room I'd reserved. All the blood and fingerprints will be gone. They can't pin Lisa's death on me." He laughed.

What about mine? How did he plan to explain my murder? I had no time to ponder the rationale of a madman because Justin lunged forward, wielding the cleaver high over his head. Putting my legs in motion and holding my arms straight out, I ran in what I am sure looked like to Justin an intended embrace. Instead I hit the baker's rack full force with my hands and followed through with my right shoulder. The contact jarred me to the bone, but worked. The mixers clanked together, and I knew with a hard twist the heavy cargo would unbalance the shelving. I gave it my all. It worked. Metal clanged. The metal rack started to topple over. Lighter-weight appliances banged onto the floor. If the mixers missed Justin, the littered floor should slow him down. Taking the only chance I had, I turned and started to run for the door. I didn't get far when a body slammed into me. Strong arms wrapped around my shoulders, trapping my arms to my sides. We fell and slid past the work counter and almost to the doorway where I'd planned to exit. Had the mixers missed Justin? Had he slid or rolled over the counter to avoid the litter of small appliances? Fighting for my life, I kicked and squirmed, trying to break free. It was no use. I was facedown to the floor, pinned under body weight. I held my breath waiting to feel the sharp sting of stainless steel piercing my skin.

"Stop fighting me." The words a whisper in my ear.

Pamela? Had I heard the voice right over the continued clanking of metal hitting the tile floor?

"I've got her covered."

Definitely Pamela. I stopped struggling.

"You can let her up," Sheriff Perry said. "Her diversion worked. Justin's out cold from a knock on the head by a kitchen mixer. There won't be any gunfire with a chance of a ricochet." He let out a low whistle. "I never thought kitchen utensils and appliances were such deadly weapons."

Him and me both.

Chapter Twenty-two

Shannon and I stood behind the counter on the make-shift set of *Cooking with the Farmer's Daughter* and smiled into the camera. Dressed to complement each other, Shannon wore a jean skirt and russet Western-cut gingham blouse with pearl snaps, while I wore a gold long-sleeved T-shirt with a denim vest and jeans, both embroidered with sunflowers. Shannon's blond tresses were clipped back from her face with ringlets trailing down her back. My stylist skinned my dark hair into a high ponytail.

Eric decided we should prepare an appetizer for our audition tape instead of a full-fledged meal, which would also work for her appearance at my live taping.

"We have shown you two ways to hard-boil eggs," Shannon said. "The traditional boil that I prefer and the oven-baked method Courtney loves."

Taking over, I said, "And two ways to make the yolks creamy and delicious with either Greek yogurt or olive oil instead of mayonnaise." I glanced at Shannon, then back into the camera. "Now we are going to show you how to dress those eggs up for an informal dinner or potluck."

Shannon took over. "Or elegant hors d'oeuvres for a cocktail party or other festive occasion like a holiday dinner."

"If I was taking the eggs to a church potluck, I'd garnish them with crumbled, crispy bacon." I pinched bacon bits I'd fried up earlier from a bowl and sprinkled them generously on top of six eggs. "Another garnish that is colorful and nutritious is chopped sun-dried tomatoes." I repeated the garnish gesture on the remaining six eggs in front of me.

"Those look delicious and would be a hit at any potluck. To dress up the eggs for brunch, try a small piece of thin-sliced smoked salmon." Shannon used small tongs to lift the salmon and arrange it on six eggs.

"Remember, if your garnish is salty, like bacon, salmon or capers, cut back on the salt in the yolk recipe." I filled in the time it took Shannon to layer a half-dozen yolks with salmon.

She continued. "As a finger food appetizer at an elegant dinner party, caviar makes a nice garnish."

I saw Shannon swallow hard as she spooned dabs of caviar on top of the six remaining eggs. I knew later when we actually had an audience and were filming the show instead of a demo tape her eggs would not be the ones she sampled.

"I hope you like our ideas for these hard-boiled eggs.

Don't hesitate to try your own ideas. You could replace crispy pancetta instead of bacon or use fresh herbs like dill or chives." We each picked up an egg and watched for Eric's cue so we'd say the catchphrase in unison. He pointed and we said, "Sometimes too many cooks don't spoil the soup, they make it better."

"That looked great," Eric said. "You can stop filming." He looked our way. "And smiling. Save it for the actual show."

"I think instead of eating the eggs we garnished, we should take one from the other cook." Shannon slid her tray of eggs away from her.

I laughed out loud. My friend wanted nothing to do with fish eggs.

"Great idea! Do it during the actual filming." Eric smiled, then crossed the room to turn up the lights. "Of course, you won't be ending the episode the same way. Courtney will do her usual sign-off after thanking you for joining her in her kitchen today."

We both nodded our understanding.

"What did y'all think?" Shannon and I waited for my sound person to remove the hidden microphones from our clothing, then moved from behind the counter. We had performed to an audience, Harrison, Skylar, Pamela, Drake, Quintin, Kinzy, all the contestants including the season winner of *The American Baking Battle*, Lynne, and Sheriff Perry.

"Terrific." Harrison clapped. "People will love it." He stood and joined us in front of the kitchen counter. The other audience members followed suit.

"I think so too." Quintin smiled. "If you didn't already have a producer lined up, I'd want the project." Quintin wore distressed jeans with an emerald cashmere sweater and didn't look stiff or staunchly. This was the first time I'd seen him off duty from the show.

I flashed him a broad smile while I tamped down my guilty feelings about thinking he might have had a hand in Lisa Mackliner's murder. Something I did every time Quintin was nice, which was quite often once the shooting progressed without a distraction like murder. He'd been so gruff and determined at the beginning because *The American Baking Battle* had been his idea, his baby. He wanted it to succeed. Despite the popularity and high ratings for the show the first season, the network considered pulling the plug since it had run overbudget, bigtime. He'd made a bargain with them that if he could keep the filming on track and under budget, he'd get a Christmas show. Which he did! We'd all been notified another filming was in our future. Quintin had apologized to Skylar profusely about pulling him from the show, but when he explained his reasoning, to keep the show under budget and on the air, Skylar had easily forgiven him. After all, career wise, we wanted the show to do well too.

"I know the network will pick up your show. It was great!" Pamela sidled up to Eric and stood so close their arms touched. She and Eric stared at each other for what seemed like minutes with what looked to me like sappy smiles plastered on their faces. I didn't like their budding infatuation, but could live with it since I chickened out on having a relationship conversation with him. When Eric learned Pamela tackled me to the ground, okay intended to save my life, he'd been so happy he'd wrapped her in a hug and planted a quick kiss on her lips. I knew then if he'd ever had romantic feelings for me, they'd been diverted to Pamela.

"By the way, how are your bruises healing?" Sympathy morphed onto Pamela's features when she asked her question.

"Well"—I lifted my arm—"I am in long sleeves for a reason. They're in the ugly purple-brown stage."

"If you could stay out of trouble, you wouldn't have bruises."

I turned and pinned Sheriff Perry with a deadpan look. "Perhaps if you had made your presence known earlier, Pamela wouldn't have had to tackle me." The sound Justin and I had heard was Sheriff Perry unlocking the door between Chef Hartsall and the sous chef's area.

He had the audacity to allow a big, wide grin to spread across his face. "He was right in the middle of his confession. If I'd have made a move, I wouldn't have heard it or the location of the murder weapon."

"You're welcome."

He laughed. "You know my men found the link between Lisa Mackliner and Justin Henry. I was busy gathering evidence and getting a search warrant when you kept calling and leaving messages that I couldn't answer. I arrived as fast as I could, and if you would heed my warnings and stay out of the investigation, I wouldn't have to keep saving you. With that said, what should I be thanking you for, Miss Archer, being a hindrance?"

"More like a sitting duck." Eric edged his tone with warning.

This was the third scolding I'd received from both men. I felt outnumbered, but I wasn't going to let that stop me. "Unlike the first time, I called you with my suspicions and told you my plans."

"And we are glad you did." Pamela stepped away from

Eric and gave me a side hug. "I don't want anything to happen to my favorite cooking show host."

"Thank you." Pamela wasn't so bad after all. Not only was she a fan of my show, she was a capable security person. I'd had doubts about her abilities due to her petite frame, but after she tackled and pinned me to the ground, I'd never doubt her abilities again.

Skylar had joined the group during Sheriff Perry and my needling conversation. "What is going to happen to Justin?"

Sheriff Perry sighed. "I filled out the paperwork for a mental illness check while he was in the hospital due to the concussion from the mixer injury. He's being charged with premeditated murder. There was just too much planning involved for it to be a crime of passion." He shook his head. "A bad situation all around."

"She didn't deserve to be murdered. She just needed some help." Sadness touched Skylar's features around the corners of his eyes. Skylar, with the help of his mother, donated money to build a mental health clinic in Lisa's hometown and established a foundation so anyone who needed help could seek it.

"Excuse me."

The small group turned and welcomed Marco and a very pretty young woman into the fold. "I'd like you to meet my girlfriend, Lisa Grey."

I smiled while a flush heated my cheeks. I hoped everyone thought it was from the hot lights. I knew it was from suspecting Marco of murder.

"Could we get a picture with you?" Marco looked to Skylar. "I flew her in today as a surprise. Wow! It was a hard secret to keep. I had to steal away to make phone calls to her mom to get everything set up."

My face burned hotter. The phone call I'd overheard in the secret passageway must have been confirming plans.

"Of course." Skylar spread his arms open wide. Marco handed me his phone. He stood on one side while Lisa moved to the other. A pretty blush covered her cheeks. I knew this was a moment she'd cherish forever. I snapped several pictures and handed the phone back. They were satisfied and bid us goodbye, lost in each other's company.

I sighed. Would I ever find love? Maybe it was the wedding-themed show, or the fact that four of our contestants paired off during the filming of the baking battle. I scanned the room. Jeremiah and Afton held hands across a tabletop, while Carla and Nadine only had eyes for each other. I glanced at Eric, who stepped away from the group to take a phone call. My eyes roved the room for Drake. When they settled on him, my heart pattered. Everything about him thrilled me, his coloring, his build, the way his eyes sparkled. Yet I knew a relationship was built on more than attraction. We'd yet to have our dinner date. I didn't know if it was because Nolan Security helped Sheriff Perry wrap up the murder investigation and by the time that was done, the second season of *The American Baking Battle* was wrapped. Or if he'd only been interested in one thing. Honestly, he avoided me since he'd suggested dinner and we'd disagreed on the location.

"Hey, girl, don't look so sad." Shannon bumped my arm with her elbow. "He'll make good on that date." She waved a hand through the air.

I glanced her way. "I'm not so sure."

"Well." Shannon lifted her brows. "I still think—"

"Enough." I halted her with my open palm. I didn't need any more seeds planted in my mind about Eric. It was obvious he and Pamela had started a relationship. I didn't express my budding feelings, so I had to accept it and move forward.

She pulled a face and shrugged. "You are not a good judge of people's emotions."

Before I could tell Shannon I shared the same opinion about her, Eric called out, "Courtney!"

I sought him out in the crowd. He waved me over.

"I need to talk to you a minute." He opened the adjoining door and we entered my dressing room area.

"I have news." His expression told me nothing.

Was it personal or professional? I swallowed hard and braced myself for either good news or bad news on both accounts.

"The network decided to air your apology after the leak to the press. They edited the apology so they could put it on before your scheduled episode last Saturday."

Moisture sprung to my eyes. "Okay." My breaths became shallow. Even though my conscience was clear about my true background, my responsibility to many others who were employed by the show weighed heavy on my shoulders. "And?"

"They have received some complaints, but overall, most of your fans don't care. The fans are more concerned that the network plans to change the theme of our show to reflect your true background and training. They watch the show for the country feel. The network is assuring the fans there will be no change in your program except maybe an updated set for next season to reflect the current trends in farmhouse or country decor."

His words rolled around in my mind. "Next season?" My eyes searched his face. "We're not canceled?"

A wide smile stretched across Eric's handsome face. "We are not canceled. You may have to make some personal appearances on talk shows to further make amends to your fans, but the network has no plans to cancel the show. As a matter of fact, they have offered to extend both of our contracts for another three years."

I jumped up and down and whooped. The weight lifted from my shoulders. My smile mirrored Eric's.

"There's more."

I saw excitement dance in his eyes. "What? I can't stand the suspense!" I'd stopped jumping. My body tensed with excitement.

"The cutlery company is going forward with your product line. The knife set will be a reality by this time next year."

"Oh. My. Gravy! That is terrific news!" I threw open my arms and wrapped Eric in a tight embrace, which he returned. I pulled away and stared into his glee-filled eyes. "All my dreams are coming true, thanks to you." Without thinking, I stretched my neck and pecked a kiss to his lips.

When I pulled back, his eyes smoldered with emotion as they searched my face before resting on my lips. His eyes flicked back to mine. Before I could catch a breath, his lips descended onto mine. Soft and gentle, his lips coaxed a reaction from me. When I responded, he deepened the kiss, creating a stir of intense emotions swirling through me.

Shannon is right. I can't read emotions. What I'd seen between Eric and Pamela was normal interaction because judging by this kiss, Eric has feelings for me.

My knees weakened while my senses thrilled to the demands of his kiss. I tried to think, to categorize what I was feeling. I was powerless. I caved into the whirlwind of emotions Eric created inside of me with one last thought.

A future beyond my wildest dreams awaited me.